# Covert

### Natasha Preston

Copyright © 2013 Natasha Preston
All rights reserved.

The right of Natasha Preston to be identified as the Author of the Work has been asserted by her in accordance with the Copyright, Designs and Patents Act 1988.

All rights reserved. No part of this publication may be reproduced, stored in a retrieval system, or transmitted, in any form or by any means without the prior written consent of the publisher, nor be otherwise circulated in any form of binding or cover other than that in which it is published and without a similar condition being imposed on the subsequent purchaser.

All characters in this publication are fictional and any resemblance to real persons, living or dead is purely coincidental.

ISBN: 1484865766
ISBN-13: 978-1484865767

# ACKNOWLEDGEMENTS

Thank you so much to Mollie Wilson from MJWilson Design for creating the perfect cover for this book and to my editor Debz.

# DEDICATION

For my biggest little brother, Jamie. AKA, the most annoying person on the planet!

# CHAPTER ONE

"I'm only agreeing to this because there will be alcohol," I said and handed my heavy holdall bag to Aaron to put in the car. Lots of alcohol and because Courtney begged.

Joshua – even his name made my stomach turn – had invited us all to his parents' log cabin for the weekend. He was trying to make amends for the past, for how he reacted after the accident, but we weren't going to forgive him so easily. Courtney had forgiven him already, of course, but she never could see what a waster her boyfriend was.

"Mackenzie, please," Courtney said, pushing her fading red hair behind her ears and widening her big green eyes. Her puppy dog look. "He's trying, and it will mean so much to me if you'll try too. Please?" She pouted, adding to the effect.

I sighed. "Fine. Okay. I'll play nice." *Two nights, that's it!*

"We all will," Megan added. "Right guys?" Aaron and Kyle nodded along, agreeing to put their differences to one side – for the weekend at least. "Where is Josh anyway?"

"Picking up his brother." Courtney rolled her eyes. "Blake wants to see him again, so Josh invited him along this morning. Although technically the cabin belongs to Blake too so there's not much anyone can do to stop him coming with."

I arched my eyebrow. We didn't know Blake, and if he was anything like Josh the weekend was going to be a nightmare. "The estranged brother?" I asked. I had seen him a grand total of two times, and that was years ago and only in the car while his parents did the kid swap.

Blake had moved away with his dad after their parents' divorced. Josh stayed with their mum, so they didn't get to spend much time together growing up, which was probably a good thing for Blake.

Courtney pushed her hair behind her ear again. It never stayed there, so I didn't know why she bothered. "They're hardly estranged." They'd spent little time growing up and rarely saw each other; I'd call that estranged.

"Why is he crashing his brother's party?" I asked.

"He's lonely?" Kyle offered, making a sad face.

Courtney leant against the car. "No, he just wants to spend time with his brother. They both want to."

Great! If Blake was like Josh then I would be coming home for sure. I didn't even want to breathe the same air as Josh, so I sort of hoped Blake was a dick too and I could leave. My list of reasons to hate Josh extended past the car accident and how he behaved afterwards. My list went back years.

The wind blew my lightweight, long chestnut hair in my face. I brushed the strands from my eyes just in time to see a metallic black Mitsubishi Warrior – the only car I knew without reading the back because it was Kyle's favourite subject – pull up beside me. *Here we go.*

Josh sat in the passenger seat, nearest to me. Beside him was his brother. They didn't look much alike. They both had the same colour dark brown hair and blue eyes but apart from that they looked totally different. Luckily for Blake.

I looked away and walked around the side of Aaron's car, wanting to put as much distance between me and Josh as possible. Even just seeing his face made me want to punch him. Courtney was smart, but when it came to him she was as thick as a post.

Josh got out of the car and said, "Hey guys. You remember my brother Blake?"

Megan shook her head. "Nope, but hi."

Blake walked to the front of his truck and casually leant against the bonnet as if he was bored. "Hey," he said, nodding.

He wore chunky black boots, dark jeans and a black jacket, making him look almost mysterious and maybe a little dangerous. His dark brown hair stuck out in all directions like he didn't give a crap – which I assumed he didn't anyway – and flopped down his forehead. Bright blue eyes scanned the group, checking us out one by one. He had something about him that made me feel almost uncomfortable.

His eyes looked like they saw everything and I didn't want him to see everything.

"Let's just leave already!" I said, opening the car door and climbing inside. The sooner we get there the sooner we get back. I sounded like my parents on Christmas Eve when they would try getting me to go to sleep as the clock ticked dangerously close to midnight.

"Err, Mackenzie," Courtney said. "You're in the car with me."

My face fell. I knew what that meant. "What?"

She stepped forwards and leant in the car so we could talk privately. "You're coming in the car with me, Josh and Blake."

"Yeah, I'm not," I replied, folding my arms over my chest like a spoilt teenager being told no.

"Please? Look, I know you're mad at him, and I understand why, but will you try? I really think you two need to spend the car trip together."

"We really don't, Court."

"This weekend is going to suck if you're being pissed at Josh the whole time."

I frowned. I wasn't the only one that didn't like him though, so why was I the only one being forced to make the extra effort? "His brother's weird," I whispered as if that was going to change Courtney's mind.

"Blake is harmless."

I was quickly running out of excuses. Sighing in defeat, I replied, "Alright! But if he pisses me off I'm switching cars."

Courtney held her hands up. "Okay, okay. Thank you."

"We're taking Blake's car then."

"Yeah, they must have decided to bring Blake's instead. I can see why." Courtney was a car person; she knew all the different types and models by sight. I couldn't even tell if something was wrong with one – unless the engine actually fell out.

"Blake's driving?"

"His car so I guess." She shrugged, watching Josh with a look that made me want to shake some sense into her.

"I call shotgun then," I replied. If I have to be in the same car as him, it certainly won't be next to him. I was aware that I was behaving like a child, but I didn't care. Josh had crossed a line, and I wasn't going to forgive him. Actually, Josh had crossed about a million lines.

I got in the passenger side before Josh had a chance to say or do anything. He could shove it if he thought I was moving. Blake smiled a little awkwardly and started the car. He didn't ooze confidence when it came to the female race, which I found ridiculous from looking at him.

We didn't know each other at all, so we quickly fell into an awkward silence. I bit the inside of my cheek and twiddled my fingers. *Say something!* We had never actually spoken to each other before. That was about to change though; we had a two-hour car ride to the Lake District ahead of us.

"So why do you hate Josh?" he asked.

I was a little surprised by his bluntness. It was no secret that I didn't like him, but I didn't expect his brother to come straight out and ask it. "Um, because he's a dick."

Blake raised his eyebrows and pursed his lips, thinking. Finally, he nodded once. "Okay then."

"You don't see him much, do you?"

"Not really. Growing up my parents couldn't get on long enough to sort out proper visits for us. Most of the time, when they finally got around to it, they did a kid swap for a day or weekend. I think I can count on one hand the number of times I've seen my mum in the last twelve years."

"That's really sad."

He shrugged as if it was nothing and it didn't hurt him. "That's how it goes sometimes."

"Yeah but still…" I shook my head. I couldn't imagine not seeing my mum every day, as crazy as she drove me sometimes. Blake must feel abandoned by her if she never made the effort, and maybe that was how Josh felt about his dad? Wow Josh and feelings, that was odd to think about and probably untrue.

Josh and Courtney got in the car, and I fell silent. There was a tense atmosphere; like there always was when Josh was around. He knew I wished he wasn't with Courtney, and I think he liked that I did. He loved things like that. Bastard.

"I don't mind you sitting in the front, Mackenzie," he said sarcastically. I clenched my fist.

"My car, bro, and I'd rather sit near a pretty face than your ugly mug," Blake responded.

Smiling to myself, I grabbed my bag of Chupa Chups lollies and offered Blake one. I should probably have been annoyed at the 'pretty face' comment, but that was overshadowed by him calling Josh ugly. Blake took an orange one – my favourite – and gave me a wink.

"Not sharing, Mackenzie?" Josh said.

I took a deep breath, resisting the urge to jam the plastic stick into his eye. "Sure," I replied, holding the bag out. He took two but only did it to annoy me, so I said nothing.

"Okay, everyone, please play nice," Courtney whined. "This weekend is going to be epic so will you all make up!"

"You know I've not got a problem with any of them, babe," Josh replied.

I wanted to punch his smug face in. Courtney would believe him, of course. She was blind to what a total idiot he was. "Whatever," I muttered, clenching my jaw.

We reached the cabin with no blood shed, so I was rather pleased with my levels of self-control, so far. Courtney seemed to keep Josh in check by flirting with him the whole way. I couldn't wait until she saw through him and all his crap. I was going to make sure I had a front row seat when she dumped his arse.

"This is it?" I asked, looking up at a huge, double-story cabin out of the window. It could easily sleep about ten people.

Blake cut the engine and smirked. "What did you expect, the Ritz?"

"No. This is amazing. I didn't think it would be this big."

"Three years ago I would have made a sexual innuendo joke."

"All grown up now, are ya?"

"Nah, that was just when I noticed Josh trying to act the big man, and I realised how lame it actually sounds."

I grinned and got out of the car. I liked Blake. Why did we have to get stuck with the idiot brother? Kyle and Aaron bundled bags out of the boot, and Megan stared up at the enormous house. You could tell from the overgrown plants and faded window frames that no one had been here in a while. Josh and Courtney had spent all last weekend here doing it up, but I think they just cleaned the inside.

The cabin was set in the clearing; the woods surrounded both sides and back and a gorgeous – hopefully shit free – lake ran along the front. It was so beautiful I didn't understand why you wouldn't use it as often as you could. Why wouldn't their parents want to keep coming here?

"You happy to be back?" I asked Blake as we walked to the front door at a snail's pace.

He shrugged as if he didn't care again. The last time he was here was when his family was 'whole'. "Just here for the piss up."

*Of course you are.*

Josh unlocked the door and turned to us. Kyle rolled his eyes, guessing what was coming, and I tried not to laugh. We

– nineteen, twenty and older than us Blake year-olds – were about to be given rules. "Courtney and I have worked hard getting the cabin ready for you all, so I would appreciate it if you would respect the place and not leave it looking like a tip."

I bit my tongue as laughter bubbled up, racing to my mouth, desperate to get out. How pathetic and pompous. None of us were going to trash the place, and he knew that. Courtney stood beside him like lady of the manor, eating it all up. I loved that girl, but she needed a good slap to knock some sense into her.

Josh opened the door and walked in ahead of Courtney. Gentlemen my arse! She didn't even care; she followed him like a little lap dog.

Wow. I walked in, and my jaw dropped.

"I'll grab the bags," Aaron said, heading back out of the door behind Blake. I looked around, and despite being in the same room as Josh; I was excited for the weekend.

The cabin was beautiful, albeit a little dated. The view of the lake from the lounge window was to die for. The sun shone down on the water's surface making it glisten. Whatever happened, I was going to ignore Josh and enjoy myself. We all needed to let off some steam after the accident.

"I'm going to explore. Anyone wanna come?" Megan asked, bouncing up and down like a child. Her short, spiky, over hair sprayed bob barely moved an inch. She had already thrown her bag by the bottom of the stairs, which was about as much unpacking as she did.

I handed the box of wine to Courtney, who was lugging the food and drink from the lounge to the kitchen. "Don't fancy getting lost in the forest, thanks," I replied.

Aaron put the last bag down. "I'll come." He walked out the door before anyone could stop him and make him help. I watched them walk into the woods. The bright midday sun shone down on Aaron's white-blonde hair, making it glow.

"Going for a walk." Kyle shook his head at them. "Crazy. Hey, Blake, where'd you put the beer, man?"

"In the oven," he replied dryly.

I tried not to smile but failed miserably. I wasn't sure what Blake was doing here; he didn't seem to have a good relationship with Josh at all and he didn't seem to want to make it better either. He could see through his brother's crap though, so he was cool in my book.

Kyle's mouth thinned in a tight smile, and I could tell he was fighting the urge to say something back. He turned and walked away, I imagined seconds from biting his head off.

Blake and I were left in the lounge, alone again. I didn't know what to say. The silence was awkward again, but it didn't seem to affect him at all. Nothing seemed to affect him!

"So did you come here much when you were a kid?" I asked, filling the silence.

He looked over his shoulder, half-smiling. "You're asking if I come here much?"

"No, I'm asking if you *came* here much."

Blake turned his body to face me. He had this cockiness about him too but for some reason it wasn't as off putting as Josh's. "We came here a lot before our parents separated. After the divorce, the place stayed empty, until now."

I didn't know what to say. "I'm sorry."

"Why? People divorce all the time." Before I had the chance to say anything else, he walked outside. He was definitely more affected than he let on.

"Beer, Kenz?" Kyle asked from behind me.

"You know it's eleven in the morning, right?"

"Yeah," he replied, tilting his head, waiting for me to explain.

I smiled and took a beer from his outstretched hand. "Never mind."

Kyle and I sat on the sofa while Josh and Courtney messed around putting things away in the kitchen. "You think we should help?" I asked.

"I offered. You know what Josh is like!"

Control freak. We wouldn't do it the way he wanted. How many different ways there was to put food in a cupboard, I didn't know! This was 'Josh's' place though, and we were made very aware that we were his guests.

"I'm going to need a lot of alcohol to get through this weekend."

Kyle nodded in agreement and raised his bottle. "Let's keep it coming then."

I clinked the top off the bottle against his and took a swig. Alcohol was definitely the answer when dealing with Josh. I hated spending any time with him at all; he made my blood boil.

Kyle and I had just finished our third bottle when the rest of the guys joined us. "Wow this looks fun," Aaron said, grinning at the bottles and bottles of alcohol spread out over the coffee table.

"Yep, Kyle and I thought we should have it all at arm's reach. Cheers," I said, raising my half-full bottle.

"Well if we're doing this, we're doing it right," Aaron replied, picking up his bottle of Absolut Vodka. "Everyone's in, no pussying out. Josh, shot glasses my man!" My smile grew.

"Err, guys, I don't want anyone throwing up in my house," Josh said in his annoying, stuck up, I'm better than you way. I had a very sudden, very childish urge to drink until I puked at least three litres of vodka. Everything he wanted I wanted to do the opposite. I knew that was dangerous though. I knew I couldn't – and I wasn't stupid enough to do it – but I damn well wanted to.

"Fucking lighten up, man," Kyle replied, his alcohol-laced voice and eye roll made Josh glare and his jaw tighten. He didn't like to be challenged. Josh was right and perfect, always. To him anyway, everyone else thought he was a dick.

Kyle lifted a freshly poured shot glass and raised it to Josh, his own little fuck you, before knocking it back. I smiled and did the same. And then I regretted it because Josh's eyebrow arched, and I knew exactly what he was thinking.

# CHAPTER TWO

An hour after drinking we'd eased off a bit or we'd all be flat on our faces before it even got dark. Well I certainly would be anyway. Josh and Courtney had gone off to their room for a bit of privacy, which just meant Josh wanted sex. Megan and Aaron were cleaning up in the kitchen and Kyle had been in the bathroom for so long that I vowed never to use that one again.

Blake stretched his legs out, kicking his booted feet up on the coffee table. He didn't fit in. He drank with us and joined in with conversation but it was weird. There was an atmosphere with him and Josh that went beyond the usual dislike of Joshua that the rest of us had.

They didn't get along so why on earth would Blake invite himself?

"What do you do back home?" I asked, trying to get to know a little more about him other than his favourite alcoholic drink.

"Worked here and there."

Okay it was like getting blood out of a stone.

"You're not very chatty, are ya?"

He flicked his eyes to me without moving his head, and I jumped. "What's the point?"

"To get to know people, to make friends, to not live like a hermit."

I was rewarded with a charming smile.

"You think I'm a hermit?"

"Aren't you?"

"No," he replied. "I don't spend much time alone at all."

The spark in his eye told me everything and I turned my nose up in disgust. "Different girl every night?"

"Not every night."

"Previously broken heart or just not grown up yet?"

"What?"

"I just want to know why you use women."

"Can it not just be because I like sex but don't want a relationship?"

"Not usually. I get it now though."

"Get what?"

"Get why."

He rubbed his forehead and muttered, "Women. What do you think you get, Mackenzie?"

"You don't want a relationship because you watched your parents divorced. You have a bad example because it's no secret that the split was a difficult one."

He sat frozen for a minute and I knew I'd hit the nail on the head. Mackenzie one, Blake zero. "You don't know what you're talking about. I haven't met anyone I wanted to see exclusively before, that's all."

"Whatever you say."

His eyes narrowed to the point where they were almost closed.

"Sorry. I didn't mean to offend you."

"I'm not offended."

God this guy was weird. He was also sexy as hell. So much so that he made every other boy I'd ever fancied look like a gargoyle.

"Wanna get out of here for a bit?" I asked.

"You don't seem like the type to offer that," he replied. The spark in his eyes was back.

"Get your head out of the gutter, you know that's not what I mean."

I thought he'd say no but he stood up and arched his eyebrow when I didn't move. "Was that a trick question, Mackenzie?"

"No," I replied, standing. "I just didn't expect you to go for it."

"There's a lot about me you probably wouldn't expect."

Yeah, I didn't doubt that for a second. He was confusing and moody and everything about him screamed complicated. There was also something about him that made me more forward than I'd ever been with a man.

I followed him out of the cabin and along the path. He headed into the woods by the river.

"So what's your damage? Or are you as perfect as you look?"

"I'm not sure how to take that," I said, and he shrugged. I was sure 'perfect' was meant sarcastically. "No damage. I'm boringly normal."

"No dark secrets you're hiding?"

I almost lost my footing. My throat closed up, almost choking me. Had Josh told him? "No, no secrets."

"Liar," he muttered.

I planted my feet and once he'd taken two more steps, he realised I was no longer beside him and turned around.

Rolling his eyes, he said, "Oh come on, Mackenzie, everyone has secrets."

"Not dark ones."

He stepped closer. I stood tall as he approached. Twigs snapped underneath his boots until he stopped almost toe-to-toe with me. I tried to ignore my ridiculous reaction to him being so close. His muscular frame and come to bed eyes really did make me want to go to bed.

I bit the inside of my cheek. He was entirely too close and too far away at the same time.

"The secrets you hide from yourself are always the most dangerous."

"I'm not hiding anything from myself."

"You're too straight."

I let that sink in for a minute, or I tried to. When it still made no sense I said, "What?"

"Perfect friend, perfect daughter, perfect student. I can see it all in your eyes. When do you let go? When do you let off steam? You're going to go crazy before you're thirty."

"You know nothing about me."

He'd hit a little too close to home and I didn't like it. There were things about my past I didn't like, mistakes I'd made that I wish I could take back. I tried to compensate by being everything that was expected of me. It was pretty tiring. The most annoying part was Blake, a guy I'd known for five bloody seconds recognised that more than my friends and family. Either he was really good at reading people or he'd read my diary.

"I don't know specifics but you've got frustrated teen tattooed all over yourself."

"And what have you got tattooed over yourself?"

Arrogant arse was my guess.

"Japanese rising sun."

"Huh?"

He pulled up his t-shirt sleeve revealing a black tattoo of half a sun.

"What's that mean?"

"No idea, just liked it."

Chuckling to himself, he walked off again.

"You've known the others for years?" he asked once I'd caught up with him again.

"Yeah."

"Kyle and Aaron didn't seem that happy about me crashing your weekend. Megan either actually."

I shrugged. "They're cool. They like the dynamic we had pre Josh best. I do too, and they've just got used to us being a group of six. They can be kind of protective, Aaron especially. That guy would do anything for his friends; he'd take a bullet for us. Not that I wouldn't. Once a guy grabbed my arse after I'd told him not to and Aaron knocked him out, literally."

"He sounds more psychotic than protective but put whatever label you want on it."

"I will," I replied, narrowing my eyes. His theories about me, although true, annoyed me but I could handle. What I didn't like was him speaking badly of my friends.

"So tell me, a group as close as you lot…"

I knew where that was going. "Not me. Josh and Courtney, as you know. Aaron and Tilly had an on/off relationship."

"You never? Not even once?"

"Nope. Girls and guys can just be friends, you know?"

"Sure, just seems odd. I've been around groups of friends and there's always a few that have had drunken sex. Or at least oral."

Or at least oral? If I wasn't disgusted at the casual way he just threw it in there, I'd laugh.

"Sorry, no dirt here."

"Wow, you lot really are as straight as they come. You planned board games for this evening?"

"No! Sorry, Mr Excitement. What do you do for fun?"

It took my brain longer than it should have to process him whipping around, grabbing my wrists and shoving me against a tree, trapping me with his entire body. I was momentarily stunned. My body wanted to arch into him. I wanted to feel his skin against mine, his tongue in my mouth, his breath on my neck.

What the hell was wrong with me? Him. It was him with his outrageous good looks and mystery.

Forcing myself to get it to together, I swallowed hard and whispered, "Sex is the only fun you have?" I stifled a moan as his lower body pressed against mine that little bit harder.

"No, sex is the most fun I have." His eyes, now on fire, looked right though me, to the things that I hid away and still he stayed pressed against me, jaw tight as if he was finding it hard not to take me against the tree.

I wasn't the person that instantly wanted someone. I had to build up to that, get to know them first but Blake made me want to throw all my rules out of the window and give alfresco a try. I was too much of a wimp to make the first move but if he kissed me I was pretty sure that'd be it.

Blake suddenly shoved away from me so hard I almost collapsed.

"What?" I asked.

"What're the odds of you freaking afterwards?"

"High," I replied. Having sex with Josh's brother, who'd I'd only really met today, in the middle of the forest was probably a bad idea. I couldn't quite get that through to my racing pulse and overheated body though.

"Thought so. Come on, I'll show you where I shoved Josh in the river and broke his arm."

Blake gave me a tour of the woods surrounding the cabin, telling me stories from his childhood. I didn't really learn that much about him though, he told me a lot but everything was fact-based and somewhat impersonal. Still it was nice to know the brothers hadn't always been so hostile towards each other and there was a time when Josh hadn't been a complete arsehole.

We took a leisurely walk back to the cabin, neither of us in a huge hurry to continue the drinking that was undoubtedly happening. Every so often his hand would brush mine and the earlier hunger for him came back and smacked me in the face. He was so different to the ordinary guys I usually went for. There was mystery and a darkness that was so totally alluring it scared me a little. Blake was just so much more. I'd known the guy for a few hours and I was already hooked. If I was sixteen I would be writing Mackenzie loves Blake in my notebook by now. It was pitiful really.

"What're you hoping to get out of this weakened, Mackenzie?" he asked. The cabin was in view now and part of me wished we had longer to go. He was cool to hang out with and it helped that he was drop dead gorgeous with a body to die for.

"I'm just hoping to get through it."

"That bad with Josh?"

"Yep. It's okay though; I can deal for a few days. It'll be good to chill with Court, Megan, Aaron and Kyle." *And you.*

"What're you hoping to get out of this weekend, Blake?"

He shrugged. "Nothin', just had some time to kill."

# CHAPTER THREE

I laughed hysterically into the cushion until my stomach muscles screamed in protest. Everything only remotely amusing was heightened when you were drunk – Kyle falling over was hilarious. He didn't even go all the way down, it was more like a stumble, but I was drunk, so it didn't matter. My stomach was full from the enchiladas we'd all cooked and devoured. There were way too many enchiladas, but it seemed to do sod all to soak up the alcohol.

My walk with Blake had caused a few eyebrow raises from Megan and Aaron. They seemed to think he was a bit of a dick but that was probably just because he was related to Josh and they hadn't really spoken to him yet.

"Oh my God, we're gonna be so hung over tomorrow," Megan whined. She wasn't as drunk as she acted, but she had always been like that. Look at me wobble and then she would blatantly make herself trip over her own feet. She didn't like being drunk and losing control, but she didn't like to be the odd one out, so she pretended. Everyone knew she pretended, and I think she knew that too, but we all went along with it and laughed at silly drunk Megan wobbling down the road.

"More shots," Aaron announced, pointing to the empty shot glasses on the table. I had lost count of how many we had done so far, but as much as we had already drank; it was still a pretty slow night. My friends and I – minus Megan –

could really put it away. Blake was surprisingly sober. I suspected he drank quite a bit in his teenage years because he had the same amount as us but wasn't too drunk, he could still walk in a straight line.

As the shots kept coming, with all of us taking it in turns to pour the drinks and run back to the kitchen for the chilled vodka, I started to feel ill. Megan brought some Italian liquor with her and made us to finish up the bottle because as she put it, 'if I take that crap back with me my mother will disown me'. I could see why Laurel didn't want it back, it tasted of lemon and burned on the way down, like what toilet cleaner probably tasted like. We also polished off Aaron's bottle of spiced rum.

I groaned and craned my neck. My body felt heavy and weak. I was getting to the sleepy part of being drunk, although I could usually go a lot longer.

"Does anyone else feel weird?" I asked.

Megan giggled. "What, drunk?"

"Sort of, I guess," I replied, pressing my hands to my face. *Please don't throw up.* As much as I would've loved to, all over the new throws Josh had bought especially, I hated being sick, the taste and feel of it rushing up my throat made me panic. "I'm just gonna lay down for a minute." *Keep still and don't move a muscle.* Things that moved were sick. I just had to be a statue until the waves of nausea went away.

"And I'm going up to bed," Megan said. "I'm tired and probably going to have the hangover from hell tomorrow." I nodded against the sofa cushion and mentally punched myself. *Do not move, Mackenzie.*

"Err, Megan, down here tonight," Josh snapped. Ah, Courtney's idea that we should all sleep downstairs. Why it mattered where we were when we were unconscious, I did not know. Of course, Josh would have to back her up. Not because she was his girlfriend but because he would be able to say he tried. It would make him look good. He couldn't care less if Megan slept outside. Arsehole.

"Shut up, Josh," she said, forcing her words to slur.

"This isn't your house, in case you forgot."

Aaron scoffed. "How could she forget? You remind us every five minutes!"

"Josh, why does it bloody matter where everyone sleeps?" Blake asked. Thank you! "Just go up, Megan." I smiled as Megan stuck her tongue out at Josh and stumbled up the stairs. *Again, I like Blake.*

"What's your problem?" Aaron said, slumping back against the end of the sofa from the floor. "Ever since Tilly and Gigi died you've been a complete prick."

Before that too.

I curled up, not wanting to talk about them with Josh. It made me violently angry when I thought about the things he said and done.

"What the fuck is your problem? You dumped Tilly just before, remember?"

Aaron's eyes darkened. "You know what, Josh, screw you! And I swear if you ever say her name again I'll kill you." I expected Aaron to get up and lunge for Josh. That was what he would have done. Why didn't he do that? I frowned. He was too drunk to move as well? Didn't usually stop him.

"Stop!" Courtney shouted. "End it now."

I clenched my fists. How could she not see what a dick Josh was? Aaron shook his head and took another swig from his bottle of vodka, finishing the last drop. I wanted to leave, but I couldn't even raise my arm. My eyes suddenly weighed a ton. I felt like crap. The room spun, and I felt as if I was floating. Snuggling into the sofa with a deep groan, I drifted.

It only felt like minutes later that I was woken up by the bravest human on earth. "What?" I growled.

Blake's very amused expression was the first thing I saw when I reluctantly opened my eyes.

"Your top," he said.

I propped myself up on one elbow and looked down. It was still on so I didn't know what he was going on about. "What, Blake?"

"It's..." He traced his finger along my hipbone where. There was a small slice of skin on show where my top had ridden up an inch or two. I tried to breathe normally but my senses were overloaded. He was all I could see and smell and his fingertip rolling over my skin was doing things to me that made my eyes roll back.

I looked around to see if anyone else was awake. Kyle and Aaron were still on the floor. Courtney and Josh must have gone upstairs. Hypocrites.

"You woke me up to touch my stomach?" I asked as calmly as I could.

"No, I woke you up to see if you've known me long enough to let me take you to bed?"

I bit my lip. "Why me?"

He frowned. "What?"

"You do casual, which means you do girls that do casual. I don't. Why me?"

After a minute of pondering my question, he replied, "I don't know."

"You want this to be a forget it happened in the morning deal?" Although it was practically morning. My head was swimming. I felt heavy and a little disorientated. A quick glance at the clock told me I'd barely been sleeping five minutes.

"I don't know. I doubt I'll forget it happened in the morning."

"Then what do you want, Blake?"

If he said 'I don't know' again I was going to swing for him.

"I want to take you upstairs. That's all I know right now."

Could I live with that? I didn't need a marriage proposal but I liked to think that I was more than just a one-night screw. There was something about Blake and about the way he made me feel that I couldn't ignore.

I sat all the way up and my lips brushed his. The hand that was on my stomach snaked around to my back and his other curled around my neck. The second his lips firmly covered mine I knew that this wasn't just a one night thing. It might not turn into anything at all but we'd definitely have more than tonight.

I cracked my eyes open and they were immediately stung by the bright morning light streaming through the windows. Groaning, I ran my hands over my face. I felt like I'd been hit by a bus. My head throbbed and every time I swallowed I felt as if I was downing sawdust. I felt worse than I did when Blake woke me up but that may well have been because Blake was waking me up.

I had never had a hangover so bad before. Last night I had drunk a lot but nowhere near enough to feel as awful as I did. Beside me, Blake lay on his side with one arm and one leg thrown over me. It was the first time he looked peaceful. Whatever weighed on his mind was gone when he slept.

My experience with the morning after a one-night stand was minimal. I knew the rules were to generally get the hell out as soon as possible but in this situation that was impossible. We were spending the weekend in the same secluded place. There was no need for any awkwardness though, we were attracted to each other and acted upon that. We were also adults.

Pushing myself up, I flopped, almost falling back against the mattress. I had no energy. The curtains were open and the sunlight burned my eyes. I needed water and pills. I also needed to throw up the remaining alcohol that was still sloshing around in my system. Never again. Ever, ever, ever again!

My movements woke Blake. He removed his hand from across my stomach and rubbed his face. "I feel like shit," he said.

"Join the club."

He peeked at me through his fingers. "How do you not look like hell in the morning? I mean you've got that hot, post-sex bed head thing happening but that's just turning me on."

"How can you feel like crap and still want sex?"

Moving both of his hands from his face, he replied, "You've seen yourself, Mackenzie."

I didn't think I was anything great but I loved how he saw me. Everyone wanted someone to think they were special.

Blake's words wrapped around me, making me feel much more for him than I should at this point. It wasn't love but it was something I wanted to explore and give a chance. If I didn't feel so awful I would lay right back down and get lost in him again.

"I…" I what?

Chuckling quietly, he shoved himself up and reached for his jeans. "I need food and a strong coffee. Do you know what everyone has planned for today?"

Following his lead, I grabbed my clothes and started to get dressed. "We're going down to the lake to swim and hang out. Aaron's decided to feed everyone barbecue food all day then we're making a bonfire in the evening."

Blake stilled and looked over his shoulder. "You're making a fire in the middle of the forest?"

"A small bonfire, we're not setting trees alight."

"Purposefully," he muttered. "I'm overseeing that."

"Oversee away. I'm sure Aaron would love the help."

"So you'll be down at the river all day?" he asked, pulling his t-shirt over his head. His muscular back was just as painfully perfect as the front. He must work out because there was no way that body just happened.

"Yeah. You'll come too, right?"

I knew he wasn't exactly one of us but there was an opportunity for as all to be friends if he'd give us the chance. The thought of him spending the day alone bothered me much more than it should.

"I'll come. I was thinking more of sneaking off for a while."

I buttoned my jeans up and folded my arms. "You're insatiable."

Blake slowly stalked towards me. I held my ground, determined not to show him how on fire I was at that longing in his eyes.

His gaze rode over every inch of my face. "Can you blame me?"

As I was about to say screw the food but wave of nausea flowed through me. I needed to eat soon and soak up the alcohol. I also needed a large glass of water and a couple painkillers. Blake wasn't going anywhere and neither was I so we had plenty of time to explore each other's bodies later.

"We can find many opportunities to sneak off but right now I need to eat some greasy food or I'm gonna feel like shit all day."

Straightening his back, he gripped my arms. "Well that definitely sounds like a plan and I definitely don't want you feeling shit all day so…" He dropped one arm completely and let the other slide down my skin until he reached my hand. With a little tug, he towed me out of the room and downstairs.

We stopped at the bottom of the stairs to assess the damage. Bottles, shot glasses and packets of all kinds of snacks littered the coffee table and floor around it. There were more empty bottles of alcohol than I remembered. No wonder we felt rough.

Blake stood behind me, his chest pressed right against my back and one hand on my hip. I liked the contact a lot.

"Well this explains the drilling in my head," he murmured, leaning down to nip my neck. Spinning around, I slapped his arm, laughing. His boyish grin made my heart swell. It was good to see him act his age.

A door upstairs opened and closed. I stepped around Blake to watch Megan hobble down. She looked as good as I felt. Lightweight!

"Kenzie?" she whispered. "I think I'm dying."

Laughing quietly, I replied, "You too, huh?"

"Jesus! How much did we drink?" she muttered, leaning heavily against the bannister as she made the final steps downstairs. She hadn't drunk much, but it was still more than she usually did.

"We're getting old," I joked. "We can't handle it anymore."

Kyle was sprawled out on the floor with his mouth wide open, breathing deeply, his jet-black hair stuck out in all directions like a bird nest. Aaron was curled up beside him, sleeping in the foetal position. They couldn't handle it either.

Blake watched us with curiosity I didn't quite understand. I had a feeling he didn't have many close friends, which was a shame because beyond that I don't care attitude was a great guy. From what I'd seen anyway.

"Where's Josh and Courtney?" Megan asked.

I shrugged and replied, "Must be up already. God, Megan, I need pills."

Kyle's eyes flicked open and widened as he saw how close Aaron was to him. I felt so rough I couldn't even laugh when he shoved him away, making Aaron wake with a gasp.

Aaron looked up, dazed. "What?" He rubbed his eyes and winced. "Christ!"

"I'm making tea. Everyone in?" I said, receiving grunts in replace of a yes and a look of disgust from Blake. I smiled, remembering he'd mentioned what drink he needed to function. "Coffee for you."

I walked into the kitchen; my head was swimming, everything looked a little fuzzy. A sea of red flashed in front of my eyes, and I blinked hard.

*I'm really losing it.*

Opening my eyes again, I stared at the floor and slowly registered what I was seeing. Bright, thick blood stretched from behind the island to almost the middle of the kitchen.

I stopped and gasped. There was so much blood. My heart raced and the ends of my fingertips tingled. The metallic smell hit me in the face, filling my lungs and making me gag. I started to shake, I and got that out of body experience people claimed to have when something was too unreal to be real.

"Courtney?" I whispered, not even hearing my own voice over the ringing in my ears.

Someone's chest pressed into my back. "What the…" Kyle whispered, stepping around me. "Stay back, Kenz."

Blake was right behind Kyle. "What's going on?" he asked.

Against Kyle's orders, I stepped around the kitchen island and my stomach lurched. "No," I cried, pressing my hand over my mouth as bile rose in my throat. Courtney and Josh lay on the floor in a pool of crimson blood.

# CHAPTER FOUR

I closed my eyes and then very slowly opened them again, expecting and hoping what I had just seen was figment of my imagination. But the image didn't change; Courtney and Josh were still there, lying motionless on the floor.

Megan let out a high-pitched scream that didn't sound like it belonged to a human. *This isn't real. I'm dreaming. I have to be dreaming.*

"Courtney," I whispered again, my voice drowning in a sea of Megan's continuous sobs and screams. "Josh!"

They didn't answer. Of course. My mind reeled. How? Who? Why? My body trembled violently from the shock. My fingers gripped the counter, nails digging into the wood. I couldn't move. I was frozen in place and completely unable to look away.

Aaron dropped to his knees; his arms hovered over Josh as if he wanted to touch him but was too scared to. "Shit," he spat. "Do something someone! Call an ambulance!"

It looked too late for that. Courtney's once almost red lips were a pale off-pink colour, and her skin was dull and grey. A stream of dried-on blood stretched from her ear to the floor.

"Who did this?" I sobbed, wishing I could close my eyes. Why couldn't I look away?

Kyle spun around. "Shit, she's right. Where is he? Or they?"

*No, no, no. Are they still in the house?* Fear gripped my throat.

Blake gulped; he stared at his brother, never looking away from his face. Josh's eyes were still open but had rolled back. He looked how I always imagined a dead body would look. "Where's who?"

"The bastard who's just murdered our friends!" Kyle spat. They wouldn't still be here; no one was stupid enough to hang around.

I dropped to my knees, ignoring the bickering going on behind me. My heart was flying in my chest. *This isn't happening.* Courtney didn't look like Josh; her eyes were closed. She wasn't dead. I just had to get her to open her eyes and everything would be okay.

"Court, wake up." I reached out and brushed her faded red hair from her face. She hated when her fringe fell in her face like that. "We need an ambulance," I said. "She needs help. Someone help her! Please!"

Tears welled in my eyes, impairing my vision until Courtney was just a blur. I heard someone drop beside me. "Kenzie?" It was Megan. "She's gone, Kenz. We need to... I don't know. We need to do something. Get up," she said, tugging on my arm. "Come on. Someone is out there. We need to get out of here now."

"No one is going anywhere!" Aaron shouted. "Kyle, call the police. Megan and Kenz, get the fuck out of this room and Blake... just don't leave this house."

I watched Blake straighten up, grateful of the distraction from Courtney's lifeless body. His face hardened, eyes narrowed. "Why did you say that? Why can't I leave?"

Aaron arched his eyebrow as if to say *well duh*. "Come on, it doesn't take a genius to figure it out."

"To figure what out?" Blake spat. Megan stood up, pulling me with her. She gripped my hand and squeezed until I felt my bones grind against each other. I already knew where Aaron was going with this. He thought it was Blake.

"The delinquent crashes the trip and we wake up with two dead bodies on the fucking floor!" I wasn't sure why he had suddenly became a delinquent in Aaron's eyes. Loner didn't equal criminal.

Blake took two short steps forward and stopped chest to chest with Aaron. He cocked his head to the side. "That's my brother laying down there. Watch your fucking mouth."

"Stop it!" I shouted, shoving between them, finally finding something inside to snap me back. Tears poured down my face too fast for me to be bothered to wipe them. Our friends were dead – murdered – and they were arguing like kids. "What the hell is wrong with you, Aaron? This isn't helping so both of you stop." I turned to Kyle and said, "Call 999!" He already had his phone glued to his ear. I dropped back to my knees. "Should we do something? How long do you think it's been? Aaron, you know CPR. Try. Please."

"Mackenzie, I can't bring her back."

*Try!*

I knew that. I knew he couldn't. Of course he couldn't. She was stone cold and white as a ghost. It wasn't as if she had just collapsed. Courtney was dead, but what did it say about us if we didn't at least try?

Their blood stained the bottom of my jeans, creeping up and turning the blue denim dark red. I watched as it very slowly rose. My friend's blood was over me. My body shook to the point where my muscles ached. I wanted to wake up.

I always thought movies went over the top with blood shed, and they did, but there seemed to be so much I felt as if I were in a horror film. If we were in a horror film though, there would be blood up the walls and over every surface. I looked around and saw it was only on the ground, surrounding their lower bodies.

"There's so, so much blood," I whispered and stroked Courtney's hair. Her face was still perfect – apart from the trickle by her ear – most of the blood was below her chest and had spread towards her legs. "Do you think they died before? They did, didn't they?" I asked. My voice hitched as I sobbed.

Aaron knelt down, rubbing my back. "Before what?" he asked, speaking to me like he would a baby.

"Before they... bled out." Died.

"Yes," he replied, pulling me up.

He didn't mean that yes. That yes was to console me. Whether she died quickly or not didn't change the fact that she died an awful and painful death. I heaved; the metallic smell and gory site was too much. They were dead. Gone. My heart shattered at the knowledge that I would never see my best friend again. I pressed my fist to my mouth and heaved again. Aaron understood; he yanked me into his arms and hauled me off to the bathroom.

I flopped to the floor, and Aaron lifted the toilet seat up just in time for me to empty the contents of my stomach into it. Gripping the side of the toilet, I threw up until nothing was left.

When I finished, I sobbed hysterically and collapsed against the wall. I felt as if someone had stabbed me too, right through the centre of my heart. I was terrified. It was all so unbelievable, surreal. It was something that happened to other people.

"Do you want to stay here?" Aaron asked.

Fear gripped me. I looked up and grabbed his hand. "I don't want to be on my own."

"Okay, it's okay. Come on." He helped me stand up. I turned the tap on and rinsed my mouth out, the after taste of bile and alcohol made me want to throw up again.

"I need to go back in there, but you can stay in the living room."

"No, I want to be with everyone." I held onto his hand as if it was my only lifeline. Aaron walked back slowly. *Just don't look.*

My stomach clenched as we walked into the kitchen. I let go of Aaron when we reached the island. From where I was I couldn't see them, and I wanted to keep it that way.

"The police are on their way," Kyle said. He was still on the phone to emergency services. "I don't know!" he growled into the phone "We woke up and… they're dead." His face paled.

None of us really knew what to do. I had never felt so helpless before. We had called 999 but should we do something else? Was there even anything else? We should have tried CPR. Even though I knew they were dead and nothing could bring them back. I wanted to be able to say to their families and to ourselves that we at least tried.

If I could turn back the clock, I would have gone on that CPR course with Aaron. I should have, but I never thought I would need to. No one ever thinks they would need to. Courtney laughed at it, said it's a waste of time spending the day learning something you would never use. 'The most Aaron will ever do,' she had said, 'is put a plaster on someone's finger. I don't need a course to teach me how to apply a plaster'. She was so wrong.

I refused to look back at them laying there. The image was already burnt into my memory, and I knew it would creep up on me when I least expected it. Haunt me years and years down the line right when I thought I had dealt with it and moved on.

My body was weak, dizzy, and I felt like I was going to collapse. I needed to eat. I felt like I was hungry, but food definitely wasn't an option. I was aware that I was crying, but I couldn't feel it. I couldn't really feel anything. Numb: that was what I was.

"Why would someone do this?" Megan wailed, coughing as she tried to catch her breath. Her reaction was the exact opposite of mine. She was hysterical – the way I should be – but I wasn't. I was empty and detached.

"Mackenzie," Aaron whispered, bending his knees, so he was level with me.

I shook my head. "I…I don't, Aaron." I was aware that I wasn't making sense, but I couldn't think sense.

"Shh, I know." He pulled on my arm, and I let him lead me to the sofa in the lounge.

The door handle rattled just as I sat down, making me jump. It was only then that I heard the sirens and saw the flashing blue lights.

Someone bashed the door from outside and Blake jumped up to unlock it. I couldn't remember anyone locking it last night. Police officers burst through the door and Aaron, Blake and Kyle wasted no time in explaining. They all spoke at once; their voices muddled together creating a buzzing noise that couldn't be understood.

One of the officers, a tall man with shaved black stubble for hair held his hand up. "Calm down. Where are they?" he asked, his voice thick with authority, similar to my old high school head master.

"Kitchen," Blake replied, leading the way.

"Stay here," Kyle said, looking between me and Megan before following the guys to Courtney and Josh.

I did what he said because I couldn't face seeing them both like that again. Courtney was always so warm, with a glowing tan. Seeing her pale and cold was heart breaking.

"What do you think they're doing?" I asked Megan.

She shook her head; her hands trembled on top of her lap. "I don't know. Where will they take them? To the hospital?"

To the morgue. I squeezed my eyes closed as soon as that thought entered my mind. "I don't know. Probably," I replied.

As a distraction, I fixed my eyes on the fireplace and watched the last of the flames struggle to flicker. I was afraid to look around in case the blood had spread. That was ridiculous though. It was impossible, but I still feared it.

A female officer knelt down in front of us. "I'm Detective Inspector Julienne Hale, but you can call me Julie. How are you both doing?"

I shook my head. "I don't know." Megan's reply was a strangled sob.

"I need to ask you a few questions if that's okay." Neither of us replied, so she continued, "Can you tell me your names?"

"Mackenzie Keaton," I replied. "That's Megan Haydock." She was in no state to talk; her head was buried in her knees, and her body shook as she cried. "Is there someone in the house? I didn't hear anyone. I would have heard, wouldn't I?"

"Okay, Mackenzie, just slow down."

"Why didn't we hear them? Courtney had a loud voice and her scream—"

"Alright," Julie said, placing her hand over mine. "We can do this another time; you've had a terrible shock."

"You will find who did it, won't you?"

She squeezed my hand. "We will."

Blake walked back into the room and sat on the side of the fireplace. Leaning his elbows on his knees, he tugged his hair with his fingers. He didn't show emotion, unless it was a cocky smirk, so I had no idea how deeply Josh's death had affected him. I imagine deeper than he would ever let on.

"Blake," I said softly. In my own head, I sounded ridiculous, treating him like a child. He didn't look up but cocked his head to the side, acknowledging me. "You okay?" He didn't move or reply. I suspected he didn't know himself.

"We have to wait in here," Kyle said as he and Aaron walked through the door. He shook his head and sat down beside me. Julie walked into the kitchen, leaving us with a uniformed officer that I had a feeling was assigned to watch us.

For the longest time, no one said a word. We were frozen with shock. Paramedics and even more police officers – about five or so more – came streaming past us, but we stayed still. I felt as if I were in a nightmare and needed to wake up. I couldn't think straight. Nothing made sense. Who would want to hurt them? Why just them? And why hadn't we heard anything?

"We slept through the whole thing," I said. Hearing it aloud made it even more unbelievable. "Do you think they shouted for us?"

"Don't," Kyle said, wrapping his arm around me. I fell against his side, giving in to my body's need to shut down. He stroked my hair, and I was done for. I burst into tears, shamelessly gripping his shirt.

I could feel my body shaking, and I was freezing. It was warm inside, and the fire was still lightly burning from last night, but I felt as if I had slept out in the cold.

We sat in the lounge in silence, waiting for the police to do whatever it was they did. The door to the kitchen had been closed so we could no longer see anything, and we were told not to go back in there. The room was a crime scene now. Upstairs was off limits too so we couldn't get our things, but we were told the police were taking that anyway. I didn't know why. Why were they looking for something in our stuff?

"I want to leave," Megan whispered, clenching her fists over and over and shaking her head. "I want to leave."

So did I, but we weren't allowed to. "Why didn't we hear anything?" I repeated. Surely we would have heard someone breaking in and stabbing two of our friends! "Do any of you remember?" No one answered me, so I assumed they hadn't, or they just weren't listening to me. I barely remembered anything after Josh and Aaron's argument – the one where Aaron told Josh he would kill him if he mentioned Tilly's name again. I already knew I wasn't going to tell the police that. I didn't want to get him into trouble.

Blake stood up, and everyone's eyes followed him to the front window. The police officer, our guard, turned his body to face him straight on, letting him know he was still watching. "We couldn't have been that drunk. None of us drank enough to be that out of it during a fucking murder!" he said.

"Well no one heard anything!" Kyle said.

Blake spun around. "I'm aware of that, Kyle. What I don't get is why. Or how."

The kitchen door opened, and the shaved hair detective raised his eyebrows. He walked into the room, carrying himself as if he owned the place. "We need to have a little chat."

One by one, we all shared a quick glance. That meant something. We had told him what happened – well the boys had – so why did he say 'we need to have a chat' as if he didn't believe what they had said?

I watched him silently as he walked to the fire and stood in front of it. He was the focal point of the room. Clicking his tongue, he said, "I'll get the pleasantries out of the way first, I'm DI Wright. Now with that over, the door was unlocked for us this morning, wasn't it?"

"Yes," Aaron replied, frowning at the stupid question asked.

Wright clicked his tongue again. "The back door in the kitchen is locked too. When was it locked?"

"Last night," I said, remembering that one. "Courtney locked it before we started drinking. Why?"

"Hmm, that's what I thought. Mr Harper," Wright said to Blake. "The only doors are that one," he said, nodding to the front one beside Blake, "and the kitchen, correct?"

"Yeah," Blake replied.

"I can find no evidence of forced entry, and since both doors were locked, that leaves us with another possibility."

I frowned. "What's that?"

"One of you did it." He swung his arms behind his back. "So... who wants to confess?"

My heart stopped, and my mouth fell open.

## CHAPTER FIVE

"No," Megan whispered, shaking her head.

I couldn't believe it. I wouldn't. None of my friends were murderers. We all had our issues with Josh, sure, but none of us wanted him to die. And Courtney, she was perfect, sweet, funny, and loyal. She was the best friend anyone could ask for. No one hated her. This was a random attack. It had to be. There had to be someone else.

"No. You need to keep looking. There must be somewhere they could have got in," I said, shaking my head. "Blake, you know this place better than anyone—"

Blake shook his head. "They've checked the doors, Mackenzie. I watched them. There is no other way in."

"That can't be true!" I insisted and turned to the hostile looking officers. "The windows!"

"Are all closed and locked and have been since you arrived, so I'm told," Wright replied. "No one could get into the property without breaking in."

"Please keep looking." I couldn't believe one of my friends had done it. Was it not enough to have lost them? Now we were accused of being the ones that had done it.

"They don't need to keep looking, Mackenzie. We know who did it," Aaron said and stared at Blake.

"Don't be an arsehole, Aaron," I replied. Josh was Blake's brother; he had more to lose than all of us.

Kyle stepped closed to Aaron, backing him up. "Who was it then, Kenz? Come on; was it one of your friends or the creepy stranger?"

Blake said nothing. Why wasn't he saying anything? He wasn't defending himself.

"It was none of us! The police reveal one stupid theory and you start turning on each other." I shook my head. I thought I knew my friends better than that. I thought our friendship was stronger than that. "Will you all please stop this so we can figure out what happened to Josh and Courtney? The way you're all acting is disgusting. We need to stick together, not rip each other apart."

"She's right," Megan said. "I don't believe any of you could do this."

I felt Blake's eyes burning into the side of my head, but I didn't meet his gaze. I refused to believe I spent a whole day and night with a murderer. Even though we didn't know him, I didn't believe he was capable of killing two people in cold blood.

Wright clicked his tongue. "As interesting as all this is, I need you to get into the cars now." I felt naked under his intense glare. It was clear he thought one of us did it. "We're all taking a trip to the station," he said, pursing his lips, "and then my colleagues are going to search every inch of this house." He nodded towards the front door and walked out.

I sat in a small interview room, biting my lip. My fingertips were stained black from the ink. My mouth had been swabbed, and the underneath of my fingernails scraped. I wore a grey sweats and a plain white t-shirt as my clothes were being sent off for examination.

DI Wright and a female officer he had introduced as DI Lancer sat opposite me. I refused to have anyone else with me because it would seem like I had something to hide. I gulped as Wright opened his mouth to speak.

"Tell me again, Mackenzie, what happened last night?"

I shook my head. "I don't know. We were all drinking. God, we drank a lot. The last thing I remember is Blake waking me up from the sofa and..." I was going to have to admit that we'd slept together and I wasn't sure why it was embarrassing, it just was. I licked my dry lips. "We went upstairs. In the morning we woke up and went down. That's when we found… What we found."

"Where was everyone else when you and Blake went upstairs?"

"I think everyone but Megan was still in the living room. I didn't really see, I was drunk and preoccupied. I assume they were because they didn't want to get in an argument with Josh too."

"Argument?"

"Yeah, Megan and Josh had a disagreement about where to sleep and Blake told her to go up. Oh, Josh and Aaron fought about it too."

"They physically fought?"

"No."

"What was the argument about?"

"Megan and Josh's?"

He blinked hard as if I had asked a stupid question. There were two arguments. How was I supposed to magically know which one he was thinking of? "Yes."

"Um. Courtney wanted everyone to crash downstairs, but Megan wanted a bed. Josh told Megan that it was his house, and she had to sleep where he said. Blake stepped in and told her to go to bed. It was nothing really."

"What was Joshua's argument with Aaron over?"

I bit my lip, watching the tape spinning around in the black, rectangle box, recording our conversation. "Josh said something about Aaron dumping Tilly before the accident." I frowned, was that it? "I think. He spits that out occasionally. I can't remember exactly what they said, but they shouted and then Courtney told them to stop."

"And then?"

"And then we went back to drinking."

"Why did Courtney want everyone downstairs?" he asked.

I shrugged. "She said we should all drink until we dropped. I don't think she really cared if anyone wanted to go to bed though."

"But Josh did?"

"Josh is Josh." Was Josh. He wasn't an 'is' anymore.

Wright's bushy eyebrows pulled together. "What does that mean exactly? What was Josh like?"

"He didn't really care about anyone other than himself. He liked to be the big man, and we were all supposed to be in debt to him for organising things like the trip." I dropped my eyes to the table. "And the Theme park weekend."

"Was that the one that ended in the car accident?" he asked. "Two people died that day, is that correct? Tilly Moss and Giana Beaucoup."

"Yes," I whispered. "How did you know that?" Tilly and Gigi were at the back left of the minivan, right where the lorry hit.

"It's a small town, Mackenzie." He leant forwards, resting his elbows on the table. "Josh organised the trip which led to two of your friends' deaths."

"I know where you're going with this. No one blames Josh for what happened, it was an accident." We just blamed him for how he behaved and what he said after.

"How can you be so sure your friends feel the same way? It would seem that Megan hasn't forgiven him. Aaron too."

"Not forgiving someone is one thing, murder is another. None of my friends are capable of murder."

He sighed. "So that brings us back to you."

I gulped. My palms began to sweat. "I did not murder them."

"Let's talk about your relationship with Courtney Young for a minute. You'd been friends how long?"

I frowned at his use of past tense. Insensitive bastard! "About eight years. We met when we were eleven, in the first year of high school." We had met on the first day actually.

We sat next to each other because everyone else seemed to know someone. Neither of us had been put in a form with our friends from primary school, so we stuck together.

"And in that time have you had any fallings out?"

"A few, I guess. We never argued for long though. I think the longest we've ever gone without talking was three days." It was going to be longer now. I pressed my fingernails into the palms of my hands. Tears welled in my eyes. I would never hear her laugh or sing like a cat being strangled again.

He wrote something down, and I thought he was going to ask more questions like that, but he changed direction. "How long had Josh and Courtney been together?"

I shrugged. "Um. Just over a year."

"You don't seem too thrilled by your friend's relationship with Joshua, why is that?"

"Like I said before, Josh is a selfish person. He brought her down. She was so much more outgoing and confident before him. After they got together she didn't have her own voice or opinion, she just back up whatever he said or wanted. She deserved better." His eyebrows arched. "That doesn't mean I wanted anything bad to happen to him." Not that bad anyway.

"What happened after Tilly and Giana's death? From what I can gather, that's when the feud began."

"It wasn't a feud. He said some things that were insensitive."

"What things?"

"He said that at least it wasn't him and Courtney."

"That died in the crash?"

I nodded. "Yes. Of course I was glad everyone else was okay, but I don't know how he can place anyone else's life below his own. He also said the accident was Gigi's fault anyway because she got too drunk to drive so Court had to. Apparently that meant she deserved to die."

"And you hated him for it."

I played with the hem of my top in my lap. I didn't hurt anyone, but he was constantly leading me there, wanting me to admit to something I hadn't done. I wanted to tell the truth, but I was scared to. "Hate is a very strong word. I didn't ever want anything bad to happen to him, but I wished he would break up with Courtney and get out of our lives."

"How badly did you want him out of your life?"

"I didn't kill him!" Why wasn't he listening to me!

Wright's mouth twitched, and he leant forwards. His breath blew across my face. It smelt of stale tobacco mixed with mint. "I'm not saying you did it, but do you know who?"

"No, I swear, I don't. My friends didn't though. I know that much."

"Hmm," he murmured. "Did you each have a bedroom to yourself?"

"No. Megan and I were sharing; the others had a room each." But I stayed in Blake's.

"And you unpacked as soon as you arrived?"

"I did."

"Everyone else?"

I don't know. I'm not their mum! "I'm not sure. Megan didn't, she never does."

"Hmm." He clicked his tongue. What did that hmm mean? "Who had a key to either or both of the doors?"

"Josh."

"Just him?"

"I don't know. He didn't give anyone else on that I know of. Blake might have one, it being his lodge too."

I wanted to ask why, but something stopped me. Wright was intimidating. He looked like a powerful man. Tall, muscular, take no shit attitude and probably a bit in love with himself. Like one of those kids that were told every day that they're perfect, amazing, destined for greatness. Basically, someone that would come to realise that opinion was solely their parents' and they were, in fact, not perfect and would have to deal with people who were generally better at things than them. Courtney was a little like that at first and then she got with Josh. I preferred her before.

"You stayed with Blake all night?"

"Yes."

"He was still there when you woke?"

"Yes. I woke first."

He nodded once.

"What did you have to eat while you were there? Did you cook?"

The sudden change in direction worried me. I'd never been interview by police where they thought I could have done something wrong before. "We all cooked enchiladas."

"You all cooked?"

"We all helped, yeah."

Why the hell was that important?

He gave a short nod again. "And the drinks. I suppose you all got a round too?"

"Yes," I replied slowly. There was something I was missing. And it was probably so obvious Wright was screaming at me in his head, come on, Mackenzie, I'm asking because… But I had no idea what that because meant.

"So you all drank, you fell asleep and when you woke Joshua and Courtney were—"

"Yes," I replied quickly before he could say dead on the kitchen floor out loud.

"Not a peep in the night, huh?"

"No."

He arched his bushy caterpillar eyebrow. "I think that's it for now. You're free to go back to the waiting room with the others."

Already? He looked at me and half-smiled. *He's not done with me at all.* I stood up and walked out of the room, anxious to get back to my friends and make sure they were okay. Megan's emotions ruled her, and I was worried she would be falling apart.

"Okay?" Blake asked, pulling the door open for me.

I shook my head. "Not really." Megan sat on the chair, curled up in a ball; Kyle's arms were around her, rocking her like a child. I knelt down. "Megan?"

Her body trembled. "She's not said anything since she came out of being questioned," Kyle said. "How'd it go?"

"He thinks it was one of us," I replied, looking between my friends and Josh's brother. Blake had moved to the other side of the room. He stood against the wall, looking out of the window, acting as if he was alone.

Kyle followed my gaze to Blake. "Maybe it was," he whispered. I shook my head. We couldn't turn against each other. We had to stick together until the police found out who was really responsible.

I was about to speak up and defend Blake when Wright came back into the room. His arm stretched out as he opened the door wide. "We're going to do a drug test on you too, Mackenzie," he announced as if he had just said we're going to get you a cup of tea.

"What? Why do you need to do that?" I asked. He hadn't mentioned that before. I thought they had finished with the tests.

Oh that was the *because*.

He rubbed the dark stubble under his chin. "Standard procedure, especially when I have two murdered teens and five more claiming to remember nothing. Take a seat, Miss Keaton, Mr Harper." He closed the door half way, having a conversation with someone on the other side.

Blake sat on the faux leather chairs, staring into space. I took a seat between him and Megan. "This is like a dream," Megan whispered.

"A nightmare," I countered. "Have you both been in yet?"

Blake shook his head. "Aaron went first." He looked up. "Did they tell you what they're testing for?"

"This is the first I've heard of it. Drug test though, so everything." I shrugged. "I really don't know. I've never had to do a drug test before. This is crazy." Did they test for every drug or just the most common ones? "Have you seen your mum yet?" I asked Megan.

She shook her head, sobbing. "I-I think they're all here, or they've been called, but we can't see them until we've done this anyway." Her voice wobbled as she tried to talk through crying.

Blake stood up and walked to the window again. He leant on the windowsill, deep in thought. He was going to face his parents soon, and they were going to have a lot more to deal with than getting him through this – they had also lost a son.

"Megan, come with me," Wright said, poking his head round the door.

Megan shot me a look as if to say either *wish me luck* or *help* and left the room. She looked terrified; dark circles dominated her eyes, making them shrink into the sockets.

I ran through everything in my head for the millionth time. Once I'd fallen asleep there was nothing. No noise in the night that disturbed me and I ignored. Surely if they were being murdered they would have made a noise. They had to have made a noise. Courtney would have screamed, and her scream could wake someone from a coma.

The door opening and Kyle being summoned broke me away from going over it all again. Wright was calling us himself. Why wouldn't he send an officer to do that? Did he need that much control that he did the shit jobs himself too?

I sat back and closed my eyes. There was nothing new I could remember, and it scared me that so much of the evening was either a blur or completely missing. That didn't look good. We couldn't have been drugged. No one else was in the house, unless it had been done before we left for the weekend. By who though?

"Blake, are you okay?" I asked once we were alone.

He shook his head. "Me and Josh..." Shaking his head again, he turned to me. My breath caught in my throat. He looked so haunted, almost as if he was in physical pain. *You and Josh what?*

"What, Blake?"

"This is going to kill my mum. She'll wish it was me."

I blinked in shock. Sure Blake had decided to live with his father, but that didn't mean she didn't love him as much as Josh. "No, that's not true."

I gulped. He looked as if he was in despair; his eyes were on fire. I knew in that moment he really believed what he said was true. He really believed his mum loved his brother more and would prefer him to be dead. "She wouldn't want it to be you."

"No, she wouldn't *want* it. But she would want it to be Josh a hell of a lot less."

"Blake, come with me," Wright ordered.

He walked out without another word or even a glance in my direction.

When it was my turn, I was lead into a small room with a black table like they had at the doctors. "Sit down, this won't take long," a lady told me. She didn't introduce herself.

"Thanks," I said, taking a seat.

"Roll your sleeve up."

My eyes widened. "This is a blood test?" I hated blood tests and needles.

"Yes. Roll your sleeve up, please."

I wanted to ask if it was voluntary, but I suspected not. I pulled my sleeve up and looked away, biting on my bottom lip. They were never as bad as I worked myself up to believe, but I still hated having it done. "What are you testing for?"

"Drugs," she replied bluntly.

Weren't they required to tell you what it was exactly if you asked? I didn't push it and question her further; I just wanted to hurry up and get out. I needed to see my parents and go home. What was supposed to be a chilled out, drunken weekend, messing around with my friends had ended up with murder, blood and police stations. It was as if I were on a TV show.

The needle stabbed at my skin and pierced its way through. I held my breath. I could feel a stinging pain as she extracted my blood. This is nothing compared to what

Courtney went through. I swallowed the lump in my throat. Had she been in pain long? Did she pray for death?

"Alright," she said, gently pulling the needle out and placing a cotton wool ball over the tiny hole. "All done. You can wait with your friends in the front. I believe your parents will be here soon." Thank God!

"Okay, thanks," I replied and hurried out of the room.

Wiping my tears, I stepped through the door and into the entrance area. Aaron, Kyle and Megan sat on the chairs by the front door. I sat beside a shaking Megan and rubbed my arms, suddenly feeling the cold.

"Where's Blake?" I asked.

Megan nodded to the door. "Speaking to his dad on the phone. He's in Hong Kong, apparently, and trying to get a flight back."

"He doesn't even seem that upset," Aaron said, watching Blake through the glass. "What does that tell you?"

"That he's just seen his brother's dead body and he's in shock. Same as us," I replied.

How could Aaron judge him like that? There was no set way you had to react when you lost someone you loved. Everyone reacted to grief and loss differently. I surprised myself by being too calm. When it was Tilly and Gigi I was a mess. But I saw them die. I watched Tilly cry until she fell silent and I heard Gigi whisper something unintelligible before her eyes closed. This time was different. Better and worse in different ways. This time everything was up in the air and having me and my friends accused overshadowed everything else.

Aaron shook his head. "Why do you have to try to see good in everyone?" Why was that a bad thing? I frowned. "It's pathetic, Mackenzie."

"That's enough!" Kyle said.

Aaron sighed heavily and said, "Shit. I'm sorry, Kenz, I shouldn't have said that. I guess it's not a bad thing." I could tell by how tight and tense his eyes were that it almost hurt him to apologise. Aaron was stubborn and hated to admit he was wrong. Some of his ideas had screwed him over, but he still went steaming ahead, choosing making the problem worse rather than admitting he was wrong and moving on.

Wright walked up to us, owning the room. I felt as if he was trying to pull the truth from our minds. "You're all free to go," he said, "but don't go far." Turning on his heel, he walked out. I would have thought he would keep us in, questioning us for hours. His tactics were odd and unnerving.

I stood and took a deep breath. What were my parents going to think? I knew they would believe me when I told them I didn't hurt Josh or Courtney, but would they believe none of us had? I needed them to be on my side and trust that I knew my friends.

I followed Aaron and Kyle out; Megan trailed behind in a daze. My hands shook as Kyle pushed open the door. All of our parents stood outside talking to two officers. My dad looked like he was about to punch one of them and run in to find me. Mum's eyes were red and blotchy, standing out against her unusually pale skin. I gulped as her eyes fell on me.

"Oh, Mackenzie," Mum said, her voice broken and full of emotion. I stumbled forwards; my legs barely carried me forwards and into her arms. "Shh, it's okay," she whispered softly and stroked my hair.

# CHAPTER SIX

I sat in my lounge with my parents, Megan, Aaron, Kyle and their parents, Blake and his grandparents. His dad wasn't here. I didn't know why but I didn't want to ask. His mum was a mess.

My dad, who had taken charge, sat on the footstool, facing everyone. We looked like we were having a meeting about the five of us bunking off school rather than how we were going to deal with Courtney and Josh's murder and the investigation.

The other dads and Blake's grandad had gripped the situation by both hands and were ploughing off into what should happen and what we should do. Leave this to the men. They were determined to fix things for their families.

Blake said nothing, not one word other than a grunted hi when he arrived twenty minutes ago. I felt sorry for him; he was the only one that didn't have both parents there for him, he didn't have one parent.

Megan huddled up under her dad's arm like a small child that was afraid of everything. Aaron and Kyle acted their usual we'll-fix-it-and-be-strong-for-the-girls selves. A hug wouldn't do it this time though. Kyle spent days at mine when Tilly and Gigi died trying to help me and I loved having him there but this was different, we were being accused of killing Courtney and Josh. One of us could go down for something we hadn't done and nothing would make that okay.

"We don't know if they have found the clothes the murderer was wearing or the knife used so until something turns up to prove their innocence, they are looking at any one of them," Dad said. "We need you all to be straight with us, did you let anyone else in the cabin? I know we said not to but—"

"No, Dad," I replied. Getting in trouble for having someone over was so far down on the list compared to being accused of murder. "We've told you it was just us. Aaron and Megan went for a walk and then Blake and me did. After that, we all stayed in. We drank, had some dinner and drank some more. When we woke up we found them."

"I just don't understand how you didn't hear anything," Megan's mum, Judy said.

Aaron leant forwards. "We were all out of it on booze."

I looked away as my dad's brow creased at Aaron's words. His little girl wasn't supposed to get off her face. "Hmm, was it only alcohol?" Dad questioned.

"What?" I asked, blinking in shock. Was he really asking if we were druggies? "Dad, yes!"

"It just seems very strange that anyone could be so out of it on alcohol that they heard nothing, let alone five people. We need to know now if you've taken drugs."

"Dad!"

"Mackenzie, you won't be in trouble if you have, we just need to know."

"Honestly, Mr Keaton," Blake said, "we didn't touch any drugs." Hearing Blake call someone by their title and surname was weird, too polite.

Dad nodded once. "Okay, I believe you."

"They'll realise it wasn't us soon though, won't they?" Megan whispered from between her parents.

"I hope so, Megan," Dad replied, "but until then we need to get a few things straight. Lawyers."

"I don't think that's a good idea yet," Kyle said. "That makes us looks guilty."

Dad smiled. "I agree, Kyle. It's something we need to consider and research though, but for now I think it's best that we don't hire anyone. We need to show the police and the community that you have nothing to hide."

"But shouldn't they have someone present when they're being questioned?" Aaron's mum asked.

"I'm not sure that sends out the right message," Dad said. "We want to show the police especially that there's no need for anyone else to be present. They have nothing to hide and they won't trip up because they're innocent."

The community, people that had watched me grow up and been there at my christening, birthdays, waved as I set off for prom now thought I could be a killer. I couldn't go out of the house without people staring. No one ever said anything to my face, but I could feel their words creeping over me like a swarm of ants. I had never been so disappointed in people before.

"We need to get the locals behind you more so you all need to continue going out and doing what you do. Go to the funerals as you normally would. I know some of you expressed some concern over attending, but you have as much right as everyone else to say goodbye to your friends. Don't act guilty because you're afraid of what people think." Dad paused to look at us.

"And that goes for me too?" Blake asked, frowning almost sarcastically.

"Yes," Dad replied. "I know people don't know you but don't shut yourself off because you're the most likely one to have done it."

My dad was a pretty good judge of character so the fact that he didn't think Blake was responsible backed up what I already knew. I had been told from a very young age that your gut instinct was usually right and listening to it had saved me a few times. If I hadn't listened to it about Arsehole Ashley, I would have been the one to be cheated on, rather than the poor victim he asked out when I turned him down.

"What about enemies of Joshua and Courtney?" Judy asked. "It doesn't make sense that it was random because only they were harmed, right?"

"Yeah, I guess," I replied, forcing the thought from my head. It could have been random, and Josh and Courtney were just the only ones to have caught them sneaking in. We were out of it, so there was no point in killing us too.

"Well, does anyone know of any?" she asked. "Nothing little and silly, it has to have been something big to kill for. I know Joshua made a few enemies after Giana and Tilly died, but I don't think those were anything too serious. There can't be many people with a strong grudge."

"I can't think of any that would go that far," Aaron replied.

"Me neither," I said. Kyle shrugged, and Megan shook her head. "No one at school or uni hated either of them that much."

Dad rubbed his forehead – something he did when he was deep in thought and trying hard to figure something out. It was his tax return and helping me with my university applications face. "Okay, let's go through this one more time, so we're all on the same page. When you got to the cabin you unpacked, Aaron and Megan and then Blake and Mackenzie were the only ones to leave, right?"

Aaron nodded and replied, "Yeah, we went for a walk in the forest."

"How long were you away for?"

"I dunno, about half an hour."

"It was more like forty-five minutes," Megan said, correcting Aaron.

Dad rubbed his head again. "Okay. And you didn't see anyone or anything?"

"Just trees, a shed, the other lodge in the distance and the lake."

They must have walked quite far then; there were only five lodges at the park, and they were spaced really far apart. If Blake's parents sold theirs now, they would be rollin' in it.

"Right, the rest of you were doing what while they were out?"

I bit my lip. "Drinking."

His eyes tightened. He knew I drank; they both did, but not so irresponsibly. "I see. So you unpacked and drank?"

"Yes," I whispered. "Megan and Aaron came back, we continued drinking, Blake and I went out for about an hour, then we all made dinner, ate, and drank again."

"And no one left the lodge at any point in the evening? Not even to take some rubbish out?"

"No."

"And no one came by?"

"No."

Dad sighed. "Did you see or meet anyone on the way there? Tell anyone you don't know where you were going?"

I shook my head. "No."

"Who knew where you were? Just family?"

Kyle scoffed. "Everyone, literally. We had posts and pictures all over Facebook. I think Courtney even checked-in."

"Checked-in?" Dad asked.

I rolled my eyes. "It's a Facebook thing, Dad. You can check in using your location."

"And everyone can see where you are?" he asked, raising his voice and his eyebrows. Uh oh. "Mackenzie, I—"

Holding my hands up, I felt my face heat at being nineteen and getting told off in front of my friends. "Okay, I got it. I won't do it." I had no desire to tell the whole world my every movement anyway. "Can we move on?"

He shook his head as if to say *the youth of today* and raised his hands. My dad was a hand gesturer. "So you're at a cabin in the woods that we now know anyone could have found you at. You saw no one else and let no one in. Now we need to ask ourselves who would have wanted to follow you there."

Megan's mum shook her head and dabbed under her eyes. No one had properly cried yet, besides Megan. I thought being here and going over everything someone would. We were all still in shock, but for how long? Soon enough we would have to face what was happening properly, and DI Wright had only just started. What if one of us went down for something we hadn't done? I gulped and looked up at my dad, praying the man that fixed all of my problems growing up would be able to solve this one too.

# CHAPTER SEVEN

I could feel all eyes on us. It had been that way for the last four days. Wherever I went people watched me, whispering things like 'there she is', 'it can't be her' or 'it's usually the nice ones'. Women that spent their days drinking tea with my mum while they planed yet another village fete crossed the street when they saw me.

Josh's mum, Eloise had welcomed us into her house for the wake, knowing we weren't the ones that hurt them, but his other relatives seemed quick to judge and assume. Megan gripped my hand; she hadn't looked up since we walked through the door.

I thought the police would want their bodies longer but apparently not. I was always surprised by how quickly people were buried, but I suppose you wouldn't want to leave them too long. The healing process could start once you had said goodbye – something my mum swore by. I disagreed. The funeral was the goodbye, but after you had to piece your life back together and find a way of dealing with the absence of that person. The after the goodbye was the hardest bit.

"We shouldn't have come here," Kyle whispered, darting his hazel eyes around the room. He was nervous and on edge.

I frowned. "We have as much right as everyone else. We've done nothing wrong, and we're allowed to say goodbye too."

"But his family clearly don't want us here," Aaron added, speaking through his teeth.

"We won't stay long. Just long enough to show Eloise and Blake we're here for them."

Aaron scoffed. "We should be looking a little closer at Blake."

Rolling my eyes, I replied, "Why's that?"

"Who is the most likely killer, Mackenzie?"

I shrugged. "I don't know. Some crazy guy out in the woods that somehow got in and—"

Kyle sighed sharply. "No one got in though. Aaron's right, it has to be Blake."

"It's not him, Kyle."

"Why not? What's going on with you two?"

"What? Nothing's going on. Josh is his brother. I'm sorry if I don't believe the guy we spent a day with is capable of killing his own brother!" I shook my head. Every time anyone mentioned it was one of us I became defensive. How could they think that? I worried they thought it could be me. Would that ever cross one of their minds? I hoped they knew me better.

"They're not close, and he clearly didn't like Josh," Megan said.

"Well neither did we! Look, let's not do this here. After Courtney's funeral tomorrow, we should do something else. A formal wake isn't what she would want," I said to change the subject. They didn't know that I'd slept with Blake and right now I didn't want them to. It was sort of a forgotten subject with Blake too. There was just too much going on to have that talk.

Courtney's funeral was going to be hard. I didn't want to go and be forced to acknowledge that I wouldn't see her again, but I had to. At Tilly and Gigi's funerals, me, Megan and Courtney clung to each other, supporting each other. Now it was just me and Megan, and as hard as Megan tried she wasn't good at supporting, she was too emotionally selfish.

She nodded, her hair moving today as she toned down on the hairspray, probably because she couldn't be bothered. "Okay. Can we just go soon? Please."

"In a bit," I replied. "For Josh we should stay a little while, unless Eloise asks us to leave."

Josh and Blake's dad wasn't here. He hadn't been able to get back in time and Eloise refused to wait. He was due to arrive in the UK later tonight. I felt so sorry for him missing his own son's funeral. Eloise should have waited. It was wrong and selfish of her not to. She should have put Josh before her hatred for her ex-husband. I could tell Blake wanted his dad here, he was surrounded by family, but he barely knew any of them.

Out of the corner of my eye I saw Blake get up and leave the room. "I'll be back in a minute," I said. He had barely said a word the whole morning, just one-word answers or grunts.

He was in the hallway when I found him, looking up at a large collage of pictures in a huge glass frame. Without looking at me, he said, "I'm only in three of these." There had to be over sixty pictures, and he was right, they were all of Josh with the exception of three, which included Blake too.

"I'm sorry."

"Don't be sorry, Mackenzie, it's not your fault. He was her favourite, always had been. Even when we were all together, she preferred him. It was always her little 'Joshie'. He was the last child she was going to have, so she put everything into him, and I was left with next to fuck all."

I gulped at the tone in his voice. He sounded bitter. I found that understandable though. He felt like his mum didn't love him and favoured his brother, but Josh was dead now. Stuff in the past shouldn't matter when someone had died, or perhaps I just didn't know how it felt and how deep this feeling of inadequacy ran for Blake.

I looked around, trying to casually see if anyone had heard us, but we were alone. I knew his words would make my friends think it was him even more. He may have resented his mum and brother, but that didn't make him a killer.

"She loves you. Blake, Josh is gone now; you and your mum have to support each other."

"Why?" He arched his eyebrow and looked into my eyes. I gulped at the fierceness of his smouldering blue eyes. "She was never there for me. She was *never* there."

"You've both lost so much. You should use this as a chance to bring you both closer together. Don't let Josh's death be for nothing."

"But it was for nothing. I feel like I'm at a stranger's funeral in a stranger's house." His eyes narrowed. "I don't want a relationship with her." He turned and walked back into the lounge, leaving me speechless. How could he say that? I didn't believe it for a second. He wouldn't look so beat up if he didn't care.

"Kenz," Aaron said, stroking his hand down my back.

I jumped at the sudden contact. It took me a minute to recover from Blake's words. "Yeah?" I replied, finally looking up.

"I know you're going to go off on one about Blake again, but please hear me out."

I rolled my eyes. "This is getting old, Aaron."

"Please," he repeated. Sighing, I waved my hand, agreeing to listen. "Okay. Did you know he was kicked out of his old high school?"

"So?"

"For fighting."

"Lots of guys get into fights at some point in high school. I don't think we should condemn him for that."

"Don't you think it's even a little bit strange that he, the delinquent, turns up suddenly and the next morning we wake up to… what we woke up to?"

"No, I think there was some mad man running around in the woods and saw an opportunity. Or maybe he wanted to stay somewhere not knowing anyone was in; perhaps Josh and Courtney startled him."

"I get that you don't want to believe it. I don't either, but what other feasible option is there? We know no one else got in. Will you at least consider it?"

I shook my head. "No."

Aaron sighed in defeat. "Let's go back in." I walked ahead and heard him add, 'you'll wake up soon,' under his breath. I ignored him. He could think whatever he wanted; it wouldn't change what I knew.

Aaron and I joined Kyle and Megan back in our corner out of the way. I could feel everyone's eyes on us, but I refused to look at them, knowing I would just see blame and hate in their gaze. I didn't understand how so many people who had watched us grow up could suddenly believe we were capable of murder. Thankfully I didn't know too many people here, but the few I did acted as if I could give them the plague and avoided me.

"Just a little longer," Kyle whispered, tightening his arms around Megan.

Blake entered the room again, holding a large glass of amber liquor. He sat on the opposite side, between us and his mum. All day he had barely spoken to anyone, and I noticed his family didn't make much of an effort to talk to him, except for his paternal grandparents. No wonder he felt Josh was the favourite.

"Okay, can you at least promise me to be careful around him?" Aaron said, looking past me to Blake.

My heart gave a little squeeze. He was worried about me. "Aaron, I'll be fine."

"Promise me, Mackenzie."

"I promise."

"And you'll call me if you're ever around him and don't feel safe?"

I frowned. Did he honestly, truly believe it was Blake? "I will," I whispered. How on earth was I going to get them on his – our – side? We were all in this together. He nodded once and walked away, towards Josh's cousin, Greg. I was left speechless for a second time. I felt as if I was being pulled in two directions had to pick a team. We are all on the same team!

I looked over at Eloise, and my heart broke for her. She stared at a framed picture of Josh that sat on the small end table beside her. I wanted to go over and say something, but what did you say to a woman that had just buried her son?

Blake watched his mum. He looked torn, lost even. She was his mum, but he looked as clueless as I was when it came to speaking to her. Screw this! I wasn't giving up on him that easily, and I wasn't letting him push me away like he seemed to do with everyone else.

I walked across the room, noticing his eyes following me as I sat beside him. "Hey," I said. Despite what Aaron and Kyle said, I believed him. He may be the odd one out, but that didn't mean it was him.

"Hi." He leant down, leaning his elbows on his knees. "She won't even look at me now," he said, paying no attention to our last conversation. I wasn't sure what to say. "Last night when I asked her if she wanted me to do the reading for her, she looked at me like..." He shook his head and sighed. "I don't even know how to explain the look, but I could see in her eyes that she was burying the wrong son."

Not again. "Don't say that."

"It's true. I don't blame her; she spent Josh's whole life with him. I was the one that didn't choose her."

"That doesn't mean she loves you any less."

He turned his head to the side and looked up at me. "The glass is always half-full in Mackenzie's world, isn't it?"

"Does it look half-full?"

"You're trying to make it. That's why you won't accept one of them did it," he said, nodding to the corner where my friends stood. "Josh and Courtney are dead, but if you can prove your friends are innocent... Half-full."

"You're way too cynical. Do you trust anyone?"

"Myself."

"That doesn't count."

He sat up straight and shrugged. "Then no."

"That's really sad."

"If you don't trust anyone then no one can screw you over. You're going to find that out the hard way," he said and stood up, walking out of the room.

I wrapped my arms around myself. His words hit me hard. Kyle was right; we shouldn't have come here. I walked into the kitchen to get my coat so we could leave. We all needed to be far away from here.

"Which one of you was it?" Josh's uncle, Pete spat. Pete and my dad were friends so the way he looked at me with so much hate made feel like shit. "Which one of you bastards killed my nephew?"

I shook my head, pressing my back against the marble counter. Was he going to hit me? His face was red with rage and his eyes were wide. A bubble of saliva had gathered in both corners of his mouth.

"None of us, Pete, I swear," I replied. "We wouldn't."

"You have the audacity to turn up at his funeral!"

"We haven't done anything wrong."

"Tell the truth," he hissed through his teeth. "Tell the police what you did."

"Pete, please—"

"No," he growled, making me flinch back. He looked so angry, so furious that I wasn't sure how far he would go. "There couldn't have been anyone else. If you had any decency at all, you would own up and put an end to our family's misery. Joshua deserves justice."

*So does Courtney.* "I want that too. You're looking in the wrong place, Pete. I promise you we didn't do this."

"Your promises mean nothing to me, Mackenzie. My sister might not see what you've done to her son, but I sure can. You will pay—"

"Hey," Kyle snapped. "That's enough." He wrapped his arm around me, pulling me against his side protectively.

"I'm sorry you lost your nephew, but we lost two friends, and this wasn't our fault."

"You're all liars. You'll rot in hell for this."

"Pete!" I said. It was so unlike him. The once joke-a-minute man that had me in stitches growing up was cold and hateful. "I understand you want someone to blame, I do too, but we didn't hurt him." I wasn't sure if he would ever believe me. I could tell him a million times that it wasn't us, but he was so wrapped up in what the police said and needing someone to blame that he couldn't see clearly.

"Get. Out," he said very slowly. "Don't ever come back here again."

"Come on," Kyle muttered, guiding me out of the door. Aaron and Megan stood in the hallway with wide eyes. "We're going."

I didn't see Blake before we left, a quick glance in the lounge on my way out told me no one in there had heard Pete's outburst. For that, I was grateful. I didn't want any doubt setting in for anyone else.

"What are we going to do?" I asked as we walked to Kyle's car, still holding onto myself.

No one had an answer for me because they all knew until we found out who had done it we were all screwed.

# CHAPTER EIGHT

"What the hell is he doing here?" Kyle said, frowning at someone in the distance, behind the curtain of leafless, skeleton trees at the side of the graveyard. The trees had died years ago but were never removed. I found it morbidly appropriate. Kyle's tear-stained face hardened.

I turned and though glossy eyes saw DI Wright standing just far enough away from the congregation for it to be obvious that he wasn't here to be a part of the funeral. He wore a black suit and tie, so he looked as if he belonged, but his eyes focused solely on us and not the hole in the ground that Courtney was about to be lowered into.

I shiver ran through me. Today of all days he had to show. I just wanted Courtney's funeral to run smoothly and be filled with the people she loved and cared about and those who cared about her. Wright hanging around made it all about what happened and not saying goodbye. It was hard enough without having that constant reminder that we were was in the frame.

"Can't he give us one day?" Megan said from behind me. He hadn't turned up at Josh's funeral though, so why Courtney's? Did that mean something or was he just bored today?

"He's trying to catch a murderer, Megan." Blake's voice made me jump. He stepped in front of us and looked back at Wright. "Gotta keep an eye on his main suspects."

"What're you doing here?" I asked. Courtney wasn't really anyone to him. I hadn't expected him to come.

"Paying my respects on my brother's behalf," he replied. "I decided to stay with my mum for a while too. She's a mess." I blinked in shock. He ignored my obvious surprise. He did care. "I'm actually the worse person to be around for her though. I don't do emotional women."

"I'm sorry, Blake," I said.

He shrugged. "It's okay."

"How's your dad?"

"Better than Mum but a mess too. They had the I-can't-believe-you-made-me-miss-my-son's-funeral-how-fucking-selfish-are-you-Eloise argument about three seconds after he arrived. Two seconds later than I thought so that's progress."

There was nothing I could say to that. Sorry again maybe? I was with him on that one. Eloise should have waited for Josh's dad no matter what she felt for him.

"Look, after this we're all going to the basketball court, you want to come?" From the look on Aaron's face and the daggers he was shooting at me, he didn't want Blake there, but this wasn't about Aaron.

Blake frowned. "I thought the wake was at the social club?"

I nodded. "It is, but we decided to do something else. We hung out at the courts a lot." I raised my eyebrow. "And drank there a lot. It seemed more... fitting."

Blake pulled his lip between his teeth and cocked his head to the side. Finally, after thinking it through, he replied, "Okay. Thanks."

I smiled, glad he'd accepted. He had no one around here, besides his mum, but she wasn't in any state to support him properly right now. His parents were both grieving so they couldn't give him what he needed. As much of a mysterious loner Blake was, he needed someone.

My attention turned returned to Courtney when her mum started reading her a bedtime story, the way she did when Courtney was a child. I blinked hard. My eyes filled with tears. It was her last and final goodnight. The story being read was Little Red Riding Hood, which I remembered Courtney telling me was her favourite childhood book.

I took in a deep shaky breath and my hands trembled. With every word spoken, I could feel her pain of losing her child, her only child. "This isn't fair," I whispered and started crying. Why was this happening to us? Why did we lose two more friends? I felt as if I had swallowed a football the lump in my throat was so large. This shouldn't be happening.

My legs were weak. I could barely hold myself up. Courtney was my best friend, and now I would never see her again. My heart broke as her coffin disappeared out of sight, into the ground. *No, no, no, no.* My lungs tightened. I couldn't breathe.

Blake's arm snaked around my waist. He held me close to his side.

"We'll be alright," Aaron said, glaring at Blake. "I promise."

I turned my body, burying my head in Blake's hard chest. He said nothing to comfort me and I expected that was because he didn't know what to say. It didn't matter; I just needed to be held through the crushing grief of losing such a beautiful friend.

I couldn't watch another person I loved – someone so young with so much to give – be placed into the ground. It was hard enough with Tilly and Gigi; I never imagined I'd lose another friend so soon. Grandparents and parents you kind of knew you would lose when you were still sort-of young, but friends weren't supposed to go anywhere until you were well into your eighties.

"Can we leave now, please?" I asked as Courtney's family scattered dirt on her coffin. I wasn't sure how much longer I could keep it together, and I couldn't fall apart, not while everything was so complicated and messy. When their murderer had been found, I would allow myself to grieve, until then I was determined to remain strong. They deserved justice. They needed people to fight for them not to fall apart.

"Yeah," Kyle replied, nodding towards the yellow stone path that lead to the cars. "Let's go to the courts and give Courtney the send-off she would actually want."

"Vodka and beer," Blake said, raising his eyebrow. "Classy."

Megan narrowed her eyes. "Do you want one or not?" He nodded in reply, and Megan handed him a beer. Blake was right; it wasn't classy, and it was very stereotypical teens drinking at the park, but we had a laugh messing around and playing silly games. Everything was easier back then. Uncomplicated.

We sat in a circle on the grass beside the barely used basketball court, leaving one space for Courtney unintentionally. I didn't let myself think about this being our goodbye to her. I wasn't really ready to do that yet. There couldn't be a proper goodbye until I knew the person that killed her was behind bars.

"Should we say something?" I asked. "I feel like we should."

Aaron nodded and took a swig of his beer. "Why don't we all say something about them both? I'll start. Courtney was one of the most beautiful girls I've ever known, but she wasn't cocky with it. She was modest and that added to her beauty. Josh," Aaron said and laughed. "Well Josh was punching well above his weight, and he knew it. He loved her; though, as much as some of you doubt it, he did."

He meant me. I had never doubted he loved her, in his own way. But it wasn't enough; it wasn't real and pure. He didn't put her first. It wasn't true, unselfish love. He wouldn't have done what was best for her if it meant he lost out on something. He wanted to change her. If you really loved someone you accepted the bad parts too.

"I'll go now," Megan said, taking a shaky breath. "In the first year of high school, Courtney and I didn't get along. I felt that she was trying to drive a wedge between me Mackenzie, Tilly and Gigi. It was only when my first boyfriend dumped me that I realised I was wrong about her. Mackenzie was on holiday, Tilly and Gigi were busy, and Courtney came round with chocolate and a DVD. She was a good friend, and I'll miss her so much." She smiled sadly and took a deep breath. "Josh. Well Josh said some stupid, terrible things that I'm sure he regretted, but he wasn't an evil person. I wish I had the chance to tell him I forgive him." Megan looked to me. My turn.

I put my plastic cup of neat vodka down on the floor and frowned. "I'm not sure where to start. There are so many things I want to say. Courtney and I were pretty much inseparable all through high school, and I remember how excited we were that we had the same classes every year. She was always there and never judged me, or anyone for that matter. I couldn't have asked for a better friend, and I can't believe she doesn't get to grow up with us." Tears filled my eyes and the lump in my throat I swallowed felt like a football.

"We were supposed to rent a flat together. Remember, Megan? We were going to get a posh place in a nice part of the city."

Megan nodded. "Preferably one that overlooked a football club so we could watch them run around in shorts."

I laughed and wiped my eyes. That was Courtney's idea. "Yeah."

"What about Josh?" Blake said. "Aren't you going to say something about him?"

I nodded. "Of course. Blake, Josh and I had our differences, but I never wanted anything bad to happen to him. We were friends before." I frowned. Well, years ago, sort of. "I wish I got the chance to properly sort out our differences so things could go back to the way they were." Four years ago we hung around with the same group and although we weren't good friends we did speak. And then I couldn't tolerate him. And then he couldn't tolerate me.

Blake nodded once and opened his mouth to say something when Wright sat down beside him, completing the circle. Where the fuck did he come from? He just appeared! "Didn't fancy the wake then?" he asked.

"Not their one," Kyle replied. "Can we help you with anything?"

"You could tell me which one of you murdered your friends." He looked around, pinning each of us still with his icy gaze. "No? Worth a try, hey!" He threaded his fingers between each other. "I've just had the test results back."

"And?" Aaron said, glaring at him.

Wright was too arrogant. He had something about him, an aura, which oozed conference and made it seem as if he owned everything and everyone. I got the impression that he knew a lot more than he told us, and he waited until he felt it was the right time to share the information. He probably had the test results back days ago.

"Rohypnol."

My mouth hit the floor. "The date rape drug?"

Wright's lip curled at the side. "The very one, Mackenzie. You know it well?"

"Everyone's heard of it," I replied. It was often in the news. It was the reason I got the never-leave-your-drink-alone lecture from my parents whenever I went out. We were always hearing stories about women that woke up having been drugged and raped the previous night and had little recollection of how it all happened.

My blood ran cold. Someone had done that to us.

"Someone spiked us with Rohypnol!" Blake said. His voice was much louder than usual, showing his anger and disbelief. "Who?"

Wright shrugged. "Again, I was hoping one of you would be able to help me out with that, but I won't be holding my breath."

"Wait?" I said. "Did we all test positive?"

"Yes."

"Even Josh and Courtney?" Aaron asked.

"Yes," Wright replied. "Strange, wouldn't you say?"

My heart spiked with the glimmer of hope. "But that proves someone else did it then!" We were all in the clear. We were all drugged and the murderer used that as his, or her, or their chance.

"Nothing has changed, Mackenzie. All this proves is that this murder was well thought out. Premeditated. Whichever one of you has blood on your hands; you have done a very good job of covering your tracks. I'm impressed, drugging yourself too – after the murders, of course – and hiding among your friends is incredibly cleaver. I must say this though, as clever as you are I will find out which one of you is responsible." He pushed himself up and walked away. "Be seeing you real soon."

For the longest time, no one said a word. I think we were all too shocked to speak. I looked into the eyes of each of my friends, and I just couldn't see a killer, especially not one so callous.

"Is he seriously accusing one of us of spiking the rest, killing our friends and then covering it up?" Kyle spat.

"He's crazy," Aaron added. "He should be out there looking for the real killer, not making stupid, ridiculous accusations about us!" So he believed Blake was innocent now?

Megan shook her head; tears filled her eyes. "Someone planned this. How could you hate someone so much? Courtney was… she…" Megan trailed off, taking a deep breath. She wasn't able to finish her sentence, but I knew what she wanted to say.

There was someone out there who wanted Courtney and Josh dead so much they sat down and planned the whole thing. They even went as far as drugging us to make it possible.

I took a deep breath. "Okay," I said, trying to wrap my mind around the latest bomb Wright had dropped on us. "Do any of you know someone who Josh and Court had a problem with? Even if it was something stupid, you need to say now."

This had just stepped up another level. I knew Wright would love to pin it on one of us, and his latest theory that we drugged ourselves after murdering our friends would make sense if he could magic enough make-believe evidence or motive. There was no way I was letting one of my friends go down for something they hadn't done.

No one replied. I began to grow frustrated with them. Was I the only one desperately trying to figure this out? They didn't seem to understand what would happen if we didn't find the real killer. I didn't trust Wright to put as much effort into finding the real killer as he was putting into trying to force a confession from us. Though he must be.

"Guys, come on! I need you all to help me. We can figure this out. We knew them better than anyone else. You know what's going to happen if we don't, right?"

"Yes, Mackenzie, I think we're all aware of Wright's fascination with us being the big bad, but what do you really think we can do? None of us have a fucking clue how to catch a murderer," Aaron said, raising his eyebrows. In the sun, you could barely see the light blonde hair sitting above his eyes.

I frowned. "So we should just give up and accept it?"

"No." He sighed and his shoulders hunched over. "I just don't know what to do or where to start. This is all pretty fucking new to me."

Maybe we did need lawyers?

"We start by making a list of anyone that hated either of them."

Josh's personality meant his list was going to be long. He'd rubbed hundreds of people up the wrong way in the past. Of course, not all of them would kill over it, but I had a feeling Josh's enemies would be the answer here.

I shrugged. "I can't think of anyone that hated Courtney. Do any of you?"

"Are you getting Courtney out of the way quickly so we can focus on who hates my brother?" Blake asked, reading me like a book.

"No offence, but—"

He held his hand up, and I stopped talking. "I get it, Mackenzie. I would have done the same. So... anyone hate Courtney? I didn't, barely knew the girl."

I shook my head. Kyle, Megan and Aaron replied no verbally.

"I feel like we should get a pad for Josh," Blake said, snorting in a humourless laugh.

"I'll start," Kyle said. "Well we all know the four of us had a problem with him after Tills and Gigi died, but we also know it wasn't us four. Blake had issues with his little brother, right, Blake?"

"Right," he replied. "But I didn't kill him either." He looked beside Kyle to Aaron, "Contrary to popular belief."

"Tilly's dad," Aaron said, ignoring Blake completely.

"No, he was angry but not at anyone in particular," Megan replied.

Aaron glared at her. "He said he wanted to kill whoever was responsible. Come on, we should at least consider it."

He'd said that in the heat of the moment out of pure anger and grief, but could he have meant it? "Aaron's right," I said, arching my spine and sitting up. "Think about it, we were all there in the minivan. We all survived and Tilly didn't. The lorry driver died so he couldn't pay. Courtney was the one driving and Josh was the one who planned the trip and acted like an arsehole after."

Kyle scratched at his jaw roughly. "Her dad is the only one that hates them and us, probably. He lost his daughter. Come on, there's no greater motivation to kill than revenge for your child."

In ice cold shiver ran down my spine. The theory made a lot of sense.

# CHAPTER NINE

"So why are you redecorating?" I asked Kyle as I stood in his sheet-covered room. His furniture had been moved into the centre, exposing the dark, midnight blue walls. Until ten minutes ago I had no idea he was even thinking about redecorating. He called a little while ago mumbling about needing a change and his dark room was depressing him.

"Just can't stand this shitty colour anymore."

He held up a large tin of a light but bright green paint. I smiled, well, sort of smiled. "Err…"

"You hate it?"

"I don't hate the colour. I think you will though. It's really bright for a whole room."

"I don't care. I need something bright. A complete change."

I picked up one of the many brushes he had lined along the chest of drawers. "It's certainly a change."

He grinned. "What would I do without you?"

"Paint it yourself?" I dipped the brush in the tin and slapped it on the wall. He was going to hate the colour, definitely.

"You been okay? Yesterday sucked."

Yesterday was actually one of the hardest days I had ever lived through. Not only was it a goodbye to Courtney, but it also brought back memories of Tilly and Gigi's funerals. I shrugged. "I'm alright."

"Hmm, lie."

I stopped and turned to him. "It's not a complete lie. Right now I'm doing okay."

"You're focused on the man hunt. When the killer's found you'll fall apart." I kept quiet. Kyle knew me so well. "I'm worried about that, you know. I'm worried you'll be the way you were after Tilly and Gigi died."

Biting my lip, I thought about what he said. I was a mess when they died. I didn't eat for almost a week and barely got out of bed. It was so hard to accept that I would never see them again. It still was. I knew Kyle was worried back then; he came around every day, bring my favourite foods and DVDs to comfort me.

"I'll be okay. I have you, Megan and Aaron." And Blake, sort of. The list was getting smaller and smaller. I was terrified of losing another one of them.

"You'll always have us." He held his arms out, and I practically collapsed into them. Gripping hold of his waist, I held on for dear life. It was just us four now and we had to stick together. "I'm so sorry, Mackenzie." His body shook as if he was crying, but he made no sound. Kyle was always so strong for us; he needed to be able to let it out sometimes too.

"Shh, it's not your fault. We're gonna be okay," I mumbled into his shoulder, praying that I was right.

'We're going to be okay' was one of the most overused phrases but also one of the truest. No matter what had happened, how deeply something hurt you, the world continued to spin and you continued to breathe. Things might suck for a while, sometimes a long while, but eventually you would be able to function again.

He pulled away and took a deep breath. "Anyway, we should get this painted. I think it'll take two coats."

I nodded and picked up the brush again. "Kyle, do you honestly believe Blake killed them?"

His arm moved up and down as he painted the bright green onto his wall. It took him a long time to reply, "No one got in, so yes. We don't know him, and I'd much rather believe it was a stranger than someone I've known over half my life. I get that you want it to be someone else, but I don't think it can be."

It had to be.

"Did it ever cross your mind that it could be me?" I asked, holding my breath. If he said yes it'd crush me.

Kyle laughed. "You're kidding, right? Mackenzie, you make me take spiders outside because you won't have them killed! No, I never thought it's you." I blew out a big breath of relief. His eyebrows arched. "You think it could be me?"

"No," I replied. "I don't think it's any of you."

"You have a thing for Blake," he said. It was a statement and not a question. A thing. I cared about him as a human being. I refused to believe he could kill his brother so that meant I had a thing for him? We'd had sex and he made me feel things that were all new and all frightening. But I didn't feel like I could tell Kyle that.

"I don't. Kyle, I barely know the guy."

He shrugged. "Maybe. You defend him blindly though."

"It's not blindly."

"Yes it is. You said yourself you don't know him. You're defending a guy that for all you know could be a rapist or serial killer. I'd call that blind."

"Whatever," I replied. There was no point in trying to change his mind, and I couldn't be bothered to waste my breath. Have you spoken to Aaron or Megan yet today? I tried Megan earlier, but it went straight through to voicemail."

"Aaron's at hers. Her grandparents came home from Italy to support her, probably why she didn't answer."

I nodded and made a mental note to go and see her in the morning. If Aaron was already there she wouldn't need me too, and I didn't want to intrude if her family were over.

"So do you really think it could possibly be Lawrence?" I asked as we worked side by side. If we were to take his death threat seriously after he lost Tilly then shouldn't we take Aaron's seriously too?

He lifted his shoulder and let it drop. "Maybe. I think he could have done it. If someone handed him a gun and told him he could shoot us without getting in trouble, I think he would have. He wants someone to blame for Tilly's death, and you can't blame the poor bastard."

"I know but to kill someone over an accident. I can't get my head around it."

"I don't understand it, but people justify things to themselves all the time. I can buy this because it thirty per cent off or just one more drink will be okay because I've eaten a big dinner."

"I'll kill this person because they deserve it?"

He shrugged with the same shoulder again. "I guess."

"That's stupid!"

"Kenz, I'm not saying it's not or that it's right, but it happens. Our other option is Blake, but I know what you're like so let's not argue over him."

It took us four and a half hours to paint Kyle's room twice. My arm ached, and I felt like collapsing. "Shit. It's *really* green," Kyle said, looking at the bright walls with wide eyes.

"Yep," I replied. "I'm not painting it again for at least three months so you'll have to live with it for that long."

He grinned. "Deal. Hopefully it won't look so much like I'm living in a Disney forest when the furniture is back."

"Doubt it but let's see."

We uncovered his furniture and pushed it all back into place. The walls looked no less green but at least with his chunky wooden bed, chest of draws, widescreen TV, and triple wardrobe, you saw significantly less of it.

"I hate to say I told you so…"

He smirked and nudged my shoulder with his own. "No, you don't. I wanted a change, and I got one. I can deal for a while."

"Maybe we can paint three of the walls white or something? That'll tone it down."

"Yeah, maybe."

"Okay, let's get the last things put away and then you're making me some food." He still had football trophies, posters and a few shoeboxes of stuff left in the middle of the room.

I bent down to pick up one of the shoeboxes, and the side fell open, spilling the contents onto the floor. "Damn it," I muttered and knelt on the carpet to pick up the photographs that had scattered.

"Smooth," Kyle said, kneeling to help.

One caught my eye, and my heart stopped. "Kyle, what's this?" I asked, holding up that photograph.

His mouth dropped open and closed quickly. He shrugged. "Just a picture from years ago."

I looked back at Courtney kissing Kyle and frowned. Court's hair was a fiercer red, brighter than the one she usually used, a colour that she had to get because her hair was fading and they didn't have her usual. I was the one who had dyed it for her, for the last time it seemed, just before Easter, three months ago. This was recent. "Kyle, this must have been taken in April. Courtney's hair," I said, explaining how I knew. "What the hell was going on between you two?"

We stared at each other, silently challenging the other. Kyle sighed and closed his eyes again, and I knew exactly what he was about to say. He kept his eyes shut as he very quietly confessed, "We were together."

"Together? You two were together? When? How? I don't get it…"

"Behind Josh's back. In secret. Having an affair. Get it now?"

My shoulders slumped. All the air left my lungs in one big rush. How much did I not know about my best friends? "Shit, what the hell were you thinking? Why didn't she tell me? Why didn't *you* tell me?"

"Really, Mackenzie?" he muttered dryly.

"We've known each other since we were seven, and I would have preferred to see her with you than Josh."

"Yeah, well, so would I. She wouldn't leave him. She said so many times that she would and finally, eight months later, she cut me off and chose him."

My eyes bulged. "Eight months?" This wasn't just a brief fling; it was a full on affair! It was going on through most of her relationship with Josh. I shook my head. "I don't even know what to think."

He shrugged and snatched the photo back. "Don't think anything. She led me on and screwed me over. I would have done anything for her. I loved her so much, but she chose him. I hate her for what she did to me."

I blinked in shock. Kyle was so hostile. "Don't say you hate her," I whispered. Courtney was wrong for leading him on, and I was angry with her for hurting him, but she was dead now.

He stood up and gestured to the mess on his floor. "I've got things to do."

Sighing, I got up too. That was my cue to leave, and honestly, I needed some time away from him to get my head around it. "I'm sorry you got hurt."

Kyle stared on, his eyes dark and empty. Finally, he replied, "Doesn't matter now, does it."

I turned and left his room, eager to be as far away from him as I could. My happy, mischievous, caring friend had been replaced by a bitter, spiteful stranger.

I walked to my car in a daze. Just how much did Kyle hate Courtney? Courtney and Josh? Yesterday I would have never thought he could be capable of murder but that person in his room was completely different. Was the furious person that I had just met – Kyle's darker side – capable of stabbing two people that were once friends? An affair. Kyle didn't do that. He was loyal and had morals! Well, I thought he did.

At home in my bedroom, I paced the floor, trying to get everything straight in my head. Kyle and Courtney. Together behind Josh's back. Did Josh know? He couldn't have known. If he did, there was no way he would have kept it to himself.

Aaron and Megan were at hers with her family, so I didn't want to disturb them; I wasn't even sure if I should tell anyone. I had to talk about it though. What did it mean that they had an affair? Kyle was so angry about it too. Courtney was dead and he was still mad at her.

My hands trembled as I sat down on the sofa to try and make sense of it all. It seemed like one thing after another. I had barely got my head around their deaths, being a suspect and then being drugged. This on top of all that was too much.

I looked up at the ceiling and blinked rapidly, trying not to cry. I needed to hold it in. If I started I would fall apart. Courtney needed me. Megan, Kyle, Aaron and Blake needed me.

A car pulled up outside my house, and I looked out of the window. Kyle's red Astra parked on the drive. I didn't see him get out, but I heard his door slam shut and then he rang the doorbell. Why was he here after practically kicking me out of his house? Had he come to apologise and explain? I needed an explanation, and I needed him to take back what he said about hating Courtney.

I took the stairs slowly, giving myself a little extra time to think. My heart drilled as I approached the door. I was nervous and it was pathetic. Kyle had never made me feel nervous before. I trusted him, but after the things he said about Courtney he scared me.

Gulping, I opened the door and let him walk inside. Neither of us said hi like we usually did, and he could barely look me in the eye. I played with the end of my sleeves, biting my lip and waiting. Kyle used to be someone I could rely on.

"Are your parents in?" he finally asked, looking just above my eyes.

"No," I replied cautiously. I didn't want to consider him to be the murderer, but I was.

"Good. Can we talk?" He nodded to the sofa, asking permission to sit. He had never asked before, usually he just plopped himself down wherever he felt like it.

I nodded. "Okay." I felt like I should add 'but my parents will be home soon.' I didn't want to go there though. It felt like it would be condemning him before I knew anything. He still looked like the same old Kyle that I grew up with and loved. His eyes still sparkled with mischief, and I could picture him laughing as he shouted run after knocking on our neighbours door in the dead of night.

"Mackenzie, I'm so sorry," he said as he dropped down onto the sofa.

I sat down and faced him, needing to watch his reactions and expressions. "What part are you sorry for?" For telling me you hate Courtney or for hating her?

"All of it. I was angry. Thinking about it always pisses me off. I really loved her, Kenz. It kills me to think about her choosing him all over again."

"I understand that. Do you really hate her though?"

He sighed. "Yes. But I love her too."

I shook my head. "I can't believe she didn't tell me. I thought she told me everything." We had a fairly open friendship. We talked about everything, including our most embarrassing crushes. I told her about the time I threw up in my first boyfriend's mouth! Well almost, he moved just in time but it was all over his cheek.

"She wanted to," Kyle said, frowning, "but we agreed that it would be best to keep it between us. At the start we didn't really know what was happening. We didn't plan any of it. After a while it became too hard to tell anyone."

"Does anyone else know?"

Kyle shook his head. "No."

"You didn't tell anyone? Not even after she chose Josh?"

"I wanted to."

"But?"

"But nothing."

I gulped. There was definitely something else he wanted to say. "Kyle," I prompted.

"I thought about revenge. Of course, I did. I thought of a million ways I could hurt her like she hurt me. Telling Josh, putting that photo of us on Facebook, the video of us on YouTube, well RedTube, but it wouldn't change anything."

RedTube? They'd filmed themselves?

Blinking hard to erase the previous revelation, I asked, "So you did nothing?"

"Nothing but pretend I was fine. Everything went back to normal. I didn't treat her any differently to the way I did before we started screwing around. It drove her crazy, and I realised that was my revenge. She would forever think that I didn't give a shit. That I could get over her in an instant."

I frowned. "You said you didn't want revenge?"

He shrugged. "I didn't want to waste a lot of energy on it, so I moved on. It was just a bonus that it pissed her off so much. She didn't like that I wasn't pining for her, Mackenzie."

"That doesn't sound like Courtney at all."

He shrugged and stood up. "I guess you didn't know her as well as you thought then. I gotta go. See you tonight," he said and walked towards the door. I watched him step outside and turn around. "We okay? I don't want you to be pissed at me."

"I'm not pissed. We're cool."

Kyle left, and I slumped into the cushions behind me. I couldn't tell if he was being honest or not. He was a bad liar, but I had found out things today that shocked me. Courtney was a cheat and Kyle was angry and bitter.

I was left wondering if I really knew any of my friends at all.

# CHAPTER TEN

Kyle had called me no less than nine times since he left my house yesterday. He was desperate to make me believe he had nothing to do with Josh and Courtney's death. I wanted to believe him, and deep down I did. He would never hurt anyone, but there was this other side to him that was a complete stranger to me. I couldn't help wondering if that side of him could have done it. If he'd snapped.

I pulled up outside the cabin, and my hands started to shake. There had to be something somewhere the police missed because I was going crazy letting a little doubt slip into my mind. I was hoping to find something that would point towards Tilly's dad, but I didn't know what.

Blake's truck sat in the driveway, but that wasn't surprising. He didn't really have anywhere to go and get away from his family. I was surprised that he and his mum had such a distant relationship. They needed each other now more than ever.

I walked straight into the cabin, ignoring the almost painful beating of my heart and sick, metallic taste in my mouth, and looked around for Blake.

The place was a mess. Everything had been turned upside down. Photographs were lying face down on the side table; the coffee table was now against the far wall and the sofas were clearly out of place. What on earth…

I cleared my throat as I spotted Blake by the window, staring out. His head snapped around in my direction, and he arched his eyebrow. "What're you doing here?" he asked.

Not letting him intimidate me, I shoved my hip out and stood straight. *Trying to prove to myself Kyle isn't the killer.* "What are you doing here?"

"This is my cabin. Your turn."

"Looking for…" I trailed off, frowning. What was I looking for? I slumped. "I don't know. Anything, I guess."

Blake cocked his head to the side. "You're looking for a murderer. What makes you think you'll find something dozens of police officers and detectives couldn't?"

"They don't have as much to lose as I do."

He sighed. "So dramatic."

"What happened here?" I asked, ignoring his comment.

"Police were searching for the murderers clothes. They have the knife, was one of ours."

"They do?" The knife! There must be fingerprints on the knife! "And?"

He shrugged. "And they have the knife. We all used the knives…and most of the utensils actually. Doubt they'll find much there."

Could we all have used the same one? I knew we took it in turns chopping everything for the enchiladas but what were the odds of us all touching the same knife? I tried to think back, but a lot of that night was a blur. Josh had brought two knives from home. We definitely all used a knife at one point, even if it was only to pass it to someone else, but the same one?

Blake smirked, lighting up his striking blue eyes. "So what have you got planned then? Sniffer dogs?"

"Are you going to help me or what?"

"Did I offer?" he replied, frowning.

"Fine, Blake, just stand there and look out of that window at nothing. Pretend I'm not here."

"Hard to do when you're talking at me."

"What the hell is your problem?" He was being an arsehole. "What's happened since yesterday?"

"Nothing," he grunted. "Just pissed off with all this shit. I want to know who killed my little brother, and I want all your little friends to stop looking at me as if I did it."

"And I want to know who killed my friends."

"Friend," he corrected. "You hated Josh, remember?"

I gritted my teeth. "Fine. I want to find out what happened to my friend and her boyfriend. Better?"

Ignoring me, he said, "Where do you want to look first?"

My head spun. "You're helping now?"

"Don't make me change my mind."

I shrugged. "I've no idea. You know this place better than me. If he or she didn't use the doors then what about the windows?"

"They were all closed. Properly closed from the inside."

"Yes I know that, Blake."

"Then why are you looking there?"

I wanted to punch him. He was pushing my buttons, and I was seconds from snapping. Why did no one take this as seriously as I did? I needed to check, just in case. "Just do your own fucking thing!"

Blake's eyebrows shot up in shock. Before he could reply, I left the lounge and walked into the kitchen. The kitchen was the most logical place for someone to enter, or at least exit. The murders happened in the kitchen and whoever did it would need a quick escape.

I wanted to run back to my car, drive home as fast as I could and hide in bed, but I couldn't allow myself that weakness. I didn't want to stop and think. I didn't want to face the reality of what happened.

"Mackenzie?" Blake said. I ignored him and shoved at the little window over the sink. The handle was down, and the window didn't budge. I was hoping the latch was broken, and it would open. The police would have tried that already of course.

"What?" I replied, shoving the wooden frame with as much force as I could muster. "Damn it!" I slammed my palm down on the glass in frustration. "Why won't it just fucking open!" I shouted.

"Stop." His strong hand gripped the top of my arm and pulled me back. "It's not going to magically open, Mackenzie, and you're just going to end up hurting yourself!"

I held my finger up as another thought sprung to my mind. "Maybe I'm starting in the wrong place. I should find the murderer before I find out how they did it. I mean nothing is really impossible, right?"

"Okay, Jonathan Creek, where are we starting?" If I was Jonathan Creek I would have figured it out by now. I had no clue.

"A hide out." I turned on my heel and walked out of the cabin, rubbing the ache in my chest. The killer would need somewhere around to hide in, to wait for the perfect moment. I was sure of it.

Blake's footsteps thudded behind me, crunching dried leaves on the ground. "You don't even know where you're going," he said.

"No one knows where they're going before they first go there," I replied, power walking ahead. "If you're just here to annoy me then please turn around now."

"You can't just go wondering off in the woods by yourself."

I stopped and turned around. "Why do you care?" He blew hot and cold all the fucking time. I had no idea where I stood with him. I just wanted one bloody thing to be simple.

He was right behind me, eyes burning into me. I couldn't figure him out. Blake was a mystery and a pretty annoying one. "Got nothing else to do," he whispered, giving me goose bumps.

"Liar."

His eyes narrowed, clearly disliking how I challenged him. "I want to find the killer too. No one else can give me answers, so I figure why not tag along with Detective Mackenzie and see where it leads me. Besides, I can't stand being at home." His voice lowered as he confessed living with his mum was unbearable. I could only imagine what it was like for both of them.

"I'm sorry."

He smiled half-heartedly and shrugged one shoulder. "What are you looking for?"

"A shed or cabin," I replied. "Anything the killer could have been hiding in."

"Are you expecting to find bloody clothes and the murderer's ID too?"

"Hoping, not expecting. There any more places like the one you showed me?"

"A couple more." He walked past me, headed in a different direction to where I was originally going.

He was helping? "Do you still know the way?"

"Please," he said, turning his head to smirk at me. "I'm a man."

I followed him, weaving around the trees. The deeper we walked into the woods the darker it became. "Are you sure this is the way?" I asked, wrapping my arms around myself.

"What, do you think I'm leading you into the middle of nowhere to slit your throat?"

"That's not funny, and I don't think that's what you're doing. I think you've gotten us lost. No man would ever admit to that, so I think you're taking us around in circles hoping we'll eventually come across the cabin again."

He sighed. "Just ahead you'll see a crappy old shack. We found it years ago when we were looking for somewhere to play with our water pistols."

"You needed shelter for that?"

"We needed a base. Every good military operation has a base."

I grinned, imagining Blake as a child, running around and playing fantasy games. We started walking again, slower this time. "Quite the imagination you have."

"Had," he corrected. "Life screws you over eventually."
"Pessimist."
"Hopeless optimist."
"How far does the river go?" I asked.
He shrugged. "How should I know? Far, I assume."
"That's a lot of water for evidence to be dumped in. And a lot of forest too. Do you think they've hidden it all somewhere? The clothes I mean."
"No, they're probably doing their weekly shopping in them," he replied dryly.
I narrowed my eyes. "You're a dick."
"The first is huge, you could lose anything in there, the ground is covered in leaves and crap so you could probably bury a lot in there too."
"Great. We have no hope." Finding anything seemed impossible. If Blake was right, and he knew this area better than me, the murderer could have already hidden the evidence in any part of the miles of woodland.
He pointed ahead. "There you go."
I frowned, but as I took another step I could just about see the side of something wooden. "We're here?"
"No, I took you—"
"Alright, thank you!" I rolled my eyes and muttered under my breath, "Sarcastic bastard!"
Blake grinned wide, flashing his teeth. He was a little too good at shoving everything aside. I could do it well enough to function but Blake could do it well enough to be himself.
We walked closer, and I stopped. *No way am I going in there!* The whole thing looked as if it was about to collapse. It looked like the type of place you screamed for someone not to go near in a horror film.
"It's creepy," I said as a cold shudder ripped through my body.
"It's an old shed, Mackenzie! What do you think it's gonna do?" I ignored him and nodded towards the door half hanging off the top hinge. Blake's smile grew. "Ladies first."

"Shut up and go." I didn't understand how he could continuously make jokes when what we were doing was serious. "Unless you're scared?"

He rolled his eyes. "Reverse psychology doesn't work on me. This is your crusade. You lead the way, Detective."

"Fine." I stood taller, trying to fool myself I was braver than I felt. "But for the record, you have no balls at all, *princess*." I wasn't sure what his reaction would be, whether he would continue the cocky attitude or bite back, but I didn't bother waiting around to find out. I walked ahead, closer to the run down shed.

I gulped. Cobwebs plagued the top of the doorway, but the bottom half was clear. It looked as if someone had been here recently. I peered inside, but the dust-clad windows prevented much light from streaming inside.

I looked over my shoulder and was met by an incredibly smug looking Blake. "Want me to go first, sweets?" he asked.

"Is that a genuine offer?"

He bit the inside of his mouth, pretending to think, even though we both knew he already knew the answer. He sighed. "Move out of the way." Swiping the remaining cobwebs away with his hand, he stepped inside.

"What's in there?" I whispered.

"Nothing for you to whisper for."

I took a deep breath, gritting my teeth. "What's in there, Blake," I hissed.

"Sod all. Come in."

He could have been lying, and I would walk in there to see a skeleton or something, but for some reason I trusted him. Blake drove me crazy with his attitude, but I knew he wouldn't put me in any danger. Well not real danger at least, he would probably let me do something like walk into a room with a skeleton to scare the shit out of me.

I took a small step and was half way through the door. It smelt musty inside and my nose tingled. Blake wiped the cracked glass with his hand, creating a hand length window.

A slit of light poured into small room, giving enough so we could see.

The inside of the shed was filled with dust, mud, and more cobwebs. The floor was littered with empty packets of crisps and bottles of drink. I frowned. "We're not going to find anything, are we?"

Blake scratched the back of his neck. "If you want to continue looking for someone else, I'm with you."

"But?" I prompted, sensing he had more to say.

"But I think it was one of your friends."

I gulped and shook my head. "No, it couldn't have been. They wouldn't."

"That's what they want you to believe, yes."

"No. I need to keep searching. Check the use by dates on the litter, some might be recent."

"And that will prove?"

*I don't know!* "Please, Blake," I said, pleading with him. I knew I was looking for a needle in a haystack and searching rubbish was plain ridiculous, but I had to find someone else. I couldn't accept it was one of my friends.

He held his hands up. "Alright, let's look at rubbish."

I smiled. "Thank you."

He knelt down and picked up a faded packet of crisps. I wanted to tell him that the bag had clearly been here a long time, but he was doing me a favour. "I hope your friends appreciate you."

"What do you mean by that?"

"You're doing everything you can to prove their innocence – innocence you don't even know is there – including sifting through crap. What're they doing for you?"

"I don't do things to get something in return."

"No, but perhaps you should ask yourself if it's appreciated a little more often."

"I know it is," I replied and picked up crumpled biscuit packet. Gasping, I shoved the packet towards him. "Blake, look!" There was blood on it. Not a lot, but I hoped against all the odds that it was the real murderer's blood. A frown slipped onto his forehead as he studied it.

"How long do you think it's been there?" I asked.

"How the hell should I know?"

"Well does it look like old blood?"

He shrugged. "I dunno!"

"I think it looks newish." He smirked and shook his head to say *of course you do*. "This isn't funny! Why aren't you taking this seriously?"

"Because you've got us sifting through crap! I'll humour you and we'll take this to Wright." He stood up. "Now come on before you find a dead bird and accuse that of—"

"Alright, thank you." I turned on my heel and stomped outside. Keeping my cool with him was hard, even when he was trying to help. Blake seemed to know all right buttons to push, and he pushed them every chance he got.

"Mackenzie?"

"Yeah."

"What will you do if one of them is the killer?"

"I honestly don't know. Will you help me? None of them seem overly enthusiastic about looking themselves." And I had no idea why. "I need someone," I whispered.

He frowned. "Are you gonna cry? I don't do well with hysterical women, remember?"

"I'm not going to cry. Not yet."

"You've set a timer?"

"When this is all over. Until then, I'm strong Mackenzie."

"Your friends really are lucky."

I shrugged. It's what anyone would do for the people they cared about. "So will you help?"

The corner of his mouth pulled up into a smirk, and he did a little bow. "I'm at your service, Detective Keaton."

I breathed out sharply, relieved that I had someone to go through all this with, even if that person drove me insane most of the time. I knew that together we could figure it out. "Thank you."

# CHAPTER ELEVEN

We arrived back at Blake's house, and I could tell he wanted nothing more than to leave again. He walked slowly into the lounge. His mum sat on the same chair she had spent Josh's entire wake on. The TV was on, but it wasn't being watched. She stared into space.

"Hi, Eloise," I said, looking at Blake for help.

He shook his head. This empty shell was normal for her now then. "Let's go up to my room."

I took a quick glance back at her as I followed Blake out of the room. Her eyes were bloodshot and sunken. Her hair was slick with grease and tied into a messy ponytail on top of her head. She looked as if she had checked out days ago and left her body behind.

"Is she okay?" I asked as we reached the top of the stairs and out of her way, not that she would have heard me if I had asked him right in front of her.

"Not really." He pushed the door open and nodded, gesturing for me to go in first. *He can be a gentleman!*

His room was plain and bare. A dull light blue covered the walls and there was nothing hanging from them to personalise it. The only furniture was a double bed, bedside table and wardrobe. A flat screen TV hung from the wall opposite the bed, but it looked old, probably second hand when they replaced another one in the house. I imagined Eloise buying a new one for the lounge and saying 'Oh we can put the old one in Blake's room'. It reminded me of a cheap hotel room.

"I've never spent much time here," he explained.

"It's fine." I wasn't sure why he felt he had to explain it to me. I didn't care what it was or looked like. "Have you heard from Wright?"

"Nope. You?"

I sat down on the bed. "Nope."

"Please, make yourself at home," he said playfully, teasing me. "He does that on purpose, I think."

"Not contacting us?"

He plopped down on the bed, making me bounce. "Yeah. We all think he would be on our case twenty-four-seven so he's not. Whatever we expect, he does the opposite."

"Ah, to mess with us. He's doesn't seem like a proper detective."

"I dunno," he shrugged, "I'd probably be cocky and arrogant if I was a detective." I snorted, and he rolled his eyes. Only if he was a detective? "Moving on! What fun activities do you have for us now? Digging up graves? Sifting through sewers?"

"Why don't you suggest something if you don't like what I'm doing."

"We could talk to Tilly's dad. You know, maybe something he says we tell us more, rather than looking at rubbish." He reached over, stroking the back of my hand with his thumb. It felt really nice and I hated that he was able to make me feel something good when I should be falling apart.

"I found blood, didn't I?"

"Probably from a half-dead animal, but whatever."

"We'll see. Wright is going to have it tested."

"I'll never understand why he's wasting his time with that. I thought he would laugh in our faces and tell us to leave."

"He knows I'm right."

"Either that or the blood will be from one of your friends and you would have dropped them right in it."

My world stopped spinning. What if it was? Would that mean they'd done it? No, it couldn't be. "It won't be theirs."

"Whatever you say. My money's on Kyle though."

I gulped. Did he know about the affair? "Why Kyle?"

"He has that dark eyes thing going on. They look mysterious with a hint of serial killer."

I laughed. "'Mysterious with a hint of killer'? Brown eyes doesn't make you a murderer."

"It's not the colour, just the way they look."

I shook my head. He was no longer making sense. "So… Lawrence's?"

"I'm assuming that's goldilocks' dad?"

"Yes, and how do you know Tilly was blonde?"

"I can sniff blondes out. It's a gift."

"You're a pig!"

He laughed, standing up as I did. "I do know you all, you know. Well, I know of you." Right he had seen us from the car as his parents had done the child swap. "How far away does Lawrence live?"

"Five minutes. We all live close."

"I hate small villages."

"There's nothing wrong with this village."

"Sure, if you don't mind a bit of murder every now and then," he muttered.

Taking a deep breath, I pushed his words to the back of my mind. I was grateful that he was helping me as no one else seemed bothered, but his little comments annoyed me. He made jokes to make everyone think he didn't care about anything. I had a feeling he was trying to convince himself too. If he said it enough he would believe it.

"And where you're from is so much better?"

"Towns are better. Fact. Here, everyone knows your business, and they all look at you, wondering what you're up to. In towns, people have lives, in villages people's lives are other people's lives."

"Okay then." Wow. We reached the bottom of the stairs and I frowned, concerned. "Blake, is she really okay?"

Eloise sat in the same position still, motionless. I wished we had met somewhere else. I understood why Blake didn't like it at home anymore. Usually I was good with grieving people. I could do or say something to try to help but. Not with Eloise. She gave nothing for me to work with. Crying I could handle. Angry I could handle. An emotionless statue I drew a blank.

"Has your mum eaten anything? Maybe we should make her a sandwich before we leave?" I said as we stopped outside the lounge door.

"She won't eat it even if you make something, never does."

"What about you?"

"I'm a big boy, Mackenzie, I can look after myself."

He walked to the front door, and I followed.

"You don't cook."

"I can if I want to. I can even use a washing machine."

"Wow, never knew guys like you existed. My dad still has to ask what setting it goes on if he's forced to do it."

Blake smirked. "He knows. If he pisses you off by asking every time, you won't make him do it. I would have done the same but just being me and Dad at home…"

"I've never met your dad."

He unlocked the car and opened his door. "We're not quite there yet." Rolling my eyes, I got in the passenger side. We weren't together and right now that was the last thing on my mind but we were something. "So what's this Lawrence like?"

"He was really nice before Tilly died."

"Understandable, I guess."

"He doesn't like Josh so we probably shouldn't mention you're his brother."

He scoffed and pulled out of his driveway. "Is there anyone in this village that actually did like him?"

"Courtney," I replied. "Look, he wasn't all bad and no one actually wanted him to die."

Blake's eyebrow arched. "One person did. We're still assuming it was just one person, right?"

I shrugged. "Can't say I've thought too much about that. All I know is that it's not one of my friends."

"Or more than one of your friends."

I narrowed my eyes. "You know when I first met you I thought you were alright." He was probably the most frustrating person on the earth. Blake turned his head to me and smirked. "Watch the road!"

"Where does this guy live exactly?"

I gave him the address and sat back, holding on and praying for my life. The accelerator was Blake's best friend. He didn't necessarily drive dangerously; he just liked to put his foot down, frequently.

"What are you gonna say to him? We can't exactly knock on his door and be hey, did you murder two teens—"

"I get it," I said, cutting him off. What should we say? After Tilly died I popped around to see how they all were and helped them sort out some of her clothes they were donating to charity, but I hadn't been in months. Perhaps I could use that as an excuse though? "I'll say I'm checking in to make sure they're okay, like I used to. Remember do not tell them you're related to Josh. I'm serious, Blake."

"Yeah, I got it but thanks for the child's reminder."

I refused to talk to Blake for the rest of the short journey; we would probably end up bickering, and I needed to stay calm. I was an awful liar and prayed that Lawrence wouldn't see through me straight away.

As Blake pulled up outside the yellow brick bungalow, my heart started to pound against my chest. I might be the only one willing to go out there and look for the real killer, but I was definitely the worst person to do it.

"Ready?" Blake asked.

I gulped and nodded. "Let's just get this over with." I didn't want to think about him being the killer. I had slept in that bungalow hundreds of times and eaten Lawrence's famous cheese and bacon bagels more times than I could count. How could someone I know be a murderer? Murderers were in other people's lives or on TV shows. They shouldn't exist in my world.

I walked along the path slowly with Blake tailing behind. He didn't make any stupid comments or try to hurry me. Tapping on the door lightly, I took a deep breath to try and calm my racing heart.

"Mackenzie, what a surprise," Lawrence said as he opened the door. He frowned. "What brings you here?"

I smiled, going over the reason I rehearsed in my head dozens of times on the way. "I just wanted to come by and see how you're all doing. It's been a while."

"It has." He nodded once and looked at Blake. "And you are?"

*Don't say you're Josh's brother, do not say you're Josh's brother.* I wasn't sure how Lawrence would react if he knew; he hated Josh more than anyone. Blake held his hand out, and Lawrence shook it. "Everyone calls me Spike." He slung his arm over my shoulder. "I'm Mackenzie's boyfriend."

*I am going to kill him.* I smiled tightly, gritting my teeth. Spike! Could he have come up with anything more lame? We should have discussed who he'd be in the car but I did not see 'Spike' coming.

"Spike," Lawrence said slowly and looked at me as if it to say *what on earth are you doing?* "Nice to meet you. Please, come on in."

Lawrence walked ahead, and I took the opportunity while his attention wasn't on us to slap Blake's arm. 'What the hell?' I mouthed, which only made him smile.

"You know your way to the living room. I'll make us some tea," he said over his shoulder. Blake tuned his nose up but didn't ask for coffee instead.

"Okay," I replied, turning right into the lounge. It was exactly the same as before, but they had replaced the wooden framed clock with a more modern metal one. Tilly hated that old clock and said it looked like it belonged in a retirement home. I had a feeling they changed it for her.

Blake and I waited in silence. I played with my fingers, nervously anticipating the conversation we were about to have. Beside me, Blake pressed his leg against mine and then took my hand, forcing me to relax a little.

"Calm down," he whispered.

"What if he did it?"

"I don't think he'll admit it, Mackenzie. We'll be alright."

"What if we're not? If he killed them he's capable of doing the same to us."

Gripping my chin, he tilted me so my focus was on him. "There is nothing in this world that is going to hurt you."

I wished we were back in his room because that was seriously sweet and by his own admission he didn't do or say anything heartfelt.

"What's happening to you?" I teased. I meant it as a joke but Blake scowled, thinking about it.

Lawrence came into the room and set a tray of tea and biscuits down on the coffee table. Blake and I sat up straight.

"Thank you," I said. "So how have you been?"

He sat down on the worn leather sofa opposite us. "Not too bad. Yourself?"

"Not great."

"Right, of course. I'm very sorry to hear about Joshua and Courtney." *Are you?* "You found them, didn't you?"

"I'm very sorry you saw that, Mackenzie. It must be very hard to live with."

Lawrence said the words, but they didn't seem genuine. I had always got along with Tilly's family; when she died Lawrence barely spoke to me. I knew he would have preferred it to be me instead of Tilly – of course he would – but I didn't think he would hate me for it.

Blake tensed beside me. Not now! "I'm very sorry to hear about your daughter, Lawrence. Mackenzie's told me Tilly was a great person."

"Thank you, *Spike*. She was a great person, one of the best. My Tilly was going to be a doctor. All she ever wanted was to help people."

I smiled at the bittersweet memories of her tending to us all whenever something was wrong. She would never get her dream career; the sick were missing out on an incredible doctor. "She would have been a great at it. I've lost count of the times she played doctor when someone hurt themselves. You remember when I sprained my wrist a few years ago and she insisted on checking it regularly and changing the bandage."

Lawrence laughed. "She drove you crazy if I remember correctly."

"Yeah I had to keep stopping what I was doing so she could look. There wasn't even anything to check!" I would have understood if it was a cut she could re-dress, but there was nothing to do. That was Tilly though; even if there was nothing that she could do to help she still tried and made sure.

"Aaron mentioned that too. Do you remember when he had pneumonia last year, and Tilly spent most of the week at his bedside?" Lawrence said, smiling fondly at the memory. "It was a shame they didn't have the chance to make a go of things. He's a good lad and it's clear he's in love with her." It was? Their relationship was so on and off and so rocky you could barely give it the relationship title.

"Yeah they would have been good together," I said. Now they were more mature maybe they could have been. "Aaron misses her too."

"Yes, he's here often to be close to her."

I tried to hide the surprise on my face. Aaron came here often? We all visited but not really often anymore. Had I completely underestimated his feelings for Tilly? Why were they so horrible to each other half of the time then? It didn't make sense.

"He still comes a lot? I didn't know that."

"Almost every week. He sits in her room or sometimes we look through pictures. I was surprised at first; Tilly was always crying over him or ranting at how much of a 'stupid pissing idiot' he was." I could hear her words so clearly. She had used that phrase for Aaron so many times in the past. "It really does mean a lot that he still cares for her so deeply."

How deeply? Deeply enough that it made him hate Courtney for being the unfortunate one behind the wheel of the van and hate Josh for his part? Aaron and vengeful just didn't go. He didn't hurt others over an accident; that wasn't him. That wasn't any of them.

"That's nice. I like that he does that. Tills would too."

Lawrence smiled but his lips barely curled. "She would."

"How long ago was the accident?" Blake asked, putting a little too much emphasis on the word accident.

"Eight months ago," I replied. I couldn't quite believe months had past. It still seemed like yesterday. I could still clearly hear the sound of crunching metal, smashing glass and my friends' screams. The minivan rolled over before coming to an abrupt stop in a ditch. I was in the row of seats in front of them, and if the lorry had hit just a few inches forward I probably would have died too.

"Eight months and six days," Lawrence corrected. He shook his head. "I will never understand why Giana drank."

I bit my lip. She didn't mean to get drunk. Before losing about a stone, she could drink about five or six drinks and not feel a thing. She only had two beers, and they didn't have a high alcohol volume at all.

"She didn't mean to," I whispered. It wasn't Gigi's fault, or Courtney and Josh's. Why were so many people having a hard time understanding that? It was a fucking accident!

"I believe that, but the accident happened as a direct result of Giana's drinking." The way he said Gigi's name gave me chills. It was similar to how hateful Kyle sounded when he told me how much Courtney hurt him.

We were hit by a damn lorry. The driver was irrelevant when you had an artic lorry ramming you up the arse! They never stood a chance, and if Gigi had been driving it still would have been Tilly that died. The man sitting in front of me wasn't who he used to be. He was cold and detached. His eyes were empty and face showed little emotion or understanding.

It was him. Lawrence was the killer.

The blood drained from my face. I gripped Blake's hand and stood up. "We should go. We have to meet Megan soon." Blake frowned, looking at me as if I had lost it. Maybe I had. "I'll stop by soon, Lawrence."

He shook his head, surprised by our sudden departure. "Okay."

I held Blake's hand in a death grip and pulled him through the house and out of the front door. I could barely breathe properly.

"Him," I whispered. "It was him."

Blake took charge. With one hand on the small of my back, he pushed me forwards, quickly leading me to his truck. "Get in," he said, opening the door for me. It was the only time he had done that for me; I usually had to do the door myself. Only took catching a murderer!

"It's him," I repeated when Blake was safely in the car.

"You don't know that. The way he spoke about Gigi is the way most people talk about Josh. Hating someone doesn't make you a killer, remember? Don't mess this up by charging in when you're all emotional like this," he said wiggling his fingers in my direction. "Mackenzie, do nothing for now."

"What? We can't just do nothing!"

"We don't have a choice. If it's him, there's no evidence. If he's pulled in for questioning and it's him he'll make double sure his tracks are covered. Please think about this carefully. Let's at least wait until Wright has the results on that blood back before we go to him with this."

I took a deep breath. He was right; I could screw everything up if I accused him without proof. "Wow, you're making sense."

He smiled. "Why thank you. Now, I'm going to drop you off at Aaron's and check in on my mum. Call me if you need me but don't say anything, okay."

"Yeah, okay. Thanks, Blake."

"Say that again."

I rolled my eyes, looking out of the window and smiling to myself. I had teamed up with a right-for-once idiot!

Blake dropped me at Aaron's as promised. Aaron and I walked the five minutes to Megan's house. The sun was shining, and the air was warm, it was weather that used to automatically put a smile on my face. It didn't today.

"I went to see Lawrence," I said, playing with the hem of my top as we walked, wishing I had worn a sleeveless top. The sun felt as if it was just a mile away and shone directly down in front of my face. My skin prickled with the heat. I didn't like it. The heat only added to the odd feeling I had in the pit of my stomach.

"Yeah," he replied, walking without a halt in his step or a flash of realisation in his all too cool expression. Either Aaron had nothing to hide or he did a wicked poker face. "He okay?"

Shouldn't you already know that? He was playing it down. Did he know that I knew or not? "He's doing alright."

"Showed no murderous signs?"

"No." Not really, just something he'd said and a feeling I'd had that could be nothing. My head was a mess, and I didn't know if what I thought or felt was because I wanted my friends to be innocent so badly. I was starting to question myself, and I didn't trust my instincts one hundred per cent anymore. "He told me you still visit."

He nodded once, his lips thinning into a straight line. "Oh. Well, yeah, I do."

"You really miss her still."

"Yeah. Can we change the subject, please?"

"Sure," I replied. Why? He had never had a problem with talking about Tilly before, unless it was with Josh. Just how much did he miss her and think about her?

Aaron groaned suddenly, looking over his shoulder. "He just pops up. Fuckin' psycho."

I followed where he was looking and saw Wright pull up on the side of the road. He was either tracking us or just diving around until he found us. Aaron and I stopped, knowing he would just follow if we didn't. He obviously had something to say.

Wright got out of the car and walked in front of us. He seemed so calm and relaxed in every situation. It was unnatural and unnerving. "Aaron Walker, just the guy I want to see," he said, swinging his arms behind his back. "Let's take a drive."

Aaron frowned. "Where to?"

"The station," he replied and walked back to his car, knowing Aaron would follow.

Aaron frowned and looked at me. "It's fine, Kenz, just go on to Megan's." Without another word, he got in the passenger side of Wright's car, and they drove off. Why didn't Aaron seem at all surprised?

I blinked in shock. What on earth just happened?

# CHAPTER TWELVE

I stood stock-still on the path, trying to piece together what just happened. Why was Aaron taken? And he just got into the car as if he'd expected it, known it was coming.

Aaron would have put up a fight, at least asked why. He knew why.

Pick up, pick up! I held my mobile so close to my ear it hurt. "Wright just took Aaron to the station," I said into the phone the second Blake answered.

"Oh I'm fine, thanks. How're you?"

I sighed. "Cut the crap for five seconds. What does he want with him?"

"This probably won't come as a surprise to you, but I'm not psychic."

"Blake," I snapped. "Why don't you take anything seriously?"

"I am. I don't know what Wright wants with him," he replied a little too coolly.

I bit my bottom lip. There was more to it. He was thinking the thing that made my stomach turn. "Why do I get the feeling you have a theory but don't want to share it with me?"

"Because, Miss Keaton, you take this detective job far too seriously."

"Just say it. Please."

"The blood, Mackenzie. I think the blood is Aaron's."

I froze, and felt the blood drain from my face. That was what I was afraid of. "No. It… It can't be his. Aaron wouldn't hurt anyone."

"Alright," Blake replied, and I could picture him rolling his eyes. "Just call me when you know more."

"Why, what're you doing?"

"Do you really want to know?"

"Goodbye, Blake," I said and hung up the phone. He probably wasn't doing anything at all. Frustrating idiot!

I walked the remaining two minutes to Megan's alone and tried to calm myself down. It was probably routine questioning and we would all be called back in too. I shouldn't let Wright get to me because his way of doing things was to be designed to do just that.

Taking a deep breath and plastering on a fake smile, I rang Megan's doorbell. I didn't want her to know what was going on, but I wasn't too sure why. Blake and I just sort of kept what we were doing to ourselves. Besides, he was the only other one that seemed willing to help.

Megan opened the door and visibly relaxed. "Thank God you're here!"

I walked inside. "Why, what's up?"

"My family are driving me crazy!" She slammed the front door behind her and lead me into the kitchen. "They're in the garden having tea. We'll say hi and escape to my room."

"Do you produce that stuff?" I asked and pointed to the four new bottles of whatever that Italian alcohol was we had the other night.

She turned and rolled her eyes. "My grandparents keep sending it over. They brought these with them. Mum's pissed because she only just got rid of the last lot."

"Why don't you just tell your nan you don't like it?"

"That's what I said!"

"Well I guess it's not too bad if you have something else first."

"A lot of something else first." She nodded to the French doors that lead out to the patio in the back garden. Her parents and grandparents were sitting around the cream metal table, drinking from tiny china cups and saucers. "Nan, Grandad, you remember Mackenzie, right?"

Megan's nan gasped, clasping her hands together and stood up. "Of course I do! Mackenzie, you look like you've grown!" The last time I saw them was about ten years ago so I couldn't have been older than nine, it was fairly safe to assume that I had, in fact, grown! "How are you? Your hair is darker." She frowned. "Did you dye it? Ruins your hair, you know."

I was pulled into a pretty tight hug for a pretty small woman. "Not dyed. It just darkened like my dad's, I guess."

That seemed to please her, she pulled away, smiling and stroked my hair. "Would you like to join us for a cup of tea? I was just about to make another pot," she said, grabbing the large teapot.

"That'd be great, thanks."

Megan's dad, Hank fetched two more matching cream chairs from the garage for us. "How are you sweetheart?" Hank asked.

"I'm alright."

"I've been looking into councillors for Megan, is that something you'd be interested in too?"

"Hank!" Megan's mum, Judy scolded.

He held his hands up. "After a trauma like that speaking to a professional is a sensible idea. Sometimes it's easier to speak to a stranger."

Megan mouthed 'sorry' and squirmed. It was really okay though. I knew he was only trying to help. "Thanks, Hank, I'll think about speaking to someone."

"Megan's been having trouble sleeping. Are you okay at night?" Judy asked.

"Mum," Megan hissed.

"Oh don't be embarrassed, darling, it's only Mackenzie."

"I'm okay when I manage to fall asleep," I said, taking the attention off Megan a little. "I keep seeing them." Megan grabbed my hand and gave it a squeeze. "Guess that's something we're just going to have to live with." There was no way to un-see something, unfortunately. I would do anything; give anything, to be able to erase that image from my memory.

"That will ease in time, I'm sure," Megan's nan said as she returned to the table with a fresh pot of tea. "I'm so sorry you both had to see that."

I bit my lip. Her words were exactly the same as Lawrence's, but they sounded so much different, genuine.

"Do you know what happens next? I've tried speaking with Detective Wright, but it's like getting blood out of a stone," Hank said, shaking his head. At least he was like that with everyone and not just the five of us.

"He doesn't really say much. Not anything that makes much sense anyway," I replied.

"I just hope they find out who done it soon. Absolutely absurd accusing you lot. Not to worry though, the truth always comes out in the end."

It was absurd but with no one else in the frame they had little to go on. Still, they should be actively looking for someone else rather than concentrating on us. I frowned. I didn't know for sure that they weren't. Could they be looking for someone else too? I should tell them about Lawrence now, despite what Blake said. Was Wright not telling us he was looking for someone else because he wanted to keep the heat on us, waiting for someone to crack?

"We're going to my room," Megan announced as we finished our tea.

I stood up. "Thanks."

Megan and I made our way to her small bedroom. She had insisted on having an en suite bathroom so now her room could just about fit her double bed and wardrobe in. I always felt a little claustrophobic in there.

She sat down on her bed against the back wall and hugged a pillow to her chest. "Mackenzie," she said slowly.

I sat at the end of the bed, facing her. "What?"

"My dad's right, the truth always comes out eventually, doesn't it?"

My heart rate picked up. "Sure. Why?"

"I did something."

"Go on," I whispered. The hairs on the back of my neck stood up and the tips of my fingers prickled.

"The night of the crash. I… I spiked Gigi's drink."

My mouth fell open. What did she…? "You did what?"

Megan gulped. "The accident was my fault, Kenz. I spiked Gigi's drink."

I blinked in shock. Gigi only had two beers because she was driving but after said she felt drunk which was odd, but she was on a diet, so no one really questioned it. We all thought the alcohol went to her head because she was eating less and losing weight.

Spiked. My heart dropped to my stomach. "You spiked her drink."

Megan's eyes widened. "Oh my God, Mackenzie, don't think that! I put vodka in her beer; I have no clue where to get fucking Rohypnol from!"

"Why?" I whispered and shook my head. What the hell would she have done that for?

She shook her head. "I can't tell you."

"What?" I said, almost shouting. "You can't tell me something like that and not explain. Shit, Megan! Tilly and Gigi *died*. Tell me what happened."

Courtney was the only one not drinking because she was on antibiotics. She has just passed her test and wasn't confident driving at all. With little choice and Josh in her ear telling her 'it's no different from a fucking car', she drove it. She pulled out at a junction and then we were hit.

"I…I" She stopped and gulped. "Promise you won't think any different of me?"

"Just tell me." I couldn't promise her that. She had just told me she was the reason Courtney was forced to drive; she spiked Gigi's drink! "Why, Megan?"

"Because when we were drunk we slept together," she said in a rush.

I laughed but quickly stopped when she didn't. Her expression didn't change. She wasn't joking. "You did what?"

"We slept together whenever we were drunk." She looked down at the floor. "I wanted her that night."

"But you're not gay," I blurted out and mentally slapped myself. That wasn't the most important part of what she had just told me, but it was true. I had never even heard her mention a Celeb girl crush like the one I had on Mila Kunis and Tilly had on Mischa Barton.

"I know." She shrugged. "But there was something about her. The first time was summer after we left school. All of you were on holiday or busy so me and Gigi were hanging out in her room. We were drinking Malibu and she just kissed me out of nowhere. At first I was stunned, but then I kissed her back. It was so different to anything I've ever felt before, softer and more intimate. Anyway, we didn't stop with a kiss and every other time we were drunk we'd have sex."

What the hell was going on with everyone? Was I the only one that hadn't slept with someone in our group? First Kyle and Courtney, now Megan and Gigi. "Why did it only happen when you were drunk?" God why was I concentrating on that part? She just told me she purposefully spiked someone, and I was getting all the gossip!

She bit her lip. "She said I wasn't ready to be a lesbian so nothing could happen, but you know her, she had no self-control when she was drunk. She was half-right; I'm not a lesbian, and I've never felt anything for a girl before or since her, but I wanted to be with her. It wasn't because she was a girl; it was because she made me feel things that I never knew existed."

A tear trickled down Megan's face, and I felt awful for her. "It's all my fault. She died because of me. Tilly too.

They both died because I was so selfish and wanted to get laid!"

I pushed myself up and wrapped my arms around her. "Shh, it's okay. You didn't mean for anyone to get hurt."

"B-But it's my fault. I have to tell the police. I-I have to."

I pulled away and gripped her face in both of my hands, forcing her to look at me. Her eyes were wide, scared. "Megan, that will achieve nothing. It was an accident. Maybe Gigi would have pulled out too. It was dark and foggy. No one saw the lorry."

"But…"

"Think about it. You spiked her drink. Do you know how that looks?"

She started sobbing, covering her mouth with her hand. "I know. I get it, I do. I get how it looks, but I swear to you, Mackenzie, I didn't hurt Court and Josh. Please believe me."

I wrapped my arms around her shaking body. "Shh, it's okay." It wasn't okay, but I needed her to calm down so we could talk more. "Megan, we need to discuss this. You can't go to the police. I know you didn't kill anyone. I believe you, but the police won't."

"But I didn't do anything to them," Megan replied. I pulled back so I could see her and try to make her see sense. "I should come clean about Gigi. People blame her for the accident."

"People blame Josh and Courtney too." I closed my eyes. This was definitely revenge. "There are about a million what ifs, Megan. I could have gone to the toilet and not waited and we would have been a few minutes later and missed the lorry. We could have left an hour earlier when Kyle wanted to, or pulled over at the burger van like Aaron wanted. There are so many things we all could have done that would have changed that night but you can't go back in time. It was an accident."

She nodded, wiping her nose on the back of her sleeve. Her dark eyes were bloodshot. "I feel *so* guilty."

"I think we all do. That's part of being the ones that survived. Take me through everything that happened that night."

Did I really want to hear how much I clearly didn't know Megan and Gigi too? We all kept our secrets, but I didn't think Courtney or Megan would have kept Kyle and Gigi from me. We could talk about things like that. Or so I thought.

She bit her lip and hugged the pillow tighter. "It was the last night and we hadn't been… together for a few weeks. She kept flirting with me, but when I tried to kiss her she pushed me away. Do you remember me suggesting someone else should drive back because Gigi drove there?"

I nodded. Megan had asked us during the afternoon before anyone had started drinking. I would have driven but like Courtney I hadn't long passed my test after failing twice and didn't feel confident enough to drive a minivan full of people. Gigi insisted that she didn't mind and wanted to drive back too. Her stepdad owned it anyway, so she didn't want anyone else being responsible if anything happened to it.

At the time I just thought Megan was being considerate and wanted Gigi to be able to drink on the last day. I had no idea of her ulterior motive. They never acted any differently around each other, not that I'd noticed anyway.

"When it was decided Gigi was driving back, I took matters into my own hands. Later back at the hotel she said she was just going to have a couple beerss o I put vodka in them."

"How could she not know?"

Megan smiled. "Probably because you bought the cheap, crap stuff."

I tilted my head to the side and glared. "I'm not forking out for the good stuff when you lot down it in seconds." Alcohol never lasted very long with my friends. Perhaps that needed to change. "So what happened next?"

"Well it worked. When you lot went back into the park we... Well, you don't want the details. I knew Courtney couldn't drink, so she ended up having to drive and you know the rest. It was my fault."

My head spun. I couldn't have been more shocked at her actions. "Okay." I took a deep breath. "What you did was wrong, so, so wrong, but it doesn't change anything and telling people will only make you suspect number one. If the police never find out who really did it who do you think they're going to come looking for?"

"What do we do? Mackenzie, this secret has been killing me. I want it off my chest, but I don't want to go to prison for something I haven't done."

"Talk to me about it, whenever you want. Whatever you need to say or vent, just do it to me, okay? We're not going to the police. You made a stupid, stupid mistake, but you didn't mean to hurt anyone."

Her eyes filled with tears. "I don't know what to say."

"Don't say anything. Dry your eyes and plaster on a smile. You need to be normal when you see me out."

"You're leaving?" she asked, frowning.

I need to leave. "I have to, but don't worry, everything's gonna be fine."

# CHAPTER THIRTEEN

I sat cross-legged on my bed in a daze. Two of my friends had hidden huge secrets from me. Actually, four had. I knew that if I told anyone I could land them both in trouble. Wright would definitely see both their secrets as motives. And what about Aaron? What had he been hiding for Wright to pull him in?

An awful thought kept popping into my head: What if it was them? If it was and I chose to do nothing, I was protecting my friends but preventing justice for Courtney and Josh. I loved Megan, Kyle, Aaron and Courtney equally. How could I choose?

I picked up my phone and called Courtney's cousin, Felicity. We hadn't spoken at the funeral, and I was hoping she could make things clearer for me. She grew up with Courtney. Her mum was a total flake, so she practically lived with Court and her parents until she moved away to university.

"Mackenzie," she said, picking up on the first ring.

"Hey, how are you?" I closed my eyes. Stupid question!

"I'm doing alright. You?"

"Yeah, okay, I guess. Are you busy tomorrow?"

"Not really. I'm packing to go back to uni but apart from that sod all." She was going back so soon? "You want to meet up for breakfast?"

"That sounds good."

"I'm leaving here at eight. Wanna meet at The Lion at ten past?"

"Okay. I'll see you then."

"Bye, Kenz." She hung up but I stayed still with it attached to my ear. I didn't think she would leave that soon. Courtney was practically a sister to her. Was the same thing happening to her as Blake? Did Courtney's mum wish it was Felicity instead?

"Mackenzie?" Mum shouted up the stairs. "Kyle's here, I'm sending him up."

I threw my phone down and waited for him. He had barely left me alone since he told me about his affair with Courtney. I found it unnerving. He knew I wasn't going to shout it out so why was he obsessed with speaking to me or seeing me all the time?

"Hey," he said, closing my bedroom door behind him.

I plastered on a smile. My heart beat faster as if it was telling me something I didn't want to know. "What's up?"

He shrugged and flopped down on my bed, lying on his back with his arms above his head. I smiled a genuine smile. That was so normal of him. He would always kick back with his limbs sprawled out on my bed. "Nothing much. I can't stand being at home."

"Parents driving you insane?"

"Yep. What are you up to?"

"Nothing. You?"

"Just come to see one of my oldest friends."

I narrowed my eyes. "I'm not old."

"That's right." He grinned and it lit up his hazel eyes. "You're the baby of the group."

I was turning twenty in four months. Courtney should have been sixteen weeks before me, but she would never get to do that. She would be a teenager forever – like Tilly and Gigi.

We fell into an awkward silence that we'd never had before. We met when we were kids, and kids just got on with it no matter if they knew a person or not. I wanted to ask him if he really meant the nasty things he said about Courtney, and I think he wanted to talk about it too.

"Is everything really okay? I know you're angry at how Courtney treated you. If you want to talk about it, we can."

"You'll judge me, Kenz. You did yesterday, and I can't stand it. You don't understand."

"Then make me understand. Come on, Kyle, there's nothing we can't talk about."

"Have you ever been in love?"

I thought I was in love with my ex, Danny, but he turned out to be a heartless dick. There hadn't been anyone else since we broke up two and a half years ago. I didn't ever want to put myself in the position I was in with him again. "No," I replied.

"Then I don't know if you can understand it yet. Courtney was everything. She was all I thought about. My whole life had become about her and making her happy. I thought she felt the same. We were supposed to be together. And then she turned around kicked me to the kerb. You can't ever imagine how much that hurts. I had everything ripped away from me and yes, I'm pissed at her. I hate her, and I hate that I can't stop loving her. I wish I could flip a switch and not care about her anymore, but I can't, so I'm angry until I'm over it."

Maybe I didn't understand how he felt, but I still didn't know if I could hate someone that I loved after they'd died, even if they had hurt me. Did he only want Courtney to be happy if she was with him? If so that wasn't my definition of love.

I groaned, rubbing my forehead, feeling a headache coming on. "I'm sorry, Kyle. Shit, I'm tired."

He frowned. "Sorry. I should have called before I came and unloaded that on you. I just want to make sure we're okay. I don't want what happened with Courtney to fuck up our friendship."

"It's okay, and it won't fuck us up. I'm just gonna try and get some sleep now." I hated that he felt he had to be around me all the time. Was he worried that I honestly thought he could have done it? I knew he hadn't. I was certain, almost.

He kissed my forehead as he stood up. "Night, Kenz. Speak to you tomorrow."

I smiled half-heartedly and flopped down on my bed, exhausted. "Night, Kyle," I replied, yawning. There was no way I would get a good night's sleep, but at least I would be alone and not have to deal with anyone else for a while.

In the morning I made my way to the local pub where I was meeting Felicity. I hoped talking to her would make everything clear, magically. There was still so much up in the air. Megan, Kyle, Lawrence, and how I felt about siding with someone that killed my friend. I was running out of ideas and needed a break.

I saw her as soon as I walked into the restaurant room at the back of the pub. She sat against the window, wearing a deep red summer dress and denim jacket. Her hair fell in tight blonde ringlets down to the bottom of her shoulder blades. Her appearance couldn't have been more different to Courtney's. Court's hair had been fierce red since she was sixteen. She loved the colour. The deeper into her relationship with Josh though, the duller it became. He didn't like it, so she stopped dying it and let it fade away. It was symbolic of what he was doing to her. In the last few months of their relationship, the Courtney I knew and loved began fading away too.

"Hey," I said as I approached the table. She looked around and stood up, smiling.

"Hi," Felicity replied, opening her arms for me. Well at least she didn't think I could have killed her cousin.

I hugged her back, and we sat down. "How is everyone?"

"Devastated. I don't want to leave them, but I have so much work to do." She bit her lip. "And honestly, I can't stand being there. I know that sounds so selfish, but there's nothing I can do to help. I feel so useless."

"You're not useless. I don't think anyone can do anything right now. They lost their daughter; they need time."

"And what about you? What do you need? Kyle said you're dealing with this too well."

"You've spoken to Kyle?"

She scanned the menu. "He's dropped by a few times. The pancakes are a bit hit and miss here, isn't it?"

I nodded my head. "Sometimes they're amazing and other times they suck." Why had Kyle gone round there? He was still clearly angry with Courtney for choosing Josh over him, so why go to see her family? Kyle and Aaron both secretly visited the family of the girl they loved, but why secretly?

An annoying, nagging voice in the back of my head kept screaming that he was hiding something else. What if it was Kyle? I had known the guy practically my whole life. Could I really be *that* blind? After the past few days, I really could believe that I was that blind though. I trusted them all. I thought they were being honest with me, and I thought they could confide in me.

"So what's with the super coping then? You know it's not healthy to bottle things up."

I laughed. That one I had heard far too often lately. "I'm temporarily bottling. I'll deal when they find the killer, or at least realise it wasn't one of us."

She scoffed and threw her curly hair over her shoulder. "That's a load of crap. I thought it was a joke when I first found out. No one believes it. Well no one that matters anyway."

"What will you do if they never find him? I don't know how I can live with knowing they never got justice."

Felicity shrugged. "Life goes on, Mackenzie. I know that's harsh and horrible, but it's true. I hope with everything they catch him, but if they don't it changes nothing. Courtney and Josh are still dead. Nothing will bring them back or make it okay."

"Really? If they never found out who did it you'd be okay?"

"Not okay. I want justice; it just doesn't change a thing. Don't drive yourself crazy with this. You know Courtney would probably say something like 'get a grip, Mackenzie. I'm dead, deal with it' wouldn't she?"

I smiled. I could hear her saying those words. "Yeah." But did that make it okay to cover up for one of my friends? And what about Court and Josh's families? "So how's uni going anyway? You still loving it up in Liverpool?"

She nodded. "I do. It's a great place. Where my uni is anyway! Not sure I'll stay after I graduate now though. I'm thinking of moving back when it's time to find a job." Felicity wanted to be a nurse and was three years into a four-year degree.

"There better job opportunities here?" That seemed unlikely. The closest hospital around was a forty-minute drive, and there were only three within a comfortable daily driving distance. Surely there was more in Liverpool?

"Not really but I want to be around family. I'm thinking of going into a walk-in clinic or something now. I like the one in Liverpool."

I nodded. "Sounds good. Would be nice to have you back this way." Liverpool was about two hundred miles north and just over three and a half hours away. She didn't get to visit much so it would be great to see more of her.

"What about you? Your course going okay?"

"Not bad. I'm enjoying it. Next year I'm going to look at trying to get more experience. Some son of a woman my mum knows is a counsellor in a high school. I'm going to get in touch with him and see if I can shadow him for a while next summer."

"Not this summer?"

"This year was supposed to be our last summer of freedom and we were all spending it working our way through a before-we-get-old-and-have-a-job bucket list!"

She smiled. "How far did you get?"

"We'd done Lego Land and camping, which I hated." It rained the entire two days we were away. "Paintballing, hedge maze and sort of the drunken weekend away."

"You don't want to do the rest?"

"One day maybe." For Tilly, Gigi and Courtney I would do all of the things we planned to, but there were far more important things to deal with before I ticked off any more activities from a list. I also didn't particularly want to do them anymore. It wouldn't be fun. It was now just something I felt I had to do.

"What's this Detective Wright like then? I've heard interesting things."

I raised an eyebrow. "Interesting is one way to describe him. He's like one of those eccentric detectives you see on TV. Not sure if he realises TV isn't real and that maybe he needs to be grown-up about his career."

"There are no other leads?"

"Apparently not but he's hardly forthcoming with information. We only know what he wants us to know and when he wants us to know it. I have no clue what he's thinking about the clothes."

She frowned, stirring the mug of tea that everyone received as soon as they arrived whether they wanted it or not. The owners, Mr and Mrs Graham were big on tea. "What clothes?"

"The ones the murderer was wearing. If it was one of us then it has to be somewhere, right?" She nodded. "They can't find it, of course. But he still won't accept that it means it wasn't us. Instead of looking for it so they can catch the person responsible they're pointing the finger at us."

"Are you sure? They can't ignore that."

I shrugged. "I'm not sure about much anymore. There's been no mention of it though." I scoffed. Like he would tell us even if he had found it. "I bet the first we'll hear of it is when he scrubs us off the suspect list. And Aaron was arrested, as you probably know, but I'm sure it won't be long until he's released."

"So fucked up," she said, shaking her head.
"Yep."

By the time I had finished breakfast and made my way back home I was feeling slightly better. I still wasn't sure what I was going to do if it turned out Kyle, Megan or Aaron had done it.

My mobile beeped with another text message, and I knew it would be Megan. It was Megan a lot recently. I still wasn't quite ready to talk to her, so I sent a message back telling her we would meet up tomorrow. That would hopefully give me more time to work things out in my head.

Just as I finished sending the text my phone rang and I sighed in relief as Aaron's name flashed up on my screen. "Aaron! Are you okay? I tried calling about a million times!" I hadn't been able to get in contact with him at all last night.

He chuckled. "Mum said you'd called. I'm fine."

"What happened yesterday?"

"Apparently Wright found some of my blood in the woods. It's okay though, I explained what happened."

My heart froze. It *was* his blood. "What did happen?" I asked, absolutely terrified for his answer. There had to be a reasonable explanation for it.

"Megan and I went for a walk; she found what she thought was one of those stupid crystal stone things. I picked it up and turns out it was an old, very sharp piece of green glass!"

"Oh. You never mentioned it when you got back."

"One, I'm a man. And two, it bled for a second, hardly bandage material. Wright just wanted me to clear it up. I think he'll want to speak to Megan. Can you believe he doesn't trust us?" he joked.

"Crazy, right?" I replied, forcing myself to laugh. "So everything is cool?"

"Yep. I gotta go, visiting the family soon. I'll be home tomorrow so we'll meet up, yeah?"

"Wait, you're going away?"

"Twenty miles away, Kenz, not to Mexico!"

I bit my lip and sat down on my bed. "Okay. See you tomorrow."

Aaron hung up, and I collapsed back on the mattress. He was visiting family last minute. Aaron usually did everything he could to get out of family things. Under any normal circumstances, I wouldn't even question it, but this wasn't normal. It did sound like he was running, maybe not from Wright and the police but from his friends. Was there something he didn't want us to see? Something we could see through because we supposedly knew him so well?

I dialled Blake's number and laid my mobile beside me on speakerphone. Hopefully he would make everything clearer. Or just turn it into a joke!

"Do I need to take out a restraining order?" Blake teased.

"It was his blood," I whispered. The line went silent. I waited for him to say something. *I told you so* was what I expected to come out of his mouth straight away. "Blake?"

"I'm here," he said. "Do you want me to come over?"

*No annoying I told you so?* "I don't know what I want. How can it be his?" My hands shook. "Did he do it?" He couldn't have.

"You're asking me?"

"I'm too close, aren't I? I believe them all so much that I can't see clearly. Did Aaron do it, Blake?"

"For what it's worth, I don't think so. My money is still on Kyle." I heard him rustling around in the background and then the sound of jingling keys. He was really coming over? "Just chill out, we still need to speak to Wright about Lawrence. Aaron's blood in a shed doesn't prove he's a murderer."

"Why are you doing this? You think it was one of them so why help me with Lawrence and reassure me."

"You asked me to, remember?"

"That doesn't answer my question. You could have told me to get lost, and don't tell me you're only doing to because you're bored because I know that's a lie."

He sighed. "Fine. I like that you're so loyal. You don't find that much, and it's not something I've ever had. Plus you're not that bad to look at."

"You had to ruin it," I replied. A small smile pulled at my lips even though I had nothing to smile about. "Are you coming over?"

"On my way," he said and hung up.

I put the phone down and smiled to myself. As much as Blake played the I-don't-give-a-shit card he really did care. My heart fluttered. I really did have a thing for him.

It took him half the time it should to get to my house. I wanted to yell because he had obviously driven fast, but I was too glad to see him. He let himself into my room as if he owned the place. "What did he say?" he asked, sitting down on my bed and laying back against my pillows.

"Please do make yourself comfortable." Blake glared. "He said he was out with Megan and cut his finger on glass, but he never said anything when he got back."

His chest shook as he laughed. "Guys stop boasting about their war wounds when they're about ten, Mackenzie. Do you believe him?"

"Yes," I replied.

Blake rolled his eyes and pushed himself up. He sat facing me. His striking blue eyes pierced through me. "Do you? There's no doubt in your mind? Aaron is innocent?"

The way he was looking at me was too intense. I felt bare. He was doing that see like right through me thing that made me nervous. "I believe him."

He flopped down on his back again. "Alright then. I think you're right too. It's Kyle. We should delve into Megan a little more soon."

"Megan," I repeated.

"You said once girl or guy. She had the opportunity."

It was my turn to roll my eyes. "We all had the opportunity."

"Shh," he whispered. "I'm going to have a nap. We'll resume this when I wake up."

My eyebrows shot up. What? "Excuse me?"

"Mackenzie, I am trying to sleep." He closed his eyes.

"Why do you really want to sleep here?"

He smirked. "Because I'm scared of the boogie man."

I sighed. "Fine, Blake. I know it's really because you don't feel comfortable at home and it's a weird atmosphere."

"Then why ask!"

I narrowed my eyes at him even though he couldn't see me. "You're not sleeping here all afternoon."

"Just a couple hours. Wake me when you've cooked dinner."

I gritted my teeth but couldn't help a little smile. Idiot!

While Blake slept, without snoring, so that was a bonus, I re-read The Shining so I had something else to focus on. I wanted to wake him up and make him talk through everything again, but I didn't want to disturb him, and I didn't want to drive myself even crazier.

Blake looked so peaceful when he slept. Innocent like a newborn baby. His eyes flitted occasionally and he would take the odd deep breath in his sleep. I found myself watching him more. I hated that he felt so alone. That was another reason he was hanging around with me, so he had someone. I was sure of it. I realised when he smiled a boyish smile and rolled onto his side that I was glad I had him too.

At half past ten, after I had cooked him his damn dinner, Blake went home. As much as he drove me crazy, he also kept me sane. I watched him drive away from my bedroom window and then got straight into bed.

I couldn't switch my mind off enough to sleep though. Everything was so messed up and confusing. I was also waiting on a text from Blake to tell me he was home okay. That was something that seemed to amuse and baffle him. I don't think he had ever been asked to do that before. I really felt for him. No one cared enough to want to know he was safe. My parents were always moaning at me to let them know I was okay.

My phone rang ten minutes after he left. I picked it up and saw Blake's name. He was meant to text. If he had called me just to say something annoying or sarcastic…

"Hi," I said into the phone. "You're home then?"

"Pete's in hospital."

I gasped. That was the last thing Blake needed. His brother was dead, and now his uncle was ill. "What?"

"He's been attacked."

Attacked! Jumping out of bed, I reached for my jeans I'd thrown over my chair. "I'm on my way," I replied and hung up so I could get dressed and get to him faster.

# CHAPTER FOURTEEN

I burst into Blake's room and found him sitting on his bed, staring at the plain wall. There was no doubt he heard me enter, but he made no attempt to look up or acknowledge me.

I slowly moved to his bed, wary, worried. "I'm so sorry, Blake. What happened? Do you want to go to the hospital? I can take you right now."

"My mum found him at his house. The front door was open and was lying on the living room floor. He's been hit over the head with his fucking baseball bat, Mackenzie!"

"Oh my God!" I sat down. "Do you know what's happening now?"

He shook his head. "I've just found out. My dad offered to come and get me but..."

"But what?"

"I don't know if anyone would want me there."

"Of course they do." It was me Pete wouldn't want there. "Come on, we need to go."

He looked over and I saw the pain in his eyes. "Why are you here?"

"Why did you come over for me?"

He frowned and looked back ahead at the wall. "Ah, we're friends now, are we?"

"Yes, so get used to it. Put your shoes and coat on, we're going to the hospital."

I could only see the side of his face, but his smirk was crystal clear. "Did you just tell me to put my shoes and coat on like I'm a child?"

"Well when you decide to act your age…" I rolled my eyes. "Come on, Blake. You have to go."

"I wonder who it was? Do you know where Aaron, Kyle and Megan are?"

"What?" I replied, laughing. "You think it was one of them?"

"How can you not think this is related to Josh and Courtney's murder?"

"Let's just forget that for a minute. Get off your arse and get in my car!"

Blake and I arrived at the hospital forty-five minutes later and walked the deserted corridor looking for Ward F were Eloise had informed me Pete was. "When we get there I think I should wait outside. You okay with that?"

Blake raised an eyebrow. "I don't need you to hold my hand."

"Course you don't," I replied sarcastically. "Why do you think anything I do for you is me treating you like a child? I want to be there for you too. There are no ulterior motives and I'm not doing it to get anything in return. That's just what friends do."

"Again with the friend thing. You really do like me, don't you?" He said it as a joke, but under the teasing I could tell he was genuinely asking. I don't think there were many people in his life that actually knew him and cared about him. I wished I could meet some of his friends and see what they were like. Distant from each other. Only hanging around together because of mutual interests – drinking – and not a lot else probably.

I smiled. "Yep, you're stuck with me."

We arrived at the ward, and I rang the intercom. As soon as I mentioned Pete's nephew was here we were told to come straight in. That didn't seem good to me, like they wanted to get his family in quick to say goodbye before the inevitable.

Blake held the door open as it clicked unlocked. I walked through and turned around, smirking. "Be careful, you're turning into a gentleman."

His blue eyes glared. "Next time I'm gonna let it hit your arse."

"Sure you will. Go ahead, I'll wait in there," I said, nodding towards the door with 'Waiting Room' above it in black stuck on letters.

"You really don't want to come with?"

"Blake, your family will be glad you came. You know how Pete feels about me; there's no way he would want me there. I'll be right here, and we can leave whenever you want." He opened his mouth, and I slapped my palm over it, sensing what he was about to say. "*After* you've seen your uncle."

I waited until Blake entered Pete's room and went into the small waiting room. One wall was lined with blue fabric chairs, and the other had a long wooden counter, exactly what you'd expect. There were tea and coffee making facilities, but I figured those were for family of patients to use, so I stuck fifty pence in the vending machine for a crappy plastic cup of coffee.

I sat down and pulled a *Woman's Weekly* magazine onto my lap. I wasn't sure how long Blake would stay, but I didn't think it would be that long. As much as I wanted my bed, I wanted Blake to stay more. He needed to connect with the family that were still practically strangers to him. The only family he really had was his dad and paternal grandparents.

Being the only person in the waiting room and with no other distraction, my mind wondered to what Blake had said. Was the person that hurt Pete the same one that killed Courtney and Josh? Blake thought it was Kyle, but I couldn't see any of them hitting someone over the head with a baseball bat any more than I could them stabbing two of our friends.

I kept coming back to the same conclusion: it wasn't any of them. I couldn't even force myself to imagine it was, not even to pretend. The image of one of them holding a knife in their hand, standing over Court and Josh's bloody bodies, refused to enter my mind. Blake was in a much better position, he didn't have any ties with any of them, he had a completely fresh way of looking at it.

I had only just finished my pond-water coffee when Blake walked into the room. "Let's go," he said.

"How is he?" I asked, standing up and throwing my empty cup in the bin.

"Unconscious," he replied and walked back out of the room. I blinked hard, throwing the un-read magazine down and scrambling after him.

By the time I got home, it was just after midnight, and I was exhausted. Blake had barely said a word the whole way home, and I wasn't sure if that was a good thing or not. I didn't see any of his family, but he told me they were in Pete's room. It didn't look good that they were all allowed to stay with him either. The only thing I had managed to get out of him was that his nan was glad he was there. I think they all were, but he expected the worst all the time.

From what I could drag out of him I knew that Pete was in a critical condition. His brain was swollen and he was unresponsive. A machine was literally his lifeline. It looked really, really bad.

I woke up with a moment of clarity. It was time to tell Wright my theory on Lawrence and let him decide what to do with it. We were getting nowhere. I had no idea what I was doing. I was a mess.

I knew the blood wasn't his but Aaron had explained that. The blood now meant nothing. Pete had been hurt, and the police needed to start looking at Lawrence before something happened to anyone else.

I got dressed and had breakfast with my parents, promising them all over again that I was okay. My parents were worriers and always had been. I visited the doctor surgery and A&E for the most ridiculous things. As their only child, they went a little overboard.

As soon as I finished eating I grabbed my keys and headed out to my car at the same time my parents headed off to work. I waved to them, rolling my eyes at the worry lines on my mum's forehead.

My mobile rang as I drove to the police station. I saw Megan's name and felt ill. Was I ready to deal with her yet? I had to at some point I suppose. "Hi," I said and put her on hands free so I could drive at the same time.

"Hey, Kenzie, you okay?"

"Yeah, you?"

"I'm okay. Look I think we all need to get together. I've not seen you all properly in ages, and you didn't make it the other night. Aaron and Kyle are coming to mine at seven tonight for pizza. We need to stick together and not continue to drift apart. You in?"

It all sounded so normal, like any other chilled evening. It all felt forced and fake now though. "Sure, I'm in. I'm driving so I've gotta go, but I'll see you later."

"Alright. Bye."

"Bye." I ended the call and pulled into the car park next to the police station. To my right was Aaron's car. I got out and saw him and Kyle walking towards me.

"Hey," Kyle said, giving me a hug.

I hugged him back briefly and pulled away. "Hey."

"You been called in too, huh?" Aaron asked, rolling his eyes.

Called in? "Yeah," I replied, not wanting to get into what I was really doing. If I asked Aaron what it was about he might question why I didn't know. Probably about Pete anyway.

"You at Megan's later?"

"Yeah, I'll see you there."

"Cool," Aaron replied, nodding and opening the car door. Kyle got in the passenger side and started messing around on his phone. Everything they did now made me think there could be more to it. Knowing Kyle he was probably just playing on some crappy app he just downloaded. They both gave me an effortless wave as Aaron backed out of the space and drove off.

I was just about to walk into the police station, still intent on telling Wright about Lawrence, when I saw him and Blake just outside the station's front doors. Blake was here too? I took a few steps closer so I could hear what they were saying.

"Yes...very colourful indeed," Wright said, raising one of his dark eyebrows. What was colourful?

I couldn't see Blake because his back was to me, but I could picture his bored expression. "Colourful doesn't make you a killer. What you're looking for is psychotic." Blake was 'colourful'? Why?

Wright shrugged. "Perhaps not and perhaps you're not the killer. You past doesn't prove you murdered your brother and his girlfriend. It did, however, make very interesting reading. I thank you for that; you saved me from a dull evening in alone." He nodded once and went back inside the station. It came as no surprise to learn Wright was single.

Blake turned and walked towards his the car park. He still hadn't seen me. What had he been hiding? I suppose it wasn't really hiding with him. We barely knew each other.

"Hey," I shouted and started running after him.

He turned his head to look at me briefly and carried on. "What are you doing here, Mackenzie?"

"What did he mean?" I asked, jogging to keep up with him.

Blake's eyebrows pulled together in a deep frown. "Nothing," he muttered.

"Bullshit!" I grabbed the top of his arm and pulled.

He spun around, almost knocking into me. "What do you want? You're all over the place, running around trying to solve a murder. I. Didn't. Kill. Them," he said slowly. There was no need for him to say that, I hadn't asked. Was it because of whatever Wright had dug up that he was asking?

"I believe you." He looked into my eyes, trying to figure out if I was telling the truth or not. "I believe you, Blake."

"Then drop it."

Turning around, he walked towards his truck. Not so fast! I followed, keeping up but keeping a small amount of distance. Whatever he was hiding I wanted to know. He had a police record for what?

Blake unlocked the car, and I opened the passenger door, tugging on it hard to get the damn thing to open. "What the fuck are you doing?" he asked. He sounded bored, and it made me smile. "What?"

"Get in the car, Blake." He sighed and got in. "Tell me."

He arched his brow. "I'll tell you if you tell me something no one knows about you."

"Is that what you always do? Deflect?"

His face was a mystery; he'd put up the wall. He was so good at giving nothing away when he didn't want to. "If I'm going to tell you something only my dad knows, something that I'm not proud of, I want the same in return. It's your choice."

"Fine." I chewed the inside of my mouth and looked out of the side window. I didn't want Blake to see me when I told him. My heart broke as I prepared to talk about it again for the first time since I was seventeen. Why was I about to tell him this? I gripped the sides of the chair. "Two years ago I had an abortion."

I waited for him to say something, but he was silent. I went on, "I was just seventeen and so scared. My boyfriend at the time broke up with me a week before I found out and he turned... nasty. I couldn't tell my parents because they would be so disappointed. I didn't want them to hate me. I didn't tell anyone."

"You did it by yourself?"

I nodded. "I booked an appointment at the clinic. I didn't even allow myself to think about it too much. I pretended I was going for a routine test. When I took that pill, I pretended it was paracetamol. When I felt the pains, I pretended they were period pains. The second I did it I hated myself. I still do. It was the biggest mistake of my life," I whispered, gulping, "and Josh was the only other person that knew."

# CHAPTER FIFTEEN

"Josh knew. How?"

I bit my lip as a scorching tear burned its way down my cheek. My heart felt as if it was breaking all over again.

"He saw me leaving the clinic. I was a mess. I couldn't believe what I had just done. Josh was delivering leaflets from the printers or something. It didn't take him long to work out what had happened." I swallowed. My throat was on fire, and I fought to stay in control.

"What did he do?"

I pulled my legs up, wrapping my arms around them in a bid to protect myself from the conversation. "He blackmailed me," I replied. "It was nothing serious really, mostly things like making me step out of his way when he wanted to get with Courtney, making me pick him up in the middle of the night, give him money, false references for jobs he wanted, getting me to agree to things like going on trips, things that we usually would have avoided because we didn't like him."

"Bastard," Blake muttered.

"Every time I tried to convince Courtney he was an arsehole I pictured his face – that half smirk and one raised eyebrow, telling me he knew something I didn't want getting out." I took a deep breath. "I wanted Courtney to be free of him, but I couldn't let anyone know what I'd done. I hate myself for it."

"Why didn't you tell your parents?"

Blinking rapidly, I looked up to stop fresh tears from falling. "Because I'm ashamed and because it's my biggest regret. They would be *so* disappointed in me. I would do anything to go back in time and change it."

Blake's hand stroked down my arm until he reached my hand. "You were young, Mackenzie."

"So? I was old enough to have sex. I just wish I had thought it through before I made a snap decision. Now I have to live with it."

"I'm sorry that you had to go through that alone and didn't feel you could turn to anyone."

"I make such a big deal out of everyone else keeping secrets when mine is so…" I shook my head and pressed my forehead to my knees.

"I put a man in hospital," he said.

I looked up through my eyelashes. "What?"

"When I was eighteen I was a bit of a fighter. Actually, I lived for it."

"Why?"

"I was angry."

"About?"

He smirked. "Man you're nosey."

I sat up and turned my body to face him. "Hey I told you my biggest, darkest secret that no one else knows. Your turn now, remember?" He reached up and wiped a small tear from under my eye. I stopped breathing for a second. "What happened, Blake?"

"I don't have a good relationship with my mum, you know that already." I nodded. "I was angry with her for not caring enough and angry at her for loving Josh more. My dad worked a lot, so I was alone most of the time. I didn't have many friends, not real friends anyway. A group of us would hang out on the street, drink and get into fights."

"And you questioned our class for drinking in a park."

The faintest smile pulled at the corners of his lips. "I never said what I did was classy. It was stupid. I was stupid. There was this guy mouthing off one night and I lost it. I can't even remember what he said, something stupid probably. Anyway, I went too far and when I was pulled off him, I realised why everyone was shouting so much. He was lying so still on the floor. There was a lot of blood." He stopped and frowned, remembering. "That was the last fight I got in."

"Whoa." I blinked, shaking my head to absorb what he'd told me. "You were dumb, but I understand why you were like that."

A ghost of a smile pulled at his lips. "No more psycho analysing me!"

"I imagine Wright was having a field day with that."

"Yeah. Although fighting and premeditated murder are two completely different things, I think I just got bumped to the top of his hit list."

"I wouldn't go that far, Mr Harper." We both jumped at the sound of Wright's voice. I spun around and saw him leaning against the car beside Blake's. He was standing level with the back windows, just where we couldn't see him. "I think maybe we should have another little chat." Wright turned on his heel and walked back towards the station, so confident that we would follow.

My heart spiked. "Shit, Blake!"

He shook his head. "It's okay. It'll be fine."

"But he's going to think I did it."

"He already does." Blake rolled his eyes. "Mackenzie, anyone can see you're not a cold blooded killer. You're too weak for one. You can barely open my car door."

"Shut up, it's stiff!" I shoved the door open – which was easy from inside – and got out. Blake followed me, laughing to himself. How could he be so calm? I was so sure he was going to arrest me the second I walked into the building.

I heard my pulse throbbing in my ears as I stepped into the all too familiar station. Wright smiled and clicked his tongue. "Mackenzie, follow me." Blake's fingers brushed my arm as I walked. I wasn't sure why. Was his gesture to tell me it would be okay?

I sat down in the small, boring magnolia coloured room. A black desk separated me from Wright. He closed the door and sat down. Leaning on the table he said, "You know the drill," and nodded to the tape recorder, which he flicked on, giving the date and my name. "So tell me about this blackmail."

"It wasn't blackmail really. Josh never made me do anything. I just wasn't allowed to tell Courtney what he was really like."

His bushy brow arched. "Which was?"

"I've told you before."

He shrugged. "Humour me."

I sighed. Telling him what I said before now seemed like a bad idea, but I had no doubt that he remembered what I had said, so I had to repeat it. "Josh was selfish and thought everyone owed him something. I knew he would try to control Courtney. He did control her. She could do better than him."

"But Josh didn't allow you to voice your opinion?"

"Well... No, he didn't." I bowed my head. "In the end I told Courtney that if she liked him he couldn't be that bad, and it was her choice. I didn't want to, but I didn't want anyone to know that I had an abortion."

"And that's why you killed him?"

I gasped and sat up straight. I knew that was coming. "No!"

"Josh was the only one who knew. He was the only one that could reveal your secret. With him out of your way, no one would ever know. His death has solved your problem, hasn't it?"

"I didn't kill him, and if I did why would I kill Courtney? She was my best friend. I would never kill anyone over a secret. I swear."

"Here's what I think happened," he said and paused for a second to see if I was going to challenge him. "I think there was an altercation between you and Joshua and you lost control. Courtney witnessed it and to silence her you stabbed her too."

"No, that's not what happened. I didn't do it." I knew I should remain calm, but it was so hard to do when someone was accusing you of something you didn't do, something so cold and cruel.

"Where were you yesterday at around eight at night?"

"At home."

"Was anyone else there?"

"Blake was until about half ten and my parents were in all evening. I didn't hurt Pete."

He held his hands up and smiled. "Just asking."

"Blake was with you all night?"

"Yeah."

"The whole time?"

"Yeah. Well…"

Wright raised his eyebrow and leant forward. "Well?"

"I mean he was in my house the whole time, but I wasn't with him." Wright stayed silent, waiting. "I went downstairs to make dinner and Blake stayed in my room, but he didn't leave the house."

"How can you be sure of that?"

"I would have seen him walk past the kitchen to get out."

"Back door?"

"That's the French doors off the living room, and my parents were watching black and white films all night. They would have seen him."

"So there was no chance he could have snuck out and back in again?"

"No," I replied. There was of course. I was cooking for about half an hour, and there was a chance while I was preoccupied that he could have. I didn't want to tell Wright that because I knew he would call Blake back in. There was no way he tried to kill his uncle.

"Did you leave the house?"

"No," I replied.

He smiled, and I thought he was going dig further about how I could have, but he didn't. "Let me run through what I think happened at the cabin once more, shall I." It wasn't a question. I didn't really have a choice. "I think you killed Josh because he was threatening to expose your secret. Courtney witnessed the attack, which meant you had to kill her too. Peter Sheffield somehow – I haven't quite worked that part out yet – found out what you'd done, so you tried to kill him too."

"I bet you said the same thing to Blake."

He smiled tightly, narrowing his eyes. "Blake's motive was different."

I blinked, shocked. Why was he admitting he'd accused him in the same way too? I couldn't figure him out. Whatever I thought he would do or how he would react he always did something completely different.

"You're free to go now, Miss Keaton."

I was? I didn't stay to question it. He worked differently; everything he did was designed to confuse you and shake you up. I stood up and left the room, refusing to allow Wright know he was getting to me.

I walked quickly through the station and out of the door. It was only when I passed the front desk that I remembered Lawrence. Would it look like I was just clutching at straws after Wright revealed his theory yet again? He would probably see it that way. Sighing in frustration, I pushed the door open and strolled out towards the car park.

"Hey."

I jumped at the sound of Blake's voice. He leant against the brick wall, one leg slung over the other as if he didn't have a care in the world. "What are you still doing here?" He frowned. "Were you waiting for me?"

"Don't get too excited," he replied. I had a feeling that Blake didn't often think about doing things for other people, or he just never had the opportunity to. "Wanna go for a drive and talk? I'll bring you back to your car later."

I smiled. "Sure."

Blake pushed himself off the wall, and we walked silently towards his truck. I wanted to ask what happened in the station, and I bet he wanted to ask me, but neither of us said a word.

He started the engine and pulled out of the car park. I could tell he was trying too hard not to look at me. "How did it go?" he asked, keeping his eyes on the road.

"He thinks I killed Josh and then Courtney when she witnessed it." I shook my head. "I don't know why he's doing this. My friends are dead and—" Sobs burst from my chest. Covering my face with my hands I cried until could barely breathe.

Blake squeezed my knee but said nothing. I could tell he really was no good in situations like these, but I appreciated him trying. "Don't take me home," I said and gasped for air.

"Where do you want me to take you?" I shrugged in response, taking deep breaths to try to calm myself down. I felt like I was drowning. "Err, you can come to mine I guess."

## CHAPTER SIXTEEN

"Who do you think it is?" Blake asked, staring up at the ceiling as we lay on his bed. I liked being at his house, as weird as that seemed. We barely knew each other, and this was Josh's place, but I felt relaxed. My parents fussed around me, and I didn't feel that comfortable at Kyle or Megan's anymore.

It took me half an hour to calm down. Blake had barely said two words to me the whole time I was crying but he stroked my hair and that was all I needed.

I shrugged. That was a question I asked myself every few minutes and every answer was always the same: *I don't know.* "I don't want it to be any of them."

"You'd prefer it to be me."

"No," I replied, knowing he would think something like that. He was way too hard on himself. I hated that he felt the outsider in his family. I honestly didn't want it to be him, but I knew I probably should want that over one of my friends.

He pushed himself up on his elbows and raised an eyebrow. "Of course you do."

"I don't, really. I don't want it to be anyone I know. There has to be another explanation."

"But there isn't, is there? We both know Lawrence is pretty pissed off, but it's not him."

Deep down I knew that, but I couldn't admit it aloud and make it real. I had known them all for years and didn't want to accept one of them did it. Believing it was Blake would be easier but for some reason I couldn't. I'd lost count of the amount of times I had protested their innocence out loud and in my head – convincing myself.

"Eventually you're going to have to accept that it was one of them."

"Who do you think it is?" I asked. He had said Kyle before, but his reasons were ridiculous.

"I don't know." He pulled his arm from beneath him and flopped back on the mattress. "No one's saying much. I still think Kyle, but I don't know. I'm not ruling the other two out just yet."

*They have said much, just not to you.* I had learned things about my friends recently that shocked me. Everyone had a reason for wanting to hurt Josh and Courtney. Should I tell Blake and see if he could figure it out from what I knew? He wasn't as close as I was; perhaps there was something really obvious that I was missing because I didn't want to believe any of them were responsible.

"Blake," I said slowly, still mentally debating whether I should say anything or not.

"Yeah?"

"There are some things about Megan and Kyle you don't know." I felt like the biggest bitch in the world. I was pretty much selling out my friends. I wanted to protect them, but another part of me wanted justice for Josh and Courtney.

He frowned, but he didn't make any attempt to move. He wasn't surprised. "What things?"

"They had a reason to kill them," I whispered.

He remained still, too still. "Go on."

I don't want to. Sighing, I resigned myself to the fact that I had to follow through and tell him since I had started. "Josh blackmailed me. You resented him," I said, making it clear we had reasons too. I didn't want him to jump to conclusions when going by motives it could easily be one of us too. "Megan spiked Gigi's drink, which forced Courtney to drive and crash, and Kyle was having an affair with Courtney."

"Courtney was cheating on Josh?"

"Yeah. Kyle said it ended a few months ago, but it went on for about five months."

He snorted. "Cocky, arrogant bastard probably deserved it."

My eyes widened, and I fought to hide my shock. "Blake!"

"Oh come on, you're thinking the same thing. Something like that would have deflated his ego a bit. I'm just disappointed he never knew. What about Aaron?"

"What?" I frowned. Complete one-eighty! "What about him?"

"What's his deep, dark secret?"

"He doesn't have one."

His eyebrow arched. "Of course he doesn't."

"You think he does?"

"What I think is that nothing would surprise me anymore. Everyone has at least one skeleton in their closet, and you need to ask yourself why Aaron is still hiding his."

"It's possible there is nothing, or nothing to do with Josh and Courtney anyway."

He sat up and was too close. "Mackenzie, you're far too naïve and far too trusting."

I sat back, putting a little space between us. I was flat against the wall, so I hoped he didn't move anymore. "So I've been told."

"People will take advantage of you."

I wrapped my arms around myself, feeling vulnerable. "Sorry for not wanting to believe my friends are murderers," I muttered.

"I'm not saying it's a bad thing, but you need to be careful. Your need to see the best in everyone is going to bite you in the arse. You can't see things clearly because you're blinded by the faith you place in people, even strangers."

"Are you talking about you?"

"Yeah, me too. You believe I didn't kill Josh and Courtney, but you know so little about me, other than I resented my brother and put a man in hospital."

I gulped. "Are you telling me you did it?"

He sighed. "No, Mackenzie, I'm telling you that you couldn't tell if I was. Which one of them is the most likely?"

"I don't know. None of them."

He smiled and cocked his head to the side. "There you go. You know it's one of us, but you refuse to face it. You know them more than anyone else. You know which one of them is the most likely, even if you won't acknowledge or accept it." I bit my lip. Was he right, did I know? "Gut instinct, Mackenzie, who is it?"

"I don't know, Blake!" I hopped off the bed and paced his room. He watched me walk silently; his bright blue eyes followed me back and forth. "I don't know."

"You do."

"No, I don't!" I shouted. "Stop it you... you arse!" He broke out into a full smile filled with amusement. "I want to punch you right now."

"Look, I'm not trying to piss you off—"

"Then stop pissing me off."

"You want my help or not?"

I shook my head and walked out of his room. "No. I'll walk to get my car."

Blake didn't follow me as I felt his house, but I didn't expect him to, he wasn't the running after a girl type.

I didn't see or speak to anyone the following day. My hope was that I would be able to see things clearer without having anyone influencing my thoughts. That didn't happen. I couldn't force myself to truly believe one of them did it. Not even Blake.

"Sweetheart?" Mum said, poking her head around my door. "We're going out now. Are you okay? Do you want to come?"

"I'm fine, Mum."

She leant against the doorframe and folded her arms over her chest. "Promise you'll call if you need anything?"

"I promise, but really, I'm okay."

"Are you seeing anyone today?"

I narrowed my eyes. Where was this going? "And by anyone you mean?"

"Just any of your friends."

"No, I'm not feeling very sociable today." Was she asking about Blake? Why was it that if you so much as mentioned the same guy twice to your parents it meant you were dating them! "I'm just going to lounge in bed and watch crap on TV."

"Okay." She smiled and grabbed the door handle, ready to close it again. "We'll see you later."

My phone had beeped more times than I could remember with missed calls and text messages. I'd blown everyone off, and although I felt bad for letting them down, I wanted to be alone too much to care. The secrets Kyle and Megan hid from me kept picking away. Why didn't they tell me? And Blake telling me Aaron was covering something up forced me to consider he could be right.

I wanted to go and see Aaron, but I didn't. I wanted to see Blake, but I couldn't handle another one of his theories or lectures. I wanted to be alone, but at the same time I didn't. There was something else to consider now too; Pete had been hurt, possibly because he found out who killed Courtney and Josh.

Groaning, I gripped my hair and flopped down into the mattress. Why couldn't it just be clear? If it was one of them then not only were they keeping it from me they were also allowing me to be a suspect. How far would they let it go? If I was somehow charged, would they let me go to prison?

Someone that I had spent about eight per cent of my time with for most of my life could be hiding themself and their terrible secret behind me. That wasn't friendship. I would never put myself before someone I love. Was I too gullible and too trusting?

Somewhere between overthinking and throwing random objects in frustration, I had a moment of clarity. I was being lied to by someone. Actually I had been for a while, thanks to Kyle and Megan. I had to look at things the way Blake did, well, not exactly how he did. I had to distance myself from them. I needed to at least know what was going on with them.

Jumping off my bed like a small child, I grabbed my phone and keys. It was time to start demanding answers rather than digging my head further into the sand. Whatever Aaron was hiding, I was going to find out. I was also going to delve into Kyle and Courtney, and Megan and Gigi's relationships. There had to be more there.

I got in my car and backed out of the driveway. It was time to visit Aaron whether I wanted to or not.

# CHAPTER SEVENTEEN

I arrived at Aaron's and thankfully his car was the only one in the drive. My heart was in my throat and butterflies swarmed my stomach. I hoped he wasn't hiding anything, but I already knew differently. Before the murders I thought I knew everything about my friends, now they seemed more like strangers.

It took me a while to want to get out of the car. I had one friend left that I still knew; that would probably change very soon, so I wanted to savour the moment. I wanted at least one person that wasn't hiding things from me.

I had a secret too, so I didn't know why I was so upset about theirs. Our secrets seemed on a different level somehow. Theirs were different. Mine only hurt me. Perhaps if they knew mine they would feel the way I did though.

The front door opened, and I knew I had been sitting in the car too long. It would look odd that I was outside so long. Aaron stepped onto the lawn. "Kenz, what're you doing?" he asked, speaking loud enough so I could hear over the sound of the engine.

I turned the key and opened the door. "Sorry, was in another world!"

He frowned. "You okay?" Aaron looked so innocent. He was all angelic blue eyes and blonde hair. I couldn't imagine him doing anything bad, ever.

"Yeah. Are you?"

"Sure. You skipped Megan's."

I shrugged, stopping in front of him. "Didn't really feel up to it."

He reached out and stroked his thumb under my eye. "You're not sleeping well."

Raising my eyebrow, I replied, "Do I look like shit?"

"No!" He rolled his baby blues. "Just a little tired. Come in."

"Your mum out?"

"Yep, you've got me all to yourself. Go on up and I'll bring chocolate and tea."

I smiled. He still seemed like my Aaron. "You know me so well."

Just as I curled up against Aaron's pillows my mobile phone beeped with a text message. 'Check his drawers under the mattress. Text BACKUP if you need me and I'll fire up the Batmobile!'

I shook my head, grinning to myself. Blake was an idiot. I had called him on the way, telling him how I intended to find out what was going on. We'd completely plastered over our fight yesterday. We moved on without mentioning it at all. I should have known he'd send something stupid like that.

'Catwoman doesn't need help.' Punching a reply, I put my phone down and waited for him again.

'Do you have a Catwoman costume?????'

I flipped my phone over and laughed quietly. Typical man!

"What're you laughing at?" Aaron asked as he walked into his room with chocolate bars stuffed in his pockets and a cup of tea in each hand.

"Nothing," I replied, sitting up to take my mug. Aaron didn't have a very high opinion of Blake, so I didn't want to start a conversation about him. "Thanks." I sipped my boiling hot tea, not caring how it burned my tongue and set it down on the bedside table. "What's been going on then?"

Aaron sat down and scooted closer to me. He frowned at my question. "What's on your mind?"

"Why do you think there's something on my mind?"

"You're doing that lost in thought thing."

I bit my lip. How was I going to ask him what his secret was without it being obvious? "Nothing much. What's been going on with you? We haven't talked in forever."

He shrugged. "Not a lot really. Tilly's birthday is soon."

"I know," I whispered. "I miss her."

"Me too. I just wish we could have gotten our shit together. Now I'll never know if we could have made it work or not."

"Aaron, you two were a nightmare. I think if you'd have tried when you were both a lot older and done with other people then maybe. Neither of you were ready for anything serious so young."

"We weren't, I don't think. I still love her though. I wished we had that chance to turn it into something more serious."

Aaron's confession of love surprised me a little. They had never said they loved each other when they were together. At least they had never told me they had. I didn't believe he really loved her. They hurt each other time and time again.

"Do you want to do something for her birthday?" I asked. For Gigi's birthday I had made her a cake and we all got her cards. It was silly really but even though they were gone I still wanted to mark the occasion somehow. They still deserved a celebration.

He shrugged. "I'm going to get high and reminisce about the good old times."

"Get high?"

"Come on, Mackenzie." He rolled his eyes. "You've never done it?"

"No," I replied.

"Such a good girl," he muttered under his breath loud enough for me to hear. "Well you're missing out. It's very good when you don't want to give a shit about anything."

I couldn't have been more shocked if he'd pulled his jeans down and pissed on the floor. We never really spoke about drugs, but I assumed none of them had done any. "Did Tilly?

"Sometimes. Screwing on a high is outta this world." He ran his fingertips up my arm. "I have some weed if you wanna give it a go."

"What the hell, Aaron!" I shouted, snatching my arm away. Standing up, I spun around. "I don't know what's wrong with you but don't try that crap with me. I'm not going to smoke pot and sleep with you! Do you know me at all?"

"Alright, alright," he said, raising his hands above his head. "Just thought we could cheer ourselves up." That wasn't Aaron. He wasn't like that. Arsehole and Aaron didn't go together. How he was acting was completely out of character.

"If you want to cheer me up be the normal Aaron that makes me laugh and feeds me chocolate!" I shook my head. "I'm going. Call me when you're you again." What was wrong with everyone right now? I felt like my friends had been abducted by aliens and had a personality transplant. They were all acting fucking weird.

Aaron didn't follow me as I left his house. I didn't even care that I hadn't found out his deep, dark secret. There was something wrong with him if he thought I was going to sleep with him like that. One thing that ate away at me as I drove was the drugs thing. We were drugged that night. Aaron had hidden smoking weed from us, what else? Was he on something now?

Without thinking about where I was going, I arrived at Blake's house and frowned. Why had I come here and not gone home? I used to absentmindedly go to Kyle's a lot. He was the one I went to when something went wrong. *Well, Blake can hear all about it and try figuring it out!*

I rang the doorbell and waited. As soon as the door opened I pushed past him. "Come in," he muttered behind me. Ignoring him, I walked upstairs to his room. His mum wasn't in again, or if she was she was hiding out somewhere.

Maybe she was at the hospital with her brother still. His footsteps following me were all I heard. No more sarcastic comments. He must be tired.

"He tried it on!" I said, dropping down on his bed and throwing my hands in the air.

"What? Aaron?" He raised his eyebrow and smirked as if to say I didn't know he had it in him.

"Yep. Oh, and he does weed!"

"I hardly think that's confession of the year."

"He does drugs."

"I wouldn't tar weed smokers and Rohypnol spikers with the same brush."

I frowned. "Do you do weed?"

"No, but I know it's not exactly on the same level."

"I know that too but doesn't that mean he would be able to get hold of Rohypnol?"

"Anyone can get hold of anything."

"I couldn't. I wouldn't even know where to start. What do you do, hang out on a dodgy street and ask whoever looks like a criminal?"

Blake raised his eyebrows. "Promise me you won't do that."

"Why? Is that how you do it?"

He chuckled. "No, that's how you get yourself raped and murdered, little miss innocent. Seriously your naivety is worrying."

"Well I'm sorry I don't know how to score drugs!"

He flopped to the bed, laughing his head off, a proper from the belly laugh. "We need to move on," he said, shaking his head and grinning so wide I was surprised his face didn't crack in half. "So now you think it was Aaron, hey?"

"That's not what I said."

"Pretty much is. You think he can score Rohypnol. You're considering it, aren't you?"

"I don't like you anymore, Blake." He smirked. "I don't know what to think," I replied, sitting cross legged on his bed.

He looked up at me; his blue eyes were icy and intense. "You know, Mackenzie. Stop fighting it so hard and open up your mind. Distance yourself from your feelings for your friends."

"I tried that today already and it doesn't work. You're distant, why can't you just tell me!"

"Distant. Not oracle," he replied dryly. "Anyway, I've told you what I think, and you dismiss it."

"Because you think it's Kyle!"

"Well now I think it's Aaron."

I gulped and my heart started working overtime. "But..." I whispered, trailing off.

Blake rose at the same time his eyebrow arched. "You think so too."

"I think if he was into that whole weed... scene then maybe. He still loves Tilly, or what he thinks is love anyway. Whatever's going on he's seriously screwed up right now."

"Why did you say it like that?"

I shrugged. "They weren't good together. Not for longer than a few weeks. Everything ended in an argument and them breaking up. I know they both liked each other or they wouldn't keep going back for more, but I don't think it was love."

"Is that motive enough then?"

"Is anything motive enough? People kill randoms because they enjoy it or because they looked at them a funny way. That's not the important part. If it was Aaron it was driven by revenge and that has always been strong motive."

"Maybe you should be a judge or—"

I clicked my fingers in front of his face and said, "Stay with me." We didn't have time for him to go off on one about something stupid. "You think Aaron, so I think we should look into it more."

"I'm a little hurt that you're using me that way."

I frowned. "What way?"

"You think it could be Aaron too, but you're using me as an excuse to run down that road. Everything else I've said you've dismissed or told me I'm an idiot."

"Not everything," I said, playing with my fingers. He was right. We both thought it, but I couldn't quite bring myself to admit it out loud.

"New rule; if you're going to use me in the future it will only be when we're both naked."

I stared blankly. "I knew you were no gentlemen, but that is pushing it."

"Baby, you won't hurt my feelings."

"No, but I'll hurt yours when I'm left frustrated and complaining about your lousy performance in the sack." He lunged for me, making me yelp in surprise. "Blake!" I shouted as he pinned me to the bed, holding my wrists against the mattress.

"You're just being mean now and since you've cruelly insulted me and mocked my performance, which you know is rockin' since you came like a train, scratched the fuck out of my back and moaned my name every five seconds, we're going to have sex again and then you're going to apologise."

I giggled from beneath him. "Thanks for the offer but I'm busy."

"What part of that did you take as being an offer? Clothes off, Mackenzie."

I sighed. "See, that is why I know you'd suck right now. How unsexy is it when someone tells you to take your clothes off like that?"

"I kinda like it."

Yeah I kind of did too but he didn't need to know that.

"Because you're a man. You kiss the crap outta a woman and remove her clothes as you go. You can have that tip for free. Let me know if it works," I replied, pulling my arms to try to get him to release me. "Come on, you're heavy and we have things to do." I frowned and looked up at him. What was taking him so long? "Hello?" I called to his lights-on-but-no-one-home face.

"You might have something there," he whispered in reply and lowered his head.

"Blake!" Eloise shouted from downstairs. "Blake!"

He jumped off me and spun towards his door. I only had time to push myself into a sitting position before she burst into the room. "He's dead," she sobbed, falling to the floor. "Pete's dead."

# CHAPTER EIGHTEEN

I dropped to the floor beside the shaking, broken mess that was Eloise. She had just lost her son and now her brother, and she looked as if she was about to die too.

Blake looked at me, lost. "Mum," he said as if he was just calling her to ask what was for dinner.

I reached out and wrapped one arm around her back, scooting closer. "I'm so sorry, Eloise," I whispered, pulling her closer to me. She fell limp into my lap and cried. Her whole body shook violently. "Shh, it's okay. Are you alone?"

"Yes, alone," she croaked, sobbing her words. She said alone as if she had lost everyone important to her. Her alone meant more than just no one had brought her home. *You still have Blake.* Why hadn't anyone picked her up? Did she drive home in that state? We would have gone to get her.

"Okay," I said. "I'm going to put you to bed and then me and Blake will sort everything out."

She didn't reply, but she didn't try to stop me when I hooked my arm under hers and lifted her up. Blake stepped in and helped, doing most of the lifting, and we carried her to her room. Practical things Blake could do, but not the emotional stuff. Eloise was dead weight, making little effort to hold herself up, but he carried her with ease.

"Blake, don't you... don't you do anything stupid. Don't you get yourself killed," she cried, taking deep breaths between words.

"I'm not going anywhere, Mum," he replied, frowning in discomfort. It would seem that the only emotions Blake could deal with were fickle ones, nothing deep and meaningful. He must love his parents, every kid did, even if they made mistakes.

Eloise cried hysterically the whole way and didn't stop when we laid her in bed. She hugged her pillow, pressing her face into the cotton as she broke down. I felt for her, huddled up in the foetal position, crying her heart out.

"Do you need anything?" I asked, stroking her hair.

"N-No. Look a-after him."

"I will," I promised her. "Shall we stay?" She shook her head and curled up tighter. "Okay, we'll check on you soon." Standing up, I nodded to the door, telling Blake to leave too.

"How do you know what to do?" Blake asked as we closed his mum's bedroom door. He looked like hell. He had no idea how to deal with things, especially women.

I wrapped my arms around his waist. His body tensed. He didn't know what to do, again. Now I knew he wasn't exactly a cuddly person, but he must have hugged people before, right? I started to feel awkward and was about to pull away, but he very slowly lifted his arms and snaked them around my back.

"I don't really. I just did what I would want someone to do for me. All you have to do is look after her."

"I've never had to do that."

"You do now."

"So when you fall apart I need to remember to put you to bed."

I pulled back, but he didn't loosen his grip so I could only just see his face. "I'm falling apart?"

"Not yet. You're not done protecting everyone yet."

I wasn't looking forward to facing everything. Pushing it away was much easier but I knew it couldn't last. I didn't really want it to last because I knew how unhealthy it was, but I was enjoying being whatever version of a normal teenager I still was. Blake helped with that; he kept me sane, and although he was a few years older than me; he certainly didn't act it.

"You're sticking around then?"

"I'm not sure what I'll do yet. Back home I don't have much going but at least it's home. Whatever I decide I'll wait to tuck you into bed though."

"You really do care, don't you? As hard as you try to push everyone away and be Mr Independent, you do care."

"I don't care; you just have this way of bulldozing your way into someone's life and fucking staying there."

I smiled. "That was sweet on some level."

He narrowed his eyes. "I don't do sweet."

"Too late, you were sweet. Inside you're made of little pink marshmallows."

"Why pink?"

"They're cuter."

"You think I'm cute?"

I pulled away, rolling my eyes. "No, I think you're an idiot." When I looked back at him, he had the biggest school boy grin I had ever seen. "Whatever, Blake. Stop distracting me." People were being murdered around us and we were messing around. Only he could turn me into my old self when my friend was dead and we were possibly on someone's hit list.

"I think we should follow Aaron, Kyle and Megan."

I smirked. "You wanna stalk my friends?"

"No, I think Pete found out who killed Josh and Courtney and they killed him. Whichever one of your friends did it they're getting desperate. If they think people are starting to find out they might do something, go somewhere, that'll lead us to the truth."

"We're going on a stakeout?"

"Yep. We need a different car."

"Hire car?" I replied, getting excited. It scared me how well I was able to distance myself from what was going on. "Can we hire one though?"

"Why can't we?"

"Don't you have to be a certain age? Twenty-five in some places."

He snorted. "Please, I have fake IDs that put me well into my thirties. I'll sort the car and pick you up at six tomorrow night. This needs to be sorted out before…"

"Before?"

"Before someone else gets hurt."

"Watch out, you're caring again."

"I meant me getting hurt."

I grinned and raised my eyebrows. "Sure you did."

"Go home, Mackenzie."

"Okay," I replied. "When your mum wakes up remember to—"

"Alright, alright, stay for now!"

I followed him back into his room and we sat on the bed. "You okay?" I asked. His uncle had just died, surely he felt something.

"Dunno really. I didn't know him." He frowned. "I barely know any of them."

"Did you want to know them?"

"Are you going to psycho analyse me again?"

I smiled. "Maybe."

"I wanted to, of course I did. That's not how it always goes though. My parents split and so did our family. There were times growing up when I wanted Mum to be in my life, properly be in it not just the odd phone call every couple months, but she was busy raising Josh and had her own stuff to deal with."

"That doesn't mean she was allowed to be less of a mum to you," I replied, feeling angry for him. No matter how far apart they were she should have been the best mum she could have. A phone call every few months wasn't being a parent.

"Mackenzie, it's cool. I'm a big boy."

It wasn't cool, but I dropped it because Blake wasn't known for spilling his heart, and I didn't want to fight. "What does this mean for us?"

"Wright is going to try pinning Pete's death on us too. Whoever the killer is, they've just entered serial territory."

"What?"

"Serial killer, Mackenzie."

"How do you know that?"

He sighed, shaking his head. "Three murders and you're serial. Although I think that might only count if there's time between so Josh and Courtney might count as one."

"Okay, I don't wanna talk about that. What if we're next?"

He cocked his head to the side. "You know that's the first time you've put yourself before your friends." It was what? "Don't look so confused. A few days ago you would have said something like what if you're all next, now it's just us."

"Because I don't know which one of…" I stopped, shocked at myself. *Which one of them is the killer.* I sat back against the headboard and pulled his cover over me. It was one of them.

Blake shifted, moving up the bed and under the cover like I had. "Do you want me to speak to Wright about Lawrence? Maybe—"

"No," I said, cutting him off. "It's not Lawrence, is it?"

Taking a deep breath, he replied, "No."

"Shit," I whispered. Blake's body shook as if he was laughing, but he didn't make a sound. "I'm so stupid."

"You're not stupid, you're loyal."

I snorted. "Same thing."

"Stop doing that. You're putting yourself down for being a good friend. Don't ever feel bad for not wanting to believe any of your friends could be murderers."

"Okay, fine. I won't feel bad, but I would like to be able to see through people a little better."

He nodded. "Yeah that you suck at. If it helps I'll tell you when someone is lying to your face."

I turned my body to face him. "Do you care?"

Rolling his eyes, he replied, "Yes. Happy?"

"Happy about?"

"Not happy. Women," he muttered. "I care about you. There."

My eyes widened; I didn't hide my surprise well. I expected him to say he cared about his family, not just me. Opening and closing my mouth, I fought to buy some time so I could think of something to say. Mr Heart of Steel had just told me he cared about me. Specifically me. And now I was more attracted to him. My little thing for Blake had become a big thing for Blake.

"Hmm, not often you're speechless. Why does it surprise you so much? I told you about your bulldozing didn't I."

"You're trying to make it sound like nothing."

"You know it's not nothing."

"Yes I know that, but you're trying... Never mind."

"Just a heads up, I'm going to kiss you now."

My breath caught in my throat. "Blake, Pete has just died. Your mother is distraught in the next room, and we're possibly next on the hit list."

His eyes were on my lips. "All the more reason to then. It's what people do in helpless situations like this. Don't you watch movies?"

I didn't have time to reply before his lips grazed mine so lightly it tickled. He pulled back, looking into my eyes, giving me time to stop him. I couldn't speak; I could barely think, so I pressed my lips to his, showing him what I wanted. Screw it, if it was good enough for the movies...

I knew it was probably a bad idea, but what I felt when he kissed me – the burning fire – spurred me on. No one had ever kissed me as passionately as Blake did. His hands rested on my hips and then he picked me up as if I weight nothing and set me down on his lap.

My hands quickly found his hair. I grabbed fistfuls and pulled gently, it was softer than I expected, but Blake didn't seem like the conditioning type. Usually I could show a little restraint and self-control, but with him it was lost. He moaned into my mouth and pushed us up, throwing us back on the bed with him above.

His tongue brushed my bottom lip and dove into my mouth. I tightened my grip of his hair and pulled his head impossibly closer.

"Blake," I hissed out as he let me up for breath while he kissed the soft skin below my ear. The sound he made in response was almost a growl. My heart missed a full beat. "We shouldn't be doing this." I said the words but even I didn't believe them.

"Yes we should," he murmured against my sensitive skin, making me tremble. I felt his smile. "You don't want to?"

I closed my eyes, letting the hot, burning sensations of his lips on my body take over. "I want to," I replied, panting.

He stopped and hovered above me. "But?"

"But your mum might need us."

I watched his eyes darken. It looked like he was having a serious internal debate. When he found the answer he sighed. "Rain check. This will happen again."

"You're very confident."

"About this I am." He rolled off me and I scrambled up to the pillow end of the bed again, lying down. He raised his eyebrow. "Getting comfortable."

I nodded. "I'm staying here tonight. Your mum might need me. If you have issues about sharing a bed you know where the sofa is."

His eyebrow rose higher. "I'm the one that would have to sleep on the sofa?"

Yawning, I replied, "Yep. Night, Blake."

"Guess I'm texting your mum then," he muttered as I closed my eyes. I was glad he remembered because with all the kissing my brain was pretty much fried. I smiled as I drifted off to sleep.

I woke to an empty bed and found Blake and his mum in the kitchen drinking tea. I made sure they were okay and then excused myself to go home. I had to check in with my parents and spend some time with them before Blake and I stalked my friends in the evening.

Throughout the day, Blake and I had texted. He promised me that he would pick me up with a hire car. I waited by the front door for him to arrive. I had butterflies in my stomach. Well, they actually felt more like birds flying around in there!

As I heard a car pull up, I shouted bye to my mum and dad and went outside. The butterflies soon fled as I set eyes on the car he had hired. I stopped and blinked, positive it was my eyes playing tricks on me.

"Are you for real?" I asked when the car didn't turn into an inconspicuous saloon.

He frowned. "What?"

I gestured to the car – a bright red convertible something. "This! We're supposed to be undercover."

"Ah but I figured they would never expect to see us in a flashy motor. Well actually be more undercover in this than some boring Focus." He tapped his head as if he'd thought of something amazingly clever.

I closed my eyes and rubbed my forehead, feeling a headache coming on. "I genuinely don't know what to say to you, Blake."

"Thank you maybe?"

"I'm not thanking you for being stupid," I replied and got in the car. "Can you at least put the roof up?"

"Later. Wanna pretend we're Bonnie and Clyde?"

"Just drive," I replied, sighing in discouragement and throwing my backpack on one of the tiny back seats. "What do you think we're going to find?"

"Probably about as much as we've found already, sweet FA, but what choice do we have? Everything is ten times more serious now. We can't just sit back and wait for the police to find out. Pete's dead and we don't know how far the murderer is going to go to protect themself."

I wasn't sure if I believed one of them would kill me or not. They all had their issues with Josh and Courtney but as far as I knew I'd never pissed them off, not enough for any of them to want to end my life. Would that matter though?

Had it gone past who they cared about now? Would they kill me to save themself? And Blake, they didn't know him and they didn't like him.

"Do you really think they would want to kill us?"

"I'm not taking that chance."

I shook my head. "We're discussing this as if we're talking about deciding on a day's outing."

"Would you prefer me to panic?"

I rolled my eyes. "No."

"Mackenzie, this is all we have left. It's find who done it or either end up six foot under or be wrongfully imprisoned. I don't know about you, but I don't fancy option B or C. Like you said before, there will be time to grieve later. Right now we fight. Okay?"

"Okay," I replied. That was what I'd been doing all along, only now I was more trying to prove Blake and myself were innocent, rather than Megan, Aaron and Kyle. Out of all of them Blake was the only one I was one hundred per cent sure about now.

"We'll drive to Megan's – you need to direct me, by the way – and check out what's going on there first. Please remember we're here to catch a killer so keep your hands and lips to yourself for the next few hours."

I rolled my eyes. "Take a left at the end of the road and get your head out of your arse." His smirk lit up his whole face and he was carefree Blake.

# CHAPTER NINETEEN

"This isn't as fun as I thought it'd be," he moaned, reclining his seat and throwing his arm over his forehead.

"And you expected?"

He shrugged with one shoulder. "Megan carrying a suspicious shaped black bag or a rolled up rug. Truck load of Rohypnol being delivered."

"You'd make a shit detective."

He looked at me out of the corner of his eye and raised his brow. "Oh, sorry, do you know who it is then?"

"That's not the point. I'm looking beyond the obvious."

"The obvious being Aaron?"

Sighing, I looked out of my window and back at Megan's house. Blake was exasperating. "Who had the time to drug our drinks?" I turned my body back and pulled his arm away from his eyes. "Why're we assuming it was the drinks that were drugged?"

He frowned. "You think it could have been the food?"

"Maybe. We all helped cook."

"We also all got drinks at some point in the evening too."

"Yes I know, but it's a possibility and there were only two people that finished up the dinner." My mind reeled with the new possibility.

"Who was that? Aaron and…?"

I gulped. "And Josh."

Blake stilled, and I waited for his reaction. After a minute, he frowned. "A murder/suicide. That doesn't explain Pete though."

"Perhaps that was random. You know Pete, always shouting his opinions out down the pub. Maybe he pissed someone off and they snapped. Maybe they used Josh and Courtney's murder to cover up Pete's. Come on, it's a possibility."

Pete was punched once for telling someone they were a 'fucking idiot' for supporting the Liberal Democrats and that they should be supporting Labour. And there was the time that he snubbed Mrs Jackson's choice of name for her son. Angel. He said not only was it a girl's name, but it only belonged on a stripper. I thought it was cute.

"You're asking me to believe my brother murdered his girlfriend and then himself."

I gasped. "What if he found out about Kyle and Courtney?"

"Then wouldn't it make more sense to kill Kyle?"

I shrugged. "I donno. His mind was obviously messed up. Blake, it could have happened. Call Wright!"

Closing his eyes, he groaned. "No, Mackenzie. Remember Lawrence? We were wrong about him." *We think we're wrong about him.* "I don't want to do anything that'll make it seem like we're desperate and looking for anything to get us out of it."

"We are desperate."

"We don't want him to know that. We need to think it through a little more first."

"Okay," I replied. "Then we'll go to Wright, yeah?"

"Let's just see how tonight goes and talk it through some more. We'll go tomorrow if we need to." He smiled at me and looked out of the window. "Hey, hey, hey," he said in a rush and nodded to Megan's house. She ran to her car, ripping the door open. "Now where's she off to in a hurry?"

"Start the car!" I hissed as Megan sped off. The idiot was too busy watching he was slow doing the following part.

We followed Megan to the churchyard and parked behind a tall transit van. Why was she here? And she rushed too, desperate to get here as soon as possible. For what?

Deep in the graveyard I saw exactly what she was in a rush to get to. Kyle was waving his hands around, shouting something that I couldn't hear. He stumbled and arched his back, off his face and clearly angry about something.

"Shit, what's he doing!" I shoved the car door open and leapt out. Blake's footsteps were right behind me as we ran towards Megan and an angry Kyle.

"Kyle!" I shouted. Megan was the only one to look up; he didn't even seem to hear me.

"I don't know what's he's doing," Megan said. "He called me ranting about what a whore Courtney was and that he wanted to dig her up!" I froze in shock. That wasn't Kyle. He did say things like that; he didn't even think things like that. How messed up had the affair made him? "I don't know what to do, Kenz."

"She's a bitch," Kyle spat, taking a few steps towards me. It was the first time in my life that I was actually scared of him. I had no idea what he would do either. Why was I always the one people expected to fix things? *Because you're always trying to fix everything*, my mind, in Blake's voice, told me.

Blake stepped between Kyle and me and Megan. "Calm the fuck down. So she picked him. Man up and stop acting like a little bitch about it." Tactful! I glared at him, but he didn't see me.

"You don't have a clue!" Kyle roared. "You pathetic loner, you don't have a clue what it's like to love someone. The only person you give a shit about is yourself."

*That's not true.*

"What?" Megan said. "What the hell is he going on about? He was with Courtney?"

"Kyle, that's enough!" I yelled, ignoring Megan's confusion. It was obvious now so she would catch up on what she had missed. "What's wrong with you? You've lost it. How much have you had to drink?" He was noticeably stumbling, which was unusual for him, unless he was off his face, and his eyes were bloodshot.

"She chose him, Kenz. How could she choose him?" His eyes narrowed and his lip curled in fury. "It's all her fault. It was all her fault."

"Kyle, don't," Megan said. Her voice was weak; she sounded as if she had just been kicked in the stomach. "Courtney's dead. It wasn't her fault and you shouldn't talk about her like that." I was with Megan on that one.

"I don't care!" he shouted, his eyes fierce and distant from being so worked up and drunk. "She deserved it after what she did to me. They both deserved it!"

"They deserved death?" Megan yelled, looking at Kyle both appalled and heartbroken. I was too. My stomach turned at his words. You weren't supposed to continue hating someone you cared about when they were dead. Why couldn't anyone else see that?

Kyle squeezed his eyes closed. "I want her back. I want her with me." His shoulders hunched over, defeated. "I love her."

I stepped forward, wanting to comfort him but was stopped by Blake's arm. Kyle narrowed his eyes at him. "Oh, piss off. She's my best friend! I'm not going to hurt her." I could see by the way Blake's eyebrow twitched that he was thinking Courtney was someone he loved and he was speaking that way about her. Blake didn't trust Kyle one bit; that was clear.

"It's okay," I muttered, gently pushing Blake's arm down. I knew Kyle wouldn't hurt me. Blake made no attempt to stop me again, so I walked to Kyle and wrapped my arms around his waist. I was super-aware that I could be hugging a murderer, but at that moment he was just my lost, heartbroken, messed up friend. "You're gonna be okay," I whispered.

Kyle gripped hold of me and cried into my neck. "I don't know what I'm doing," he sobbed. "I can't think straight.

She's gone." His legs gave way and I fell to the ground with him, unable to hold his weight up on my own. "What am I going to do?"

"I don't know," I whispered, shuffling so he wasn't on top of me so much. I still hadn't figured that part out yet. Eventually, I would have to face up to what happened. I would have to let the memories back in and accept they were gone. What I wanted to do was to carry on burying it like I was now.

"It hurts," he hissed and gripped me tighter. "I can't..."

"Shh," I whispered, rubbing his back as if he was a small child. "We'll get through this just like we did when Tills and Gigi died."

Megan knelt beside me. "But this isn't the same, Kenz. Tilly and Gigi was an accident. This," she said, shaking her head, "was deliberate."

"We can't just give up," I replied. "I understand what this is, but we have to stick together. I know this is harder, but we can get through it. I need you both. Aaron too." *And Blake*, I added silently. Now was not the time to include him when they were still so sure it had to be him.

She nodded. "You're right. Why don't you come back to Kyle's with me and we can talk about all this stuff. Maybe we can figure it out together?"

"You mean find a way to pin it on me," Blake said from behind us.

I looked up at him. "That's not what she meant."

Kyle snorted, raising his tear stained face. "The hell it isn't! We all know you had a problem with your brother."

Blake's eyebrow raised, and I knew where he was going. "We all know you had a problem with my brother and since he was in the pants of the girl you love, I think your motive shoots you to the top of the suspect list."

"Alright, stop!" I yelled, squeezing my eyes closed, exasperated. "You guys have to stop this."

"Why are you always defending him?" Kyle spat, pushing himself to his feet.

"Because he's in the exact same position as us. Just because we didn't know him before doesn't—"

"Mackenzie," he said, cutting me off. "We don't know him now."

I sighed sharply. "Trust me then, Kyle."

"You're screwing him," Kyle sneered, stumbling back a step.

"No, I'm not screwing him." But I had and I was minutes from it again last night. "You need to go home. I'm not talking to you when you're like this."

"Whatever," he mumbled, walking towards the car park in a wonky, alcohol fuelled line.

Kyle refused to go in a car with Blake so I helped Megan get him in her car and she took him home. I got back in the stupid flashy sports car and closed my eyes. "Is it Kyle?" I asked Blake as he turned the engine on.

"I don't know. He's mad, but he seems more self-destructive pissed off and not murderous pissed off. Wanna check Aaron before I take you back to mine?"

"I'm going back to yours?"

"Yeah, my mum's still a mess and I don't do hysterical women, you know that."

I shook my head. "Fine I'll text my mum again. Aaron's next. Wright tomorrow."

"You think we'll find anything at his?" he asked.

"What're you expecting, Aaron to be carrying a suspicious shaped black bag or a rolled up rug?" I replied using his words from earlier.

"Ha ha," he said flatly. "Buckle up."

I did just in time for him to step on the accelerator, pinning me to the seat. We arrived at Aaron's far too quickly and parked a little way down the road. "Can we run though everything again?"

"Everything?" he questioned.

"Motives and suspicions."

"I think it was Aaron in the kitchen with a knife."

"You know one day you'll have to deal with this too, right?" Blake's defence was to joke around and make light of the situation. It was probably something he had done his whole life. I could picture him joking about what a crap mum he had, even though it must have left its mark.

"Sure. Not looking forward to your breakdown I have to say."

"Because you don't do hysterical women."

"No, because I don't want to see you upset."

"Oh," I replied, my mouth popping open.

He smirked. "Not what you expected, hey?"

"Not really."

"I'm not a complete arsehole."

Narrowing my eyes, I replied, "No, not a *complete* one."

"Okay so we have Megan. Now she had that weird liquor, an earlier walk into the woods, slept alone upstairs and has been overly hysterical the whole time. Her motive is her lesbian affair – which I support fully, by the way – with Gigi."

I rolled my eyes. Typical man. "Yeah and Kyle. Handled the food a lot and did probably more drinks runs than the rest of us though I can't really remember. His motive is jealously and anger over Courtney, obviously. Aaron uses drugs, apparently! He left with Megan, brought alcohol too and had an equal go with the food and drinks. His motive is the same as Megan's but his is weaker. I think. Or Megan's is. She didn't love Gigi."

"So she says. Your motive is—"

"Don't! I don't want to go there. I didn't do it and you know it."

"Hey, I'm just playing fair here."

Squeezing my eyes closed, I swallowed the lump in my throat. "Please, Blake. We both know what my motive would be. I can't talk about what happened again."

He nodded once, understanding just how hard it was for me to even think about what I had done. "Alright. Well we both know mine too. Shall we move on to Josh?"

"Okay," I whispered. "Josh could have found out about Kyle and Courtney. He had the most opportunity to spike the food and drinks since he was hospitality master. That's all we really have on him."

"Wait, where was the knife?"

"I don't know. The police had it but they never said where it was found," I replied.

"If it was more than a short throw away it couldn't be Josh. The blood was only in that area." Spreading as I remembered it. "He couldn't have taken it or thrown it too far if he was bleeding out."

Blake was right.

"So if it wasn't in the kitchen he couldn't have done it and it was one of them." He nodded. "Why hasn't Wright mentioned that? Surely he would have asked about that?"

Blake's frown deepened. "Or the clothes. Whoever did it had to have blood on them. Where are the clothes? Don't mention the knife to him actually. If he's not telling us it's for a reason."

"So if one of us slips up and mentions where it was he would know. I mean only the killer would know where it was, right?

"Hmm, you're not just a pretty face."

"I'm gonna ignore that. So we know everyone has a motive and opportunity but we have absolutely no evidence to prove any of it."

"That about sums it up," Blake replied, nodding once. "Aaron's door!"

I looked over and saw a guy wearing a black hooded jacket and dark jeans standing talking to Aaron. He handed something to him and Aaron handed something back in return. My breath caught in my throat.

"Bloody druggie," Blake muttered. "Well I think it's safe to say Aaron would know where to get Rohypnol."

How fast was Aaron spiralling? I wanted to run to him, flush whatever he'd just bought and slap him silly. I couldn't though. His downfall could be guilt.

"I thought you said weed and Rohypnol were two completely different things and we shouldn't—"

"Yes, Mackenzie, but how many people do you know that do a bit of weed dealing like that? And own nice flashy Range Rovers like that? Come on, that the official drug dealer's car."

"I know none. Drugs just don't appear in my world." He smiled sarcastically and nodded towards Aaron. I added, "That I knew of."

"This is pointless. Driving this around was fun but we're not undercover cops. Let's take the car back and head to mine," he said.

"Today was a total bust."

Blake stroked the steering wheel. "I enjoyed driving this."

"Oh, I stand corrected," I replied sarcastically. As long as he had fun in the car it doesn't matter that we found nothing!

He flashed a boyish grin. "Tomorrow we'll speak to Wright about your suicide theory."

"Our suicide theory."

"It'll be ours if it's right. At the minute, it's yours. Now," he said, wiggling his eyebrows, "let's chill on my bed and I'll let you take advantage of me."

# CHAPTER TWENTY

Since Blake and I had spoken about the possibility of a murder/suicide, I couldn't stop thinking about it. If no one really could have got in, or did get in, then it was my only hope of it not being one of my friends.

Why would Josh have killed Courtney though? If he knew about her affair then he would have done something to Kyle too. Josh wasn't the type of person to leave something like that. He would see it as weak if he did. He always had to be the big man. If he knew someone else had been with Courtney he definitely would have done something. Kyle would at least have had a black eye.

"I just don't get it," I said into the phone to Blake.

"To be fair you don't get any of it. Don't yell because neither of us does."

I ignored him. Half because I couldn't be bothered to bicker about it and half because I knew he didn't mean to make it sound like I was stupid. "If it was Josh there had to be a reason. I mean you don't kill your girlfriend and yourself because you're bored."

"Well normal people don't."

"Blake," I said slowly. He was going off track, again. "We need to find out Josh's motive."

"If there is one."

"I'm coming over and we're going to search his room. Is your mum in?"

"She's at my nan's sorting out Pete's funeral arrangements."

I winced. "I'm sorry." Here we were about to rifle through Josh's things when his mum was planning another funeral for her brother.

"Don't worry about it."

"You're so cool about everything."

"I can't help it. I barely saw any of these people growing up. I don't feel like I've lost anyone, and I know I sound like an arsehole right now but I can't help it."

"You don't sound like an arsehole." He was right. How could you feel more than the usual sorry for someone's loss when you didn't know the person? Blake felt how I felt when my mum's old school friend's husband died. I had met her once but never him. I was sad for her but that was it.

He sighed. "You coming now then?"

"Yeah."

"Good. Oh and since this is your idea you can be the one looking under his bed."

Porn. "Ew."

"That's what I thought. Hurry up." He hung up the phone, and I turned my TV off. I hadn't watched anything, but I liked the background noise. With my parents at work, it was too quiet in the house. I wanted noise.

I walked to my car and kept my head down as the local knitting club walked by on their way to the village hall for their weekly meeting. Before the murders they would have stopped to chat and tell me I needed to put some meat on my bones, this time they whispered to each other, stealing little glances at me out of the corner of their eye.

Mildred, the eldest and brightest purple rinse of the bunch was the first one that would call me over. Last winter she knitted me a pink and brown stripe scarf because I didn't wrap up warm enough, apparently. It hurt that she turned so easily. I was guilty until proven innocent.

Blake was waiting by his front door when I arrived. I opened the door and stepped out, frowning at him. "You're waiting for me?"

"Did Josh have something going on with Tilly and or Gigi?"

"Tilly and or Gigi?"

He shrugged. "I get them mixed up. Both their names end in an E sound."

I shook my head and walked towards him. "No, he didn't with either of them. Gigi was a lesbian, remember?"

"Megan was straight, remember?"

Fair point. "Why'd you ask?"

"Because," he replied, holding out a handful of photos of Tilly, "I found these in his sock drawer."

Cocking my head to the side, I took them from his hand and flicked through them. They were all close up pictures of Tilly. None were too odd, most natural ones as if she hadn't known they were being taken.

"Tilly," I whispered. "Why does he have all these?" There had to be at least twenty pictures. When I reached one of the bottom of her head, cut off just below her nose and stretching down to her cleavage, I shoved them back at Blake. "Why the fuck does he have those?"

"I dunno."

"Shit was he cheating too? No," I said, shaking my head at how ridiculous the thought was. Tilly wouldn't go near Josh. She almost thought less of him than I did. "They don't look right, do they? If you were posing for your bit on the side, you'd actually pose a little. Half of them look candid and the other half look like general pictures."

"General pictures?"

"Yes!" I exclaimed, sighing. "You know, a smile for a picture anyone is taking."

"Alright. Josh has general and candid pictures of Tilly. No posing." He shook his head and said, "Still don't know where you're going with this."

"Really?" I replied flatly, pushing past him so we weren't still talking on his front step. "Blake, they mean Josh had a thing for Tilly, but it was just his thing."

"She didn't have a thing."

"I'm going to hit you."

He grinned. "Okay, I'm done." He shut the door behind him and stepped dangerously close to me.

I stood my ground, not letting him know he affected me. He would love it if he knew how my legs turned to jelly when he stood just inches from me, how his voice gave me goose bumps and his smile set my body on fire.

"Lead the way," I said, waving my hand over to the stairs.

"Ladies first," he replied. His voice was low, husky and incredibly sexy.

"Ah but you're not a gentlemen." *Just go first, Blake!* I already felt weak, boneless. Knowing his eyes were on me as we walked upstairs would probably make me collapse.

His lip curved in amusement. "You're right."

Blake walked ahead. As soon as he wasn't that close to me anymore my clouded mind cleared. I shouldn't even be thinking of a guy with everything that was going on. I couldn't even talk to anyone about it because things with Megan were weird and the only other girls I could talk about boy stuff to were dead.

I stopped at Josh's open door. Blake had already gone inside, not caring that we were about to breach the privacy of his dead brother. "You waiting out there all day?"

"It feels wrong."

"Do you want to get us of Wright's little list or do you want to respect Josh's privacy?" I walked in. "That's what I thought. There's nothing else in any of the drawers. I've not looked anywhere else yet. You take under the bed, and I'll look in the wardrobe."

"Great," I muttered. Now what kind of gross shit was going to be under a twenty-year-old guy's bed? That was something I was more than happy not to know the answer to, and I needed an answer for everything.

Turning my nose up in anticipation of all things disgusting, I knelt down and lowered my head to the floor. If there was a used condom I was out! "Nothing," I said, shocked. Everyone had at least a sock that had been kicked under their bed. Josh's was clear; I could see right through to the other side.

"Huh, what a pussy. You should see what's under my bed," Blake said. I couldn't see his amused, cheeky little grin, but I knew it was there.

"No thank you," I replied and stood up. "So where does he keep the things he doesn't want anyone to find then?"

Blake shrugged, holding up a black plastic box. "In here is my guess."

My first thought was *please let there be something in there* and my second was *I really don't want to know if there is*. What if there was something between him and Tilly? Stranger things had happened. Not a lot stranger but still.

"You ready to see what deep, dark secrets my brother had?"

"Not really."

"Good," he replied as if I'd said yes. "Let's open it then." He dropped the box on the bed, steadying it with one hand as it bounced. I held my breath as Blake took the lid off.

"Car magazines. Why hide those?"

Blake cocked his head to the side and smiled as if to say *aw bless*. "Underneath," he said and lifted the two magazines that hid the real contents of the box.

My eyes widened in shock. "What the…"

"Ohhh, Joshua!" Blake exclaimed, laughing. "What were you into?" He lifted out a black gag and swung it around his index finger. While Blake was playing and picking out other items, metal handcuffs and something else that looked like it belonged in a medieval torture chamber, I was motionless and speechless.

"Okay!" I snapped. "Put it all back!"

"Oh we got pictures!" he said, waving a pouch of disposable camera prints.

I shook my head. "I don't want to. We can't."

"These might be a clue. What if some are of Tilly?"

"Then they would be with the others you found." I knew it was likely to be photos of Courtney, handcuffed, bound and whatever else they did. "And why hadn't the police found all this when they searched his room?"

"Because I might have found it in the loft last night and brought it down before you arrived."

I threw my hands up in the air, exasperated. Blake was worse than a naughty toddler. "Well why did you put it in his wardrobe, and why did you let me look under the bed?"

"I could have hardly left it on his bed, could I? My mum could have walked in and found it. And making you look under the bed was purely for my amusement." He laughed and shook his head. "The look on your face when you thought you were going to find something disgusting under there."

I took a deep breath.

"Mackenzie, we have to look. The whole point of snooping is to find something."

"Something that lead to him killing Courtney and himself, not the kinky shit that he got off to!"

"How do you know it's not all linked? Fuck knows what he was into or how deeply."

"What if it was some satanic... something."

"Not sure you have to worship the devil to enjoy a bit of kink."

I rolled my eyes. "I'm not saying that, but what if *he* did?"

"Why don't I look?"

"Oh you'd love that, wouldn't you?"

"Ain't denying it, sweets." What the hell was wrong with him? "Oh don't look at me like that. It's not my thing, but whatever tickles your pickle."

I laughed, properly laughed. "Tickles your pickle?"

"You must have heard that phrase before?" I shook my head. *No, but I wish I had!* "You poor, sheltered girl." He pulled the photos from the sleeve and his eyes widened. "Fuck."

"What? What does that mean?"

He looked up over one of the photos, pale. "You really don't want to see."

The very tips of my fingers tingled. "What is it?" I held my hand up. "No, don't show me, tell me. Is it Courtney?"

He nodded. "And some of Josh." His eyes widened and he shoved the photos back. "Okay. That's going to take a lot of therapy." Chucking everything back in the box, he shuddered and covered it with the lid.

"Blake, what were the pictures of? How bad?"

He shuddered again. "Bad. Let's talk in my room, yeah." Shit it must be bad if he can't even be in the room anymore.

"Well?" I said, closing his door.

"They did things to each other."

"Yeah I got that. What things?"

"Whipping. I saw a whip and… marks on Josh. Blood."

My pulse thumped in my ears. "Blood?" What were they doing? "Whose blood?"

"Josh's, a cut on his chest. He had the camera at arm's length, taking a picture of Courtney…"

"Courtney? Courtney doing what?"

"Licking it."

"Fuck off!" I said and laughed. *If he thinks I'm falling for that!*

"Mackenzie," he whispered. His face was straight and serious. Not joking. He was not joking! My stomach lurched. I slapped my hand to my mouth. "You might be right with your satanic thing! I know some guys get off on pain while they're balls deep but that…"

"Oh my God can you not refer to sex as balls deep again." He half smiled, not being able to completely keep the amusement from his face. "Shit." I sat on his bed. Courtney was into that stuff. She never mentioned it. Not even something like being tied up or blindfolded. We always girly chats like that. Was she ashamed?

"You didn't know about any of it?"

I shook my head. "She never said a thing."

"I'm not surprised."

"Me neither. Not about the really... odd stuff. I thought she would talk about lighter things though. Not even when Tilly admitted she loved being tied up or Gigi with her chocolate mousse fetish."

"Please tell me you recorded your sleepovers!"

I arched my eyebrow, and he held his hands up, surrendering. "Courtney never said anything. Not anything out of the boring ordinary anyway. Do you think she really wanted to do that stuff?"

"Lick her boyfriend's blood during sex? Does anyone want to do that?"

"Do you think he forced her?"

Blake shrugged. "I have no idea. I am thinking that maybe this murder/suicide thing is a definite possibility now. But I'm thinking Courtney."

"No, she couldn't."

"Think about what she was doing to Josh, Mackenzie. If you saw a way to make that stop, if she really didn't want what was happening, wouldn't you take it?"

"She could have just broke up with him."

"Maybe there was more to it than that? Think about how she would have felt if he had been forcing her to do that stuff." Disgusted and belittled. Murderous and suicidal?

I rubbed my aching head. "I have no idea what to think anymore."

"We take this to Wright and let him investigate." How could you investigate something when the murderer might already be dead? Would they ever be able to prove it?

"Yeah," I replied, sagging into the mattress.

"You okay?"

I shrugged. I honestly didn't know. Tears filled my eyes. "What if Courtney didn't want to do that stuff?"

He dropped to his knees and leant his forearms on my thighs. "I don't know what to say, Mackenzie. Saying the right shit in situations like this isn't one of my strong points."

"You don't have to say anything. Sometimes there are just no words."

"What do you want me to do?"

I frowned. What could he do? What could anyone do? What were you even supposed to do when you found out your dead friend may or may not have been taken advantage of and abused? How did she feel? Why couldn't she have told me? I could have helped her. *It might be Courtney.* "We have to go to Wright with this. Now."

# CHAPTER TWENTY-ONE

"This is a good idea, isn't it?" I asked Blake, needing reassurance as we looked on at the police station doors. He held onto Josh's kinky and frankly terrifying sex box with a tight grip, his knuckles turning white. It was as if he felt guilty that he was about to expose his brother's dark secret. I admired him for that, but we had to show Wright to back up our murder/suicide theory.

"I don't think we have much of a choice. We can't find anything definite on your friends, and this is a possibility."

It was a possibility that it could have been Josh or Courtney. I didn't particularly want anyone else knowing what they had done in the bedroom because it was clearly something Court wanted to keep quiet, but we were running out of options. I grinned. "Well at least you're admitting I'm right."

"I never said the suicide thing wasn't a possibility," he replied.

I shook my head. "Let's not get into that now." We always seemed to bicker over absolutely anything, even when we were talking about something so serious. It was actually one of the things that held me together, stopped everything becoming too much. "What do you think he's going to say?"

He snorted. "Who knows? It could literally be anything. Come on."

I followed a step behind Blake. My heart fluttered with nerves, and the palms of my hands started to sweat. Oh God.

I just hoped he wouldn't think we were only saying it to cover up our guilt. As soon as Blake told me that was likely I hadn't been able to stop thinking about him turning around and arresting us, as ridiculous as that sounded. My mind was my own worst enemy.

Wright was standing beside the front desk talking to a colleague. He turned as if he'd sensed it was us walking in. My stomach was in knots. How did he just know? The man wasn't human.

"And to what do I owe this pleasure?" Wright said, threading his fingers together over his belly.

Blake's eyes narrowed. "We'd like to talk to you. If it's not too much trouble."

"Have you come to confess, Mr Harper?"

"We want to talk to you about another possibility," I said, cutting in, feeling Blake about to bite back with something stupid or sarcastic. "If you can spare us the time?"

"For you, Miss Keaton, anything."

Cocky, sarcastic bastard! I smiled, or what I hoped looked like a smile, and followed him into the far too familiar interview room. "How has no one ever killed him?" Blake whispered in my ear.

Grinning to myself, I shrugged. He must have rubbed enough people up the wrong way, so I saw Blake's point. I wondered if he conducted every investigation the way he was doing with this one. My knowledge of policing and detective work was severely limited to TV shows, but he didn't seem professional. He was too acentric to be serious.

"Take a seat," he said, gesturing to the thinly padded metal chairs. Being in an interview room made me feel like a criminal, even though I was innocent. It was similar to when a police car was behind you on the road, you've done nothing wrong but your heart leaps and you quickly place your hands at ten and two o'clock!

Blake sat beside me, far too close. His arm brushed against mine. I wasn't sure if it was deliberate to show unity against Wright, or he just couldn't be bothered to move the chair from where it was. "So," Wright said, waving his hand, "you have the floor. Over to you."

"Um, we thought of something, and we have something to show you."

He nodded, smirking a little in a patronising way that made me grind my teeth. "Another possibility? And I see you have a box of tricks with you."

I frowned. "Yes." Was he even taking us seriously? The contents of the box would probably wipe that smug smile right off his face.

"We think that maybe Josh could have done it," Blake said. "Or Courtney."

"What an interesting theory. That would certainly be better for you, wouldn't it? That would solve all of your problems."

Yes. "Josh had jealously issues. He saw Courtney as his. Their sex life was far from comfortable old missionary. I don't know, maybe he was mad at her or something or maybe she'd had enough. Can you just look into it, please?" I said, sliding the box over to him.

He cocked his head to the side, ignoring what I had just given him completely. "You've thought about this a lot, haven't you?"

"Clearing mine and my friends' names? You probably won't be surprised by this, but yes!"

"Let me share a little piece of information just to make your own little investigation easier, rookie," he said, raising his dark eyebrows, "Josh and Courtney were both murdered. From the angle of the knife wounds, it would have been very, very difficult for either one of them to have done that to themselves, and given the brutality and quantity of stab wounds, at this point I'm ruling that out. I'm quite offended you assumed I hadn't already investigated that possibility."

Blake shrugged. "Well you don't seem to know much so you can see how we got there."

I kicked him under the table, which only made him smirk. "Look, we just want to know who did this. They were my friends."

"Except Joshua," Wright replied.

I clenched my jaw. Why wasn't he listening to us? "Doesn't mean I wanted him dead."

"Perhaps not."

"Definitely not," I snapped. "Do you have any idea who it was at all?"

Wright leant forwards, leaning his arms on the table and smiled. "I have five ideas."

Blake sighed and stood up. "That's a no then. Come on, Mackenzie, he's obviously got nothing new to go on. Want us to leave you with that so you can flick through and work out if Courtney would have been capable of stabbing so brutally after what Josh put her through, or are you still ruling that out?"

"Thank you, Blake, I'll have someone look through it and return it as soon as possible."

Blake snorted, shaking his head. "You really don't know anything, do you?"

"I do know one thing," he said just as we were about to walk out of the room.

"What's that?" I asked over my shoulder, expecting another stupid comment that would do nothing but piss us off further.

"Your friend Aaron has been talking pretty loudly about Mr Harper's motives."

My face fell. I spun around. Aaron's been talking to Wright about Blake? "What?" I whispered.

"Not surprised. Aaron's not a huge fan," Blake replied and shrugged, showing Wright that he didn't care and it wasn't getting to him. It was getting to me though. How could Aaron do that? I would never start talking about what I knew about them just to help myself out. Aaron had no proof that it was Blake so he shouldn't be saying anything. I wasn't, and I knew he was doing drugs!

Wright's smile faded so slightly I almost missed it. "Is there anything else you'd like to discuss or are you all out of new—"

"We're done," I snapped and stormed out of the room. I wanted to request a proper detective, but I had a feeling he wasn't technically doing anything wrong. He kept things from us until he wanted us to know – for whatever reason – but that wasn't a crime.

"We're screwed, aren't we? They're going to pin it on one of us if they can't find out who really did it." I said once we were back in my room.

Blake smirked. "If there's no evidence then no."

"But innocent people go to prison. What if the jury do that beyond reasonable doubt thing?"

His smirk widened. "Good thing you chose detective and not lawyer actually."

I flopped back against my pillows. "You're not funny. I hope you know that."

He rolled over, hovering above me. "Please, you think I'm hilarious."

"Yes," I said, "but probably not in the way you're thinking."

I wanted him to kiss me more than I wanted to breathe, which was ridiculous. How the hell could someone so annoying worm their in and cause such a huge impact on my life and my heart in such a short space of time?

"Really?" he whispered, inching closer. I was pretty sure if I continued teasing him he would get payback and pull away, so I bit my lip. There was plenty of time to take the piss; this was a time for kissing.

"Blake," I moaned. The neediness in my voice made me want to hit myself.

"Yes?"

"You're being mean!"

He gasped in fake shock. "I'm not doing anything."

Narrowing my eyes, I gripped the sides of his t-shirt and pulled him closer. "If you're going to kiss me just do it or—" His lips sealed over mine, kissing me deeply, fiercely. His lips moved against mine with a desperation that made my toes curl.

We didn't have long though. My mum was due home any minute, and I really didn't want her to walk in on us. She thought Blake was just a friend, and I wanted to keep it that way. Technically that was all we were right now anyway.

"Blake," I managed to murmur against his mouth. He groaned and shook his head, gripping hold of my hip and cementing my body to his. I pushed at his chest when I could barely breathe, and he pulled away smirking. "You're like some randy fifteen-year-old boy!"

His eyebrows pulled together. "Kinda feel like it again."

"Blake Harper, are you admitting you like a girl?" I teased.

"Whatever," he muttered and sat up. I hated him being gone, and I knew that was stupid. He was under my skin now whether I liked it or not. "We should go back to mine and check on my mum."

"We?"

"Not sure if I've mentioned this but—"

"'I don't do hysterical women'," I said, finishing his sentence. "You may have mentioned it once or twice. I'll come too."

Blake was quiet in the car. I watched him drive for a minute and then decided since he wasn't filling the silence with anything stupid or sarcastic I would talk to him about something that had been on my mind. "Blake, will you tell me more about your relationship with Josh?" I asked.

His lips thinned. "What do you want to know?"

"You didn't have a good relationship?"

"It wasn't the best, but then we had barely spent any time together. I think I saw him about ten times through our teenage years. We weren't really brothers, not properly anyway."

"Did you want to be?"

"I guess. I've not really thought about it much. We weren't a family; we were split up. That was fine though. Dad and I managed." He smiled at a memory. "Though we ate crap all the time. We should be at least double the size we are."

"He wasn't a big cook?"

"Not really. He can make a few things and so can I. It was more out of laziness."

"Why do you think your mum loves him more?"

"Because she does. If you have a son that you spent every day with and another you barely spent a week a year with, who would be your favourite? I don't blame her. I favour my dad, and I'm sure Josh favoured Mum. It's natural to love who you're with most, isn't it?"

I frowned. *No, not if you're the parent.* "Maybe," I replied, not wanting to hurt him. "Why did you decide to come with us? Don't get me wrong, I'm glad you did, I just don't understand why."

He turned into his street, biting the inside of his cheek. "My dad started working more and working away. When you come home to an empty house every day, your mind eventually wonders to the other half of your family. Josh and I had spent some time together a couple months before, and it was alright. I thought maybe we could be brothers now we could control where we went ourselves. Before it had always been our parents pulling the strings, and that was usually in opposite directions."

So he really just wanted to reconnect – or connect – with his brother. "I'm sorry you lost him before you had a chance to do that." Blake gulped and nodded. His jaw tightened, and I knew I had to change the subject. He didn't do emotions well. "I'm going to cook for you and your mum tonight. What's your favourite dinner?"

He blinked heavily. "Doing a conversation one-eighty. I like spaghetti bolognese. I think my mum does too."

"Sounds good." I smiled at him, and he smiled back. His eye twitched as if he was trying to figure me out. Or he was just confused that someone had asked him that.

He pulled into his drive, and that was when I noticed the police car beside Blake's mum's. "What're they doing here?" Blake muttered, frowning.

We jumped out of the car as soon as it stopped. It didn't look good, and I prayed Eloise hadn't done anything stupid. If she was dead too then what was Blake going to do? As much as he didn't think he needed her he did.

Blake unlocked the door, and I raced past him into the living room. Two officers sat on one sofa, and Eloise was on another. I sighed in relief as I saw she was okay, physically anyway.

"What's going on?" Blake asked.

The officers, who I didn't recognise, moved quickly, gabbing Blake's arms and twisting them round his back. "Blake Harper, I'm arresting you for the murders of Joshua Harper and Courtney Young. You do not have to say anything, but it may harm your defence if you do not mention when questioned something which you later rely on in court. Anything you do say may be given in evidence. Do you understand?"

"What?" I said numbly, in shock. "Why?"

Blake's jaw was tight, tense. "I get it," he bit out.

"They found it under his bed," Eloise cried, rocking on her chair.

"Found what?" I asked, desperately looking between her and Blake to make sure I didn't miss when they took him away.

"Rohypnol. He did it. He killed my Josh."

My mouth dropped open at the same time my heart plummeted to my feet. I shook my head. "No…"

The two officers shoved Blake forwards and out of the front door. It took me a few seconds to force my legs to walk. Shock planted me to the ground. When I did move, I sprinted back out the door. "Wait!" I shouted. There had to be some mistake. He wouldn't.

The officers had just opened the back door when I reached the car. Blake looked at me, and his expression – defeat – made my heart ache. "I didn't do it, Mackenzie," he said just before he disappeared into the car. He watched me as the car drove off, pleading with me to believe him, but I knew he didn't expect me to.

# CHAPTER TWENTY-TWO

The car turned out of my sight, and my heart broke. This wasn't right. Even though there was Rohypnol in his room I didn't believe it was his. He was never on edge or nervous when I was in his room. He never so much as flinched when I got in his bed. I sprinted back in the house to find out what the hell was going on. He didn't even live here. Something was definitely not right. He was set up.

"Eloise!" I shouted, gripping the doorframe for support and to stop myself running.

She sat in her chair, hugging her knees, sobbing. My frown deepened as I realised she was crying over her son being guilty. But Blake wasn't guilty. She had no faith in him at all. There was no *my son would never do that*. She sat there and told me he'd done it.

I walked slowly over to her and perched on the edge of the sofa next to her chair. "What happened?"

"They found that stuff in his room." She shook her head, wiping her tears. Her face was tear-stained and blotchy. "I can't believe it. I don't want to believe it."

"Then don't. I don't. Blake didn't do this. How did they find it? Someone had to of tipped them off."

She frowned. "They knocked on the door and asked to search his room." *And you let them!* Although if she hadn't it would have looked like she was covering something up. No one would have known though. If it was true how would anyone have known?

"Who else has been in the house?"

"Um, I'm not sure. A lot of people have come by to check on me."

My heart ached as I asked the next question, "Did Aaron, Megan or Kyle come?"

"They were here at Josh's funeral."

"But that was the only time?"

She nodded. "Yes, that was it."

I closed my eyes and tried to think back to that day. We were together most of the time, but I had flit between them and Blake. Who had gone off alone? None of them had really moved from the spot I left them in, and I was never gone too long, but they could have had enough time to get upstairs and back. Which one of them would be so bold as to bring Rohypnol to the wake and plant it in Blake's room though? I couldn't picture any of them being brave enough – or stupid enough – to do that.

"Why would Blake want to hurt his own brother and uncle?" Eloise asked, breaking me away from my endless internal questions.

"He didn't. This wasn't him, Eloise, you have to believe that. Think about it, someone tips off the police and they miraculously find Rohypnol in his room. No one's been in his room; he doesn't hang out with anyone here. Even if he did have it, no one would have known. Don't give up on him. He needs you."

"I don't know what to do." She buried her head in her knees and gripped her hair. "I have nothing left to give him."

I clenched my jaw as anger surged through my body. "He's your son! You have to find something inside." *The same something you would have for Josh.* "I'm serious, Eloise! He needs you. You can't honestly think it was him."

She frowned, squeezing her eyes closed and shaking her head. "I don't know. I just… I don't know."

*Well fuck you then!* "Whatever!" I spat, walking out before I said something that I probably wouldn't regret.

We came in Blake's car, so I had no way of getting anywhere other than walking. I didn't want to call either of my parents or any one of my friends. I still needed to find out who put the Rohypnol in Blake's room, and I was going to start with Aaron.

As I walked I kept thinking about Blake and what he was going through. It must be terrifying being arrested for something you hadn't done and not having your mum there for you. Aaron made no secret of the fact that he thought it was Blake so hopefully Wright was looking into that too. I didn't want to believe Aaron would do something like that but deep down I knew he had it in him.

What was I going to say to him? If he did it, he would know that I was there to ask him. I had to just be blunt, come out and just ask if he did it. That was the only way. If he said no, and it wasn't him, I could possibly lose a friend.

I knocked on his door and my stomach started doing somersaults. "Hey," Aaron said, his smile stretching across his face, lighting up his baby blue eyes.

I returned his smile. "Hi." He stepped aside so I could walk in. "Can we talk?"

"Sure. My parents are home so let's go upstairs."

My heart was in my throat as we climbed the stairs. I wasn't sure if I wanted it to be him more than I didn't. Blake was innocent; I knew that. But I didn't know if I wanted Aaron to be guilty just to get Blake off. I shouldn't want that. Aaron had been in my life far longer than Blake.

"So what's up?" he asked as he sat on his swivel chair by his desk.

I lowered myself onto the bed, facing him. "Blake was arrested today."

His eyebrows shot up. If it was Aaron he faked shock well. "For the murders?"

"The police found drugs in his room."

"Wow..." He shook his head. "Can't say I'm surprised."

"No. You always thought it was him."

"Well I was right, wasn't I?"

"No, you're not. They're not his drugs."

"Mackenzie, come on! How long are you going to defend the guy for? Open your eyes! I know you don't want to think badly of anyone, but this is ridiculous. We barely know the guy. On the night he randomly decides to play brothers two people end up dead. How does that look?"

It wasn't random. He just wanted a family. "I get how it looks, and I know you don't trust him, but please trust *me*. Blake didn't do this."

"So the drug fairies left it in his room, did they?"

I gulped. "No." Raising my eyes to meet his, I waited and then watched his mouth slowly drop.

"You think it was me?" he shouted, pushing himself up and frowning, hurt and angry. "What the fuck, Mackenzie! How can you even ask me that? I think the guy is a creep and yeah, I think he did it, but I'm not about to go framing anyone!"

"Okay, okay," I replied, standing and holding my arms up. "I'm sorry, but Wright said you've been telling everyone how much you think it's Blake and—"

"So you believe that arsehole and not someone you've known years? I thought better of you."

My eyes stung. He was right. I shouldn't have believed what Wright was saying. I rubbed my forehead. "God, I'm sorry, Aaron. I don't know what to think anymore. I don't know what I'm doing or how to handle all of this stuff. Everything is already so messed up and now Blake has been arrested."

Aaron grabbed my arms and bent down to my level. "You have to face up to the fact that it was him. You said the police found drugs in his room. How much more evidence do you need?"

To believe he did it, I need a confession. "It wasn't him, Aaron."

"Who was it then? Me? Kyle? Megan? We're your only other options so pick one."

I yanked my arms from his grip. "Don't you dare ask me to choose between you."

"I don't need to really. You came here asking me. I think it's clear who you think killed them."

"I don't think it's you," I replied, only half lying. "Aaron, I'm sorry. I'm just looking for answers, and I just want to know what happened."

"So do I!"

"Alright. I was wrong, and I'm sorry. I don't want to lose you too." My eyes filled with tears, and Aaron groaned.

"Don't cry. You know I hate it when you cry." He wrapped his arms around me. "What you said hurt, but I don't want to lose you either."

"I'm sorry," I whispered. "Forgive me?"

"Sure," he replied. "Megan and Kyle'll be here soon. Wanna help me get the drink and snacks for Kyle together." He rolled his eyes, smirking.

What I wanted was to check on Blake and make sure he was okay, but I knew Wright wouldn't let me see him. Maybe hanging with them would be a good idea? Maybe now I knew they all had secrets I would be able to see through them.

We sat on the floor in Aaron's room with the snacks and alcohol in the middle. It was just like any other time we'd hung out together but the atmosphere was tense. We were all together because that was what we usually did. It was hard to stick together when I felt like I barely knew any of them.

They looked haunted. I couldn't tell their expressions between a grieving friend who had been through so much and a guilty conscience anymore. Blake was right; I couldn't tell if they'd done it.

Me and Kyle were probably the closest; he had always been an open book. And Megan, I thought, had never kept a secret from me our whole lives. Aaron was the blue eyed boy, the loving sweetheart that was going to be the best husband and dad in the world one day.

I opened a bottle of some pre-made tropical cocktail – the only bottle that hadn't had the seal broken – and took a large swig. They didn't seem to worry that one of us in that room was a murderer and had drugged the rest of us. It was clear they believed it was Blake and there was no danger of being spiked again.

"To Tilly, Gigi, Josh and Courtney," Kyle said, holding his can of beer up.

*And to Pete.*

I raised the bottle, clinking it against the boys' cans and Megan's glass of neat vodka. "Getting drunk, Megan?" I asked after we had all taken a sip of our drinks. Being with them felt wrong. I wanted to leave.

"It's over now, Mackenzie. Blake's going to prison for what he did. We don't have to worry about Courtney and Josh never getting justice. I kinda think that's cause for a celebration, don't you?"

No.

"It is," Aaron replied. "To justice and finally being able to move on."

How many toasts were they going to do? They were toasting to something that was so screwed up and completely untrue.

Megan giggled and nodded her head in one big movement. A drunken nod. She hadn't had much to drink, but she was drinking neat vodka. I didn't blame her for downing the alcohol. At least if I was drunk I could stop worrying for a while. I couldn't do that though. Blake was sitting in some holding cell so I couldn't have a laugh with my friends.

"I can't believe it's just us four left. This time last year my room was filled with eight pissed, happy people. Remember you girls dancing around the room singing into empty bottles," Kyle said and chuckled.

I smiled at the memory and wished we could go back there. Things were simple and easy then. I was shocked at how much could change in just one little year. My circle of friends had been cut in half, and I had a not-really-a-boyfriend guy friend who I could possibly lose before anything had really happened. I was so tired of losing people.

"This is all so fucked up, but at least they have the person that did it. We're all okay now," Aaron said, raising his glass to me.

My hand tightened around the bottle, but I said nothing. Perhaps if they all got drunk one of them might slip up? I didn't have much hope, but it was the only piece of hope I had.

"Thank God," Megan added. "I knew we would all get through this. We just had to stick together."

Out of the corner of my eye I saw Aaron raise his eyebrows, and I knew the gesture was for me. I had pretty much accused him of being the murderer when I asked if he planted those drugs on Blake.

"I'll just be a minute," I said and left the room. They were like strangers to me now. I walked into the bathroom and locked the door so I could make the phone call in private.

Wright was on the other end of the line almost as soon as he was informed of my call. "Hello, Miss Keaton, what a lovely surprise."

"Is Blake okay?"

"Blake is fine," he replied.

"What's happening? You know it wasn't his, don't you?"

"Unfortunately, I can't speak about—"

"Cut the shit," I snapped. "We all know you do nothing by the book so don't pretend to start now."

The line was silent for a second and then I heard a quiet chuckle. "I admire your spunk, Mackenzie." Spunk! Who still used the word spunk? "Blake is being questioned."

"I figured that. You're still looking at who it really is, aren't you?"

"If you're asking me if you're still a person of interest, yes."

I sighed in relief. That meant he wasn't jumping on the Blake-did-it train like everyone else. "Good."

"I find it quite remarkable that you would prefer to still be a suspect."

"I don't want an innocent man going to prison."

"Neither do I," he replied. "The evidence we found in Blake's room has been sent for tests."

"You mean finger printing?"

"Nothing gets past you, does it?"

I looked towards where Aaron's room was even though all I could see was the mirrored cabinet on the wall. "A couple things do. You're slightly more transparent than my friends though." Lie.

"I wish I could say the same about you. Good day, Mackenzie," he said and hung up.

I walked back to Aaron's room, and they hadn't moved an inch. Taking my seat between Megan and Kyle, I picked up my drink and then thought better of it. They had been alone with it. I didn't trust them.

Aaron barely looked at me. I couldn't make out if it was because he felt betrayed or was pretending so he would seem innocent. I used to know my friends. I could tell just by an expression what they were thinking. Now I had no clue. All of us being accused had flipped over everything I thought I knew. I was left completely in the dark.

# CHAPTER TWENTY-THREE

I arrived home shortly after they started on the shots. Celebrating Blake's arrest made me feel sick, and if Aaron made one more toast I was going to punch him. Those people were strangers.

Both of my parents' cars were in the drive, which was unusual on a weekday. "Hello?" I called and closed the front door behind me.

"Kitchen," Mum replied, and I took a left, under the arched doorway.

The last time we had a kitchen talk was three and a half years ago and they were giving me the talk after I got together with Danny. I could still clearly remember the horror I felt at having them explain about contraception. Not to mention when Mum slid a condom over a banana. I wanted the ground to swallow me whole. The day I found out I was pregnant I remembered burning the remaining condoms Danny and I had. What was the point of using them if they just split?

"Sit down, Mackenzie," Dad said. He and Mum were around the kitchen table with a teapot filled with steaming hot tea and three mugs. I sat down and bit my lip, nervous.

"Blake has been arrested," Mum said, pouring tea into the mugs.

"Yes, but he didn't do it. I know he didn't."

"Mackenzie—" Dad started, but I cut him off by holding my hand up.

"Please, Dad. I know what you're going to say, but I trust him. We've spent a lot of time together, and I just know that he could never do that."

"How well do you really know him though?"

I shrugged. "Well. You're the one that always says your gut instinct is never wrong and you should always follow it."

"And don't I regret that now," he muttered behind his mug and took a sip. "We just want you safe, sweetheart, that's why we think you should stay in until this whole thing blows over." *Blows over?* He made it sound as if it was snowing outside and I should wait in until it stopped.

"Dad, I'm fine."

He pursed his lips and put his drink down. "Mackenzie, I made it sound like a suggestion, and I shouldn't have. You will stay in until the person responsible is in police custody. Do you understand?"

"I'm almost twenty."

"I don't care how old you are. You're our child and we will do whatever necessary to make sure you're safe. Hate us if you want."

I frowned. "I don't hate you. I understand why you're grounding, sort of grounding, your adult daughter, but it's stupid."

"Honey, you're our baby and we don't want to upset you, but if anything happened we would never forgive ourselves. Now if you trust Blake then I do too. You've got a good head on your shoulders, but if you're going to see him when he gets out it will be here when one of us is home."

*Oh wow, that won't be embarrassing at all!* If that's what had to happen for them to be able to sleep at night then I could deal. "Thank you for trusting me about Blake."

"Is it serious between you two?" Mum asked.

My eyes widened. "No," I said cautiously. We had slept together and kissed a couple of times. That didn't exactly equal a serious, committed relationship. I knew him as well as you could know a virtual stranger, a bit more because of what we had been through and the amount of talking we had done, but that still wasn't a huge amount.

"You're not doing that casual thing, are you?" Dad shook his head. "Mackenzie, you deserve better than that."

"Oh my God, Dad!" My face felt on fire. "That's *not* what we're doing. We're not doing anything!"

Mum frowned. "But you are together?"

"No, Mum."

"I don't get you kids nowadays," she said. "Why you have to complicate everything I will never know. If two people like each other they should just come out and say so. Such a waste of time going around in circles when you could be happy."

My parents admitted they liked each other within days of meeting and about a week later they were a couple. It didn't quite work like that these days. Now if a girl admitted she liked a guy straight away she was a bunny boiler and if a guy did it he was a pussy. There were modern day politics you had to consider. Rules you had to adhere to in order to be happy. The young people that jumped into relationships nowadays were desperate and no one wanted a *latcher*.

"Can we not talk about this, please!"

Mum put her mug down to raise her hands. "Alright. You'll let us know when you two sort it out though?"

"Yeah, will do, Mum." I took a sip of my drink, wishing it were hotter and could scold my throat to save me from the annoying aww-our-daughter-likes-a-boy looks they were giving me. "Dad, do you think you could call the police station and try to find out what's going on? Wright won't tell me much."

"You're worried about your not quite boyfriend," he said and smirked.

"If you're not going to do it—"

"No, no, I'll do it."

"You guys are being really cool about this? You don't know Blake."

"We know you. And if you trust him over three people you've known practically your whole life then he can't be bad," Dad said, standing up. "I'll make that call now." Did I trust him over them? Well yes. I had proved that many times.

Mum smiled at me when Dad left the room. A full, toothy smile that I knew was holding something she was bursting to say. No doubt it would be about Blake. I sighed. "Go on, just say it, Mum."

"Have you kissed?" she asked.

"Yes," I replied.

"Oh, I think he's the one!" My mum was an old romantic; she and dad had been together since they were teenagers so she wanted the same for me.

"Okay, we're really done now." Why did *enough* mean nothing to your family? I stood up. "I'll see you at dinner."

"You're hiding out until dinner? You shouldn't be embarrassed to talk about boys with me."

"Bye, Mum!"

My mum was also what my friends referred to as a 'cool mum'. She allowed me to stay out late and drink – responsibly and carefully – when I was underage. I never had any big fights with her growing up. I was her only child, so she put a lot of time and effort into me, much more than she would have been able to if she had to split her attention. As a result, we were close, but not as close as she seemed to think we were.

I left the kitchen and my laughing mother to hover around Dad by the sofa. "No, I know… Well is there anything you can tell me?" he said into the phone. I knew that meant he was getting nothing too. I hated waiting around and not knowing. Blake was innocent. How long would it take to prove that?

He hung up and shook his head. "Sorry, kiddo."

I shrugged. "Thanks for trying. I'm gonna go watch a couple films."

My room wasn't like bedrooms in movies where you could sneak out down the drainpipe. Outside my window was a flat brick wall and a long drop onto stones – things that would create noise if something, a person, was dropped onto them. I wouldn't be able to sneak out. Even if I could sneak out I didn't know where I would go. There probably wasn't anything I could do to help Blake anyway.

I could go back to the cabin? Would that do anything though? There was nothing there. It had been searched, a lot. The police found nothing to tie any of us to the murders. Where else did they search? The woods? They must have. Wright hadn't said anything to us, but that was no surprise.

I curled up my bed and tried to think of something, but, of course, there was crap all I could do. I felt like a joke, running around trying everything I could – which wasn't much – to catch a killer when I didn't have the first clue how to do any of it. I was one of those people in films that was so obviously doing everything wrong. So I decided that for once I would do nothing and leave it to the police. Whatever I tried backfired so I wasn't going to interfere in case I made it worse. Blake didn't need that right now.

It wasn't fair that he was in the police station being questioned endlessly when the real killer was drinking and celebrating, but until Wright saw that whatever I did would only get in the way. Burying my head in my pillow, I shut my eyes and fell into restless but much welcomed sleep.

Something woke me hours later, someone shaking my arm. I groaned and looked at my phone beside me. It showed 9:55PM. Groaning again, I turned to grumble at Mum or Dad for waking me up when Blake's gorgeous blue eyes stared back at me, gleaming with amusement.

I threw myself at him, unashamed. It took a second for him to hug me back, but when he did, he almost crushed my bones. "You're okay," I said, closing my eyes and clinging to him. "What happened?"

"My fingerprints weren't on the drugs," he said and chuckled. "And Wright knew it was a set up. It was all too perfect."

"They know that already?"

He shrugged. "Wright had it fast-tracked. They already have my prints on file, so it didn't take long to figure out that shit wasn't mine."

"Whose prints were on them?"

"Apparently they lifted some, but none are any of ours. "Sloppy work planting something that was going to be found clear of my prints. Especially from someone so calculated."

"They're getting desperate," I whispered.

"Yeah." He pulled back and looked at me with a stern gaze. "That means they're even more dangerous. I don't want you hanging out with any of them alone anymore. I know I sound like a dad now, but we have no idea what they could do next."

I rolled my eyes. "I've already been banned from leaving this house."

"Good." He sat on my bed, pulling me by the hand. "My mum came to the station."

My eyebrows rose in surprise. I honestly didn't think she would. "She did?"

"Yeah. She was a proper mum too, doing the shouting stuff I imagined she would do if Josh was in my situation."

"That's good."

He nodded. "It was weird."

"Good weird?"

"Good weird," he confirmed.

"Where's your dad?"

"Home with Mum at the minute. He wanted to make sure she's okay until I get back. They seem to be getting on. Well they've not screamed at other, so it's going better than it has been for the last fifteen years."

I was so happy for him. He deserved a mum and for his parents to get along so it wouldn't be awkward for him. "What happens now?"

"With?"

"The investigation and you."

"The first one is still on-going, which seemed to piss Wright off, so that's a bonus. And I have to pack up my room at home and move all my shit to my mum's."

"Really?" I said, trying not to sound as excited as I felt.

He chuckled. "Yeah. My dad's away more and more, so it makes sense for me to be around family. And you."

I licked my dry lips. "You want to be around me?"

He leant forwards, grazing his lips against mine. "That shouldn't surprise you. Apparently it's painfully obvious to everyone else that I like you. I want to be with you."

What do I say to that! Blake's lips pressed hard to mine and he kissed me fiercely, knotting his hand in my hair. It was a big deal for him to admit that. I pushed myself onto his lap and gripped his back, pulling him closer. Perhaps Mum had something with her just say it attitude after all.

Blake left mine at half past ten. It was when my parents were going to bed and dropped their not so subtle hint about us not being left alone together. The house was too quiet with Blake at his and my parents sleeping. I had time to think, too much time. All I wanted was to know who it was. The other four of us deserved to live our lives without being watched, judged and questioned.

Closing my eyes, I took myself back to that day, yet again. I was determined to figure it out. Blake once told me that I already knew because I knew my friends better than anyone. Recently I'd thought that was completely untrue after all the secrets that had come out but maybe that meant I now did know each of them better than anyone else.

I pictured myself the night before at Josh's house as we all dropped off some of the food and alcohol to be packed in his designated food and drink suitcases. Control freak. Josh had demanded that all the beer, bottles of vodka and fizzy drinks were be delivered to his, so we didn't have to worry about getting it all the following day. Any other drink we wanted to bring was to be brought in our own bags.

Megan and I were standing in the corner of the living room rolling our eyes at him. Aaron and Kyle were helping him stuff the bottles of booze between packets and boxes of food so they wouldn't get broken.

Most of the conversation was lost to me, but I vaguely remembered most of it just being about packing and getting 'rat-arsed' all weekend. Besides the obvious of everyone sticking their finger up at Josh behind his back, no one acted any differently.

I pictured the guys carrying the heavy suitcase out to the Kyle's car that was going to stay there the night and us girls following them. I gasped as I remembered Josh making a joke about there being alcohol to kill us. The next thing to break its way through my memory was a bottle of Absolut Vodka being slipped through the zip last minute and the crystal clear words 'If you drink that one you will be.' It was said as a joke, and I hadn't even considered that there could be a double meaning to it before now.

My blood ran cold. In front of me, my mobile started ringing. "Hello," I said numbly into the phone without looking at the caller ID.

"Hello." I recognised my friend's voice immediately. The next four words that were spoken made my blood run cold, "Mackenzie, it was me."

*I know.*

# CHAPTER TWENTY-FOUR

I put the phone down with trembling hands. I had to go there now. I had to know why. Creeping out of my room, I made my way downstairs and out of the house. Walking wouldn't take long. I contemplated calling Blake, but for some reason I didn't feel I needed to.

Even after what he had done I still didn't believe that he would hurt me. I needed to hear it, to understand before I made a decision. There might be something that could be done, some help for a friend that had obviously snapped before he was thrown in prison and forgotten.

I walked quickly with my heart firmly in the pit of my stomach. Surreal; that was the only word I could think to describe the situation. I was on my way to see my murderous friend, and I was walking eagerly as if I were going to a concert.

Taking a deep breath, I opened the front door. It was unlocked, as I'd thought. After our phone conversation, there was no way the door would have been locked. Eyes that looked up at me were the same baby blue ones that I loved so much, but they were somehow older now. They had lost their innocence.

"Aaron," I said, not sure of how to go on. What could I possibly say to him?

He sat on the sofa, turning his head away as I entered the house and shut the door behind me. Gulping, I walked over to the seating area and sat on the sofa next to his. "Why?" I whispered.

"They're all on their way," he said, staring at the wall and not me anymore.

I could smell the harsh scent of brandy on his breath. "How much have you had to drink?" Was that why he was confessing?

He shrugged. "Not enough."

Sitting near him felt normal, like we were just going to flick on the TV and watch a film. He killed two of our friends, and I was just having a chat with him! "You called Kyle and Megan too?"

"And Blake. I only want to explain this once." Not Blake! I didn't want him near here. He was the odd one out to Aaron. I trusted him with mine, Kyle and Megan's life a hell of a lot more than I did with Blake's.

He was going to have to explain it a few more times than that for Wright. Did Aaron expect us to cover for him? All this time he had allowed us to be interrogated and sat back to cover his own arse. I could never do that to anyone let alone someone I cared about.

"Why did you call Blake too? You don't need to explain this to him."

His mouth tinned into a straight line. "I'll explain when they're here."

"Aaron," I whispered. *We're friends!*

His eyebrows knitted togetehre. "Don't look at me like that, Mackenzie."

"How should I look at you?" Why wasn't I freaking out and screaming at him? I should have been. I wanted to but I still felt like I was looking down at this whole situation from afar. Aaron wasn't somebody that hurt anyone. I was desperate to find even a glimpse of my old friend inside this alien.

"I don't know. Just not like you hate me."

I almost laughed. Did he expect me to pat him on the back and tell him it was okay? What he wanted from me couldn't happen. It wasn't okay. We weren't okay. I just needed to know why he did it, and then I needed to get him help because something had obviously happened to him.

"Mackenzie?" Blake shouted, bursting through the door like he was in an action movie. "You okay?" he asked, his eyes landing on me, scanning my whole body in a second to make sure I was alright.

I stood up. "I'm fine." I was anything but fine.

Megan and Kyle arrive together, barely a minute after Blake. They both stopped just inside the door and were both as pale as a ghost. Kyle shook his head. "What's going on, man? Tell me this is a joke."

Aaron stood up and properly acknowledged our presence for the first time since Blake made his grand entrance. I took a step back. The expression on his face made my stomach turn. He looked bored, as if this was nothing but listening to one of our uni lecturers going on and on.

"It's not a joke," Aaron replied.

Megan let out a sob and pressed her hand to her mouth. "Why?" she muttered against her palm.

"Because they didn't care about what happened to Tilly and Gigi."

"What?" I said, letting out a huge puff of air. My half sigh, half laugh of disbelief. "They were devastated by what happened." Courtney cried solidly for weeks, she hadn't driven since and often told me about the crushing guilt she felt. Josh felt it too at first and even though he said some stupid, horrible things I knew that he felt guilt, and I knew that he wished it hadn't happened.

"Were they?" he sneered. "They moved on so quickly it was like they never even existed to them."

"Aaron, where is this coming from?" Kyle asked. "You know that's not true. What happened to you?"

I tried to remember if I'd forgotten something. An anniversary of one of the times he got together with Tilly. Something, anything that would explain what had tipped him over the edge. I never even knew he was struggling. He

205

was always so strong for us. Was that it? Had everything become too much for him and he snapped? I truly hoped so because that meant there was hope for him. I wanted my Aaron back.

"Nothing's happened to me, Kyle. You can't see it. None of you can. You couldn't see what they were like. They didn't care about them, they were just glad it wasn't them lying dead in the ground."

I swallowed the quickly rising lump in my throat and clenched my trembling hands. "That's not true." Courtney loved Tilly and Gigi as much as me and Megan did. We were close, like sisters. Whatever Aaron said, I knew Courtney would never have put her own life above theirs.

"Now, here's what we're going to do," he said, pulling a knife from his pocket. "I'm going to stab Blake." I almost stumbled back in shock, as if his words had punched me. What the fuck was he on? He'd clearly continued drinking after Megan and Kyle stopped but did he have drugs in his system too?

He looked and sounded so calm, as if he'd just said 'I'm going to grab Blake a beer' rather than telling us he wanted to stab him. "And us four." He pointed to himself and then between me Kyle and Megan. "Are going to call Wright and tell him that Blake tried to kill us too, but we managed to get the upper hand. It will be self-defence."

I felt sick. My vision blurred and my ears rang. There was no way Kyle and Megan would go for that. They couldn't. "Aaron, no," I whispered.

"Cut the shit, Mackenzie," he bellowed; spit flying out of his mouth. "I've had enough of this *team Blake* crap from you. We are your friends and like you've said a thousand times before, we have to stick together."

"Aaron, man," Kyle said, his open mouth still showing his shock. "We can't do that. I understand how you feel. I do. I lost the girl I love too, and I'm still sad and angry as hell, but this isn't the way to make it better."

Aaron straightened his back, holding the knife higher. "Shut up! You don't know anything, Kyle. We just have to do this one last thing, and then we can put it all behind us. Everything will be okay. I promise."

*He's lost it.* He'd become unpredictable and that was the scariest thing. My blonde hair, blue eyed loving friend was a cold-hearted killer. Whatever he said there was no way I was letting him hurt Blake or anyone else.

"Aaron," Megan whispered, stepping forward and holding her hands up. "It's alright. Everything is going to be fine, but I need you to put the knife away. We can talk about this. Sort this out. Between us five we can find a way to make this better. Right, guys?" she said, looking back at us with her eyes wide, telling us, pleading with us, to agree.

"Of course," I said. If we could just get the knife away from him, we could sort everything out.

Blake nodded and Kyle replied, "Yeah. Anything."

Aaron laughed, tilting his head back. "Do you think I'm stupid? The second he's out of here he'll go to Wright," he spat, glaring at Blake.

"No, he won't. Will you, Blake?" I said, willing him to agree and make it convincing. I could tell by the way Blake's eyes were slightly narrowed that there was no way in hell he was ever going to help Aaron, but he nodded and looked convincing enough to people that didn't know him. "See, this is all going to be alright. We'll all cover and eventually the case will go cold."

"She's right, Aaron," Megan said. "If we all keep quiet eventually this will blow over. They have nothing on you."

"No!" he shouted, jabbing the knife at the air. "The only way this is going away is if we end it now."

"Calm the fuck down!" Blake yelled. "You're not stabbing anyone else you sick bastard. Now put the damn knife down."

"What're you doing?" I said and glared at him as Aaron did the same. Was he trying to piss him off? We needed to tread carefully. "He didn't mean that, Aaron."

Aaron growled. "Oh will you stop defending him! I'll stab you too if you keep it up." He didn't mean that. His eyes widened in shock at his own words.

Something was really off here and not just the fact that this was Aaron standing in front of me wielding a knife, admitting to murder and throwing threats around. There was just something about it that didn't fit and didn't feel right.

"You so much as touch her, and I'll kill you myself," Blake replied, far too calmly. His voice tuned my blood cold. Blake, unlike Aaron, wasn't bluffing.

Aaron stepped forwards, and Blake held his ground. "You need to back off now." There was a double meaning to that. Back off away from him and from me. "I'm warning you, Harper."

I threw my hands up. "Stop it! Both of you stop!" I felt like I was forever in the middle of those two.

What happened next happened so slowly it almost felt like a dream. Blake spat something out about Aaron being screwed in the head. Aaron lunged forwards the way he had many times before when he'd gotten himself into a scrap at school. Blake punched Aaron in the face, splitting his lip. I thought that would be it but a red faced Aaron threw himself forwards again.

Megan's high-pitched scream followed by Kyle shouting expletives pierced my eardrums. It took me barely a second to register that Aaron had used the knife; there was a red glisten on it, like it had been film wrapped. Half of my stomach was pressed against Blake's back as he shielded me.

Aaron dropped the knife and backed away, wide eyed and gripping his hair. Regret.

Was it me then? Had he stabbed me? I couldn't feel anything. Not a thing. Blake looked down, his hand shooting to his side, and I felt light, as if my body had been drained of blood. I couldn't catch my breath. I was sure I was going to collapse.

It was him.

"No, no, no, no," I whispered, unable to make a louder sound. My eyes filled with tears. I pressed hard against his hand on the wound. My hands shook and I fought desperately hard to keep them still so it wouldn't hurt him more. My hand soon heated with his warm blood seeping through his fingers to mine. I couldn't lose him. I hadn't had him long but I couldn't even imagine losing him.

Kyle lunged at Aaron and pinned him to the floor. In the distance I heard Megan talking into her mobile to the emergency services in a half-hysterical, half-scream cry for help. *Hurry up. Please, please hurry up.*

"Shit," Blake hissed. "I need to sit down."

We shuffled the short distance, and I helped him onto the sofa. What did he need? What did you do when someone had been stabbed? He laid back against the cushion and groaned. His jaw was clenched and his eyes twitched as he tried not to show how much pain he was in. His chest rose and fell a little quicker than what was normal. Did that mean something bad?

"You're gonna be fine," I said, holding back a sob. "The ambulance will be here soon. How do you feel?" Shouldn't you always ask that? Didn't you need to know if they felt cold or tired? What did it mean if he did feel any of those things though? I had absolutely no medical training, not even as a first responder. All I knew was to put pressure on the wound to stem the bleeding and keep them talking. "Blake!"

He smirked through his pain. "I feel like I just got stabbed."

"Shut up." I scolded, letting out an involuntary sob. How could he still make jokes?

Aaron laid beneath Kyle, still. He looked like a statue. The only thing that made him look alive was the way he was staring at Megan on the phone. She was the one turning him in to the police and calling for help for Blake. I was terrified that he might get up and try hurting her too.

"I told you it was him," Blake whispered and winced.

I could've hit him. If he wasn't already in a lot of pain, I would have. Thankfully no one else heard over the sound of Megan stumbling over her words in the desperate attempt to tell whoever was on the phone what had happened as quickly as possible.

"Shut up," I repeated. My eyes stung with tears, but he still managed to make me smile. The idiot.

It was only a few minutes later that I heard the sirens, but they were the longest few minutes of my life. Blake sat perfectly still, breathing rapidly and deeply. He smiled at me. He was the one that had been stabbed yet he was trying to calm me down.

"You're going to be okay," I said sternly. "You are."

"I know. You worry too much."

There was a very good reason for me to worry; my hand was soaked with his blood. I could smell the blood too, it took me right back to that day and everything hit me like a ton of bricks. My vision blurred through a heavy film of tears. I felt everything, the loss of my friends, the crushing betrayal and fear of losing Blake. I felt cold.

Eight pints of blood was in the human body. I knew Blake had not even bled out anywhere near one pint, but it looked like an ocean of red. It looked like fifty pints of blood. I was barely holding it together as it was, I couldn't handle losing anyone else. I needed Blake, Kyle and Megan so much.

Paramedics, closely followed by four police officers slammed through the door. I thought I would be shoved out of the way, but they soon realised I was the one stopping the blood from spurting out. "Hello, my name's Jerry. How're you doing?"

Blake gulped audibly. "Alright." Jerry smiled, seeming to understand that Blake was majorly playing it down.

"It happened... Um," I stuttered. "Not long ago. I don't know how long it's been, but he was stabbed and it won't stop bleeding."

"Okay," Jerry said. He was a picture of calm. "Now...?"

"His name's Blake," I said, speaking for him. "I'm Mackenzie. Should I move my hand?"

"Okay, Mackenzie. No, not just yet, stay where you are and keep pressure on that. You're doing really well. Where is the knife?"

"Floor," Blake replied. "Whole. I work out, but I don't think I'm toned enough to snap a knife."

Jerry laughed. He laughed. How was he able to do that? His job? Keep the patient's mind off what was happening?

"Well, that's good. Now, Blake, I'm going to get you to completely take over from Mackenzie. I need you to press hard on the wound and keep that pressure. We're going to get you on the stretcher and into the ambulance, okay." He looked back at his colleague who was speaking to someone on her radio in a hushed voice.

What do they know that I don't? Why was Jerry wanting to get him into the ambulance straight away? Shouldn't they check him over more first, or was that normal for stab victims? Did he assume Blake was okay because he was chatting normally?

I stayed by Blake's side, refusing to find my own way to the hospital. There was no way I was leaving him. I was terrified that something more was wrong. Had the knife punctured something? I had a thousand questions that Jerry couldn't answer.

The last I saw of Aaron was when I caught a brief glimpse of him being bundled into a police car as we made our way out to the ambulance. I didn't care what his reasons were or what was going on inside his head the second he stabbed Blake. I couldn't forgive him for what he'd done to everyone I cared about. Or what he'd done to me.

I helped Blake on his bed and scowled at him. "You shouldn't be here. You need to be in the hospital." I sounded like his mum, who had also said the exact same thing. It was a little after eleven in the morning when Blake discharged himself. I had been awake for something like twenty-seven hours, and I was exhausted. Last night – or this morning, however you wanted to look at it – I had been too scared to sleep in case something happened to Blake. I watched him sleeping for hours and thanked every possible God going that he was okay.

"There's nothing they can do for me in hospital. I'd rather be in my own bed than sleeping next to weirdos snoring all night and catching MRSA."

I smiled. "Wow, you paint quite a picture. Lay down." He did and winced as he moved. "Are you in pain? You can't have any more tablets for another half an hour."

"Half an hour is nothing, pass me them, please?"

"No!" I frowned. "Not yet. The doctor said to make sure you had them at the right time."

"The doctor also said I should stay another night."

Sighing deeply, I shook my head. "You're not getting your own way with this one too. Most men don't even like taking pain medication and you're wanting it early!"

"I'm not most men." That was for sure. "Lay down with me if you're not drugging me up."

*Now there's an offer I can't refuse!* I laid down and snuggled up to his good side. It was over. Aaron was in police custody. Me, Kyle, Megan and Blake were no longer suspects. We were free to move on with our lives.

It was over.

The emotions rushed inside me and kept building and building like a balloon being over pumped. I burst with a loud sob and dug my fingers into Blake's chest, gripping onto him for dear life.

I wasn't supposed to do it in front of him. He said once that he would suck it up for me, but I didn't want to put him in a position where he was uncomfortable. I couldn't help it though. There was no going back now that I'd started.

My heart felt heavy, like it was being weighed down with rocks. "Shh," Blake murmured into my hair. I suspected he didn't know what to say. He didn't need to say anything. I just needed him to hold me. He pressed his lips to my head and whispered, "Shh, it's okay. I'm here. I'm not going anywhere. I promise."

# CHAPTER TWENTY-FIVE

"I can't believe it's been a year," I said, stroking the top of Courtney's gravestone. It had been exactly one year since Josh and Courtney died, almost a year for Pete, and twenty months since Tilly and Gigi died. Three of those were people I loved and I'd never get to see them again.

Blake sat beside me and gave my leg a squeeze. "I know, babe."

"I can't believe I've lost that many people." I turned to him and gripped the hand that was now resting on my leg. "I almost lost you too."

"Nah, was never gonna happen. Aaron was a shit aim." Gulping, I dropped my eyes to the grass. "Sorry, that was insensitive. You'd think after all this time I'd be better at that stuff. Sorry."

I couldn't help smiling. Blake hadn't changed much at all. He was still an annoying idiot, but now he was my annoying idiot. "You're better than you give yourself credit for... sometimes."

"You're just saying that because you want in my pants."

Always joking. Rolling my eyes, I turned my attention back to my friend. "You would have been rooting for him from the start." I had no doubt Courtney would have liked Blake once she really got to know him. She would have been the one sitting on my bed going on and on about how we clearly liked each other and just absolutely had to get together.

"She had taste."

I raised my eyebrow. Not really. I didn't want to say anything bad about Josh because he was dead and Blake's brother, but he wasn't a nice person. Courtney could have done a million times better.

"Say it," Blake said. "Whatever you're thinking about Josh, just say it."

"No. You already know what I think. I'm not bad-mouthing him. Not anymore." Not now he wasn't around. Everyone knew my opinion of Josh; I didn't need to keep reinforcing it. I had let it go, hating someone was exhausting and hating someone that was dead was pointless.

"Such a good girl," he muttered.

"You know why."

He nodded. "I do. Just don't know what the difference is. You think it so why not say it?"

"Because he's dead! I will not be the type of person that pisses over—" Blake's burst of laughter made me roll my eyes. Without needing him to say anything I already knew he was having a visual of me peeing. "There's something very wrong with you."

"My life would be very dull without you, Kenz." I think that was the other way around. "I never know what to say when I visit Josh or Pete. People around are chatting away, and I'm just sitting there like an idiot."

"You don't have to say anything. It's enough that you visit."

"Please," he said, smirking, "Josh is definitely up there making some snarky comment." Probably. It really didn't matter if you spoke or not. At first when I started visiting Tilly and Gigi I sat in silence. It wasn't until about a month later that I just started chatting about the things we would have talked about if they were still here. They probably knew more of the little stuff in my life than Megan.

"It seems like just yesterday we were bickering on the way to the cabin." I ran my hand over the soft grass that had grown over the muddy mound. "I can't believe it's all ended like this." My chest tightened, and I felt like I was going to cry.

"Hey," Blake said, squeezing my hand. He kissed the side of my head. "You wanna get out of here? It always upsets you."

"Sure," I replied, standing with him. I probably would have stayed longer, but I knew how much Blake hated it when I cried, and I didn't want to sit in a church yard all morning sobbing.

We walked towards the road, holding hands. I held onto him tighter than I probably should. "Where to now, Miss Keaton?"

"Megan's, Kyle's and then back to check on your mum."

"And when you've finished checking up on everyone else are we going to make sure Mackenzie's okay?"

"I'm okay. I'll cry later when I'm home alone."

"Firstly, I'm staying with you tonight. And secondly, you don't need to schedule your womanly emotions around me. Besides, I'm getting used to the over the top, complete head-fuck that are female emotions."

Womanly emotions? I laughed at his choice of words, shaking my head as we walked towards Megan's house. "Thanks for that. I really am doing okay today though. Better than I thought I would be."

Eleven months of intense therapy later, and I was doing alright. I still only trusted three people in the world: my parents and Blake. It was hard to put my trust in anyone now. I clearly couldn't read people they way I thought I could.

There was a long road ahead but I was healing. I wasn't as angry with Aaron anymore. Since that day I had seen him once. He'd explained himself, and then I left. Recently I had been thinking about going back. I had started to forgive him, and I wanted to help.

No one apart from Kyle, Megan and his parents had bothered with him. I didn't want to be one of the ones who'd turned their back on him if there was a chance he could get better.

With time, I had started to forgive him for trying to set Blake up and the accident at his house too. I wasn't there yet, but I didn't want to carry a grudge and hate around, it was exhausting. Blake didn't talk about forgiveness much but he did tell me that he wouldn't hold it against me if I wanted to be there for Aaron.

"Blake, what would you say if I told you I do want to visit Aaron?"

"I'd say you were crazy – and you are – but you have this need to help people, which is very annoying sometimes, but I love you for it. This was always going to happen, Mackenzie, I've been fine with it for a while."

Blake wasn't the overly romantic type, so he didn't say I love you every hour. When he did say them it meant so much. Sometimes I worried that the way we got together made him feel like he couldn't break up with me. Did he not say it often because he didn't love me? It was stupid. I was stupid, but I had been hard work over the last year, and I worried that he would get bored and move on to someone that was easier to be with.

"Thank you. I love you."

He chuckled. "Well yeah."

"Do you think you'll ever grow up?"

"Not if I can help it," he replied. Good. I liked how he was, immature at times and rarely taking himself or anything else seriously. He was how you should be in your early twenties, carefree and enjoying life. I just wished I could be more like that, but as he had said thousands of times I cared too much about everyone and everything.

Megan was alone in her house; I could tell that just from looking at the outside. It looked dark and empty. When her parents were home there was always something to show it, a window open, a light on, music, energy. I walked straight inside and saw her in the kitchen, sitting at the table, staring blankly at nothing.

"Hey," I said, dragging Blake to the table. She sat facing us, holding a hot mug of tea with one hand. "You okay?"

The anniversary was always going to be harder on her. She wouldn't deal with it well, she never did. Megan wore her heart on her sleeve. I cared too much, and she felt too much.

"Seriously, Megan, you're scaring me. Are you okay? Did something happen?" *Have you spoken to Aaron? Is he okay?*

He probably wasn't okay. He was in prison. Three hundred and sixty-five days ago he was taking his Rohypnol laced vodka out of the case and checking where the knives were stored in the kitchen. Would he do something today? Mark the anniversary somehow? Pray for forgiveness in the prison chapel? Aaron wasn't religious. He thought the whole idea was farfetched and often said, 'Jesus was clearly an old time Derren Brown magician'. Had his opinion changed now he needed help? I would imagine it would be hard to have no faith in anything when you were absolutely screwed.

I sat down, frowning. She looked scared and worn down. "Megan, what happened?" Blake asked, his voice was stern and demanding.

"They killed her. They killed them both," Megan said. Her eyes were wide, alert. She looked as if she had been on a caffeine binge all night, tired but wide-awake and buzzing.

"They?" Did she believe Josh and Courtney killed Gigi and Tilly now too? Had Aaron's words wormed their way into her mind? "They didn't, Megan, you know that." Not again. I couldn't go through it all again. "Come on. Don't let Aaron get to you."

"It wasn't Aaron, Mackenzie. It was me." What? *What the fuck is she talking about?*

My stomach clenched. No. "What wasn't Aaron?" I asked. My voice, failing me, was barely a whisper. I could guess. I knew, but I needed her to say it.

Megan's eyes bored into mine, showing no emotion. Nothing. They were dark, almost black and empty. "I did it.

I killed Courtney, Josh and Pete. Aaron is as innocent as you. He confessed to cover for me."

My mouth fell open as she confirmed what I was trying to convince myself couldn't really be true. Not Megan. "But... why? What?" She let him do that? My head spun. Was this really happening? *I'm dreaming. I have to be dreaming.*

"I can't go to prison, Mackenzie. You know I'm not strong; I would die in there within a week."

I closed my eyes and held my hand up. "Wait. I don't... how did Aaron know? Why did you...? How did...?" Nothing made sense. Sense was a place where one of my friends hadn't killed another and let another take the rap. I was not there, and I wanted to be there.

Beside me, Blake sat far too still, as if he was still processing what she had said and her words hadn't caught up with him yet. He was usually quick to react to a situation, normally with a stupid comment or a smirk, but he sat silently, like Megan was telling us her summer plans.

I had a million questions, but I could barely pin down one long enough to ask it. The whole situation was crazy. Megan and Aaron were crazy. I was angry, pissed off. *How fucked up are they!*

She took a sip of her tea, her eyes filling with tears, still calm. Calm, calm, calm. I envied her that. She'd done this horrible, unforgivable thing, and I was the one that was fucking livid. "Do you have any idea what it's like waking up in hospital and being told the woman you love is dead?"

I shook my head – back to Gigi? I didn't want to yell – well I did, but I knew better than to do it. I needed the truth. Aaron needed the truth to come out. And so did Josh and Courtney's families. "Megan, they didn't kill Gigi. Nobody killed either of them. It was an *accident*."

"It's hell," she said, ignoring what I'd said completely. "I couldn't even grieve properly because no one knew about us. I missed her every second of every day. I felt like I was drowning and there was no way out. There was nothing I could do to make myself feel better or to make someone pay for what happened. Justice was never served, but they both deserved it so much."

She put her mug down and reached onto her lap. The next thing she place on the table made my heart stop. A gun. I blinked hard, not believing what I was seeing. Blake's hand tightened around mine. *Finally, he's back.* My brain refused to accept Megan had a gun. How did she have a gun?

"Megan," Blake said calmly, smiling a warm smile like the ones police give someone about to jump off a building. Blake smiled as if he was her best friend and everything was going to be okay. "Hand me the gun."

"No," she replied, her knuckles turning white as she gripped hold of it hard. My eyes widened and time seemed to slow right down. "The things Josh was saying ate away at me. He was glad it was them rather than him and Courtney. How could you wish someone died over yourself?" I didn't get that either, but I wasn't prepared to kill over it.

"I don't know," I replied, just in case I was supposed to answer and it wasn't a rhetorical question.

"I kept thinking about them both rotting in the ground while Josh walked around being a prick and Courtney defended him. I couldn't stand it. Because of them, Tilly and Gigi were dead. They didn't even care. We all took responsibility and we all still feel guilt, but not them. They *didn't* care."

"Courtney did," I said, defending my friend who wasn't able to defend herself. Megan was tarring Court with the same brush as Josh and it wasn't right. She was guilty of letting Josh walk all over her, but she wasn't a bad person. She cared.

Megan shook her head slowly. "I confronted her the night after Josh said he was glad it was them. Courtney admitted she was glad she didn't die. Can you believe that?"

Yes, I could. "That doesn't mean she wanted it be Tills and Gigi." That just meant she didn't want to die. I was glad I didn't die, and I knew that was selfish, but I was. If I had a choice though, I would swap with them in a heartbeat.

"Maybe she didn't want it to be them, but they was. She chose Josh over her friends, like she had done a thousand times over."

"So that meant they deserved it?" Blake asked. His lip curled in disgust. I squeezed his hand. This wasn't going to a repeat of what happened with Aaron. We absolutely had to stay calm this time. He had to stay calm. Megan had a gun. A gun for fuck sake! Where on earth did she get a gun from?

"Yes," Megan replied.

I blinked in shock. She really, truly believed that. I wanted to run, to get as far away from her as I could, but my body wouldn't move. My heart was breaking. The girl that cried over Bambi's mum dying and the girl that was too shy to ask a shop assistant if they had the shoes she liked in her size had killed.

"There was a link. A link between Tilly, Gigi, Courtney and Josh." She held her hand up, pointing at nothing with her index finger. She'd snapped. "They were responsible for their deaths and nothing was going to happen. Tilly and Gigi would never get justice. I couldn't stand that. Two beautiful people were dead, and no one was taking the blame. No one was being held accountable."

"So you took it into your own hands? Megan, that's not justice." It was only when something dropped onto the hand Blake wasn't holding that I realised I was crying.

"You don't understand, Mackenzie. An eye for an eye. Josh and Courtney caused Tilly and Gigi's deaths."

"What did you do? Talk me through everything." *Keep her calm and keep her talking.*

"When I had made my decision to take things into my own hands everything became clear. I instantly felt better about their deaths because someone was going to pay. I knew that it wouldn't bring them back, but there had to be justice. I thought of my plan. At first I was just going to go to Josh's house when I knew they were there and Eloise was away. You know that wouldn't have been hard to find out because Josh would brag about having the place to himself."

That sounded like Josh. No matter how small and boring if it was about him it was huge and amazing.

"When he said about going away to the cabin everything changed. It was better, easier. I knew I was implementing you guys into it, but I thought it through carefully and knew none of you would be arrested. Blake coming along last minute scared me for a second, but it didn't really matter, I had enough Rohypnol."

I laughed humourlessly. Well thank God she had enough for all! "Where did you get it?" The idea of Megan getting hold of Rohypnol was ridiculous. She shouldn't know where to get any of that stuff from.

"You remember Stoner Richard from school?"

"Yeah," I replied. Rich had been suspended from school countless times for smoking weed. He was good looking and actually pretty smart, but his home life sucked and he used weed to make everything better.

"He moved on to harder stuff, doing quite well for himself actually." As a drug dealer. She shrugged. "He can get pretty much anything, so he was boasting. Anyway, I planned to drug you all, only enough so you'd be out of it until morning, I didn't want to hurt you. I put Rohypnol in the liquor and took a second bottle, which I hid in my suitcase, so I could swap them over."

"Why?"

Blake snorted. "So when the police tested the bottles it'd be clear."

Megan nodded. "Yes. And I had a change of clothes, matching. I bagged the clothes and bottle, weighted it down and ran up the river as far as I could go before I lost sight. It's all somewhere down there. After that, I had a shower, changed into my duplicate clothes and went to bed."

"You missed out the part where you stabbed our friends to death."

She bowed her head. "You know what happened."

"Who did you kill first? How did you do it? Did they fight? Did they die quickly? Why did you stab them so many times?" I asked, fighting myself to remain calm. I wanted to hit her, scream at her, strangle her. How could she? I was floating again, watching this from far away.

"Do you really want those answers, Mackenzie?"

"Yes," I snapped. Didn't I deserve that much?

Biting her lip, she nodded once and relied, "Okay. I gave you, Blake, Aaron and Kyle more of the liquor." Spiked liquor. "When you all started looking droopy eyed, I took a shot myself and gave Josh and Courtney more too. I needed them to be able to walk around after you four were out of it. It worked. I waited in my room an hour after I heard you and Blake go upstairs to be sure you were out of it. I knew you'd both crash pretty hard once you were asleep." She'd heard us go upstairs? I wanted to know what else she'd heard but that paled in comparison.

"When I went downstairs, Josh and Courtney were in the kitchen cleaning up. I think they'd been at it a while but even though Courtney said she felt like shit he wanted them to do the washing up. I told them I'd got up to get a glass of water and offered to help too."

"Courtney stumbled into the counter, laughing as she threw the enchilada boxes in the bin." Megan's eyes darkened. I barely recognised her. "She was laughing as if she didn't have a care in the world." I wanted to shake her. We had all laughed since Tilly and Gigi died. The world still turned and life still went on. That was the way it was. Just because we didn't die it didn't mean we had to live as if we had. Tills and Gigi would never want that.

"While Josh was fucking around putting the bottles that still had something in them in the cupboard, I... I stabbed Courtney. It was so easy. At first she didn't make a sound. She looked like she was screaming; eyes wide and mouth open but she didn't make a sound. I managed to stab her once more before Josh started to turn around. By that time they were both groggy, moving slowly and not fully aware of what was going on. I stabbed him before he even laid his eyes on Courtney."

I swallowed bile. "Then you stabbed them both some more?"

"Don't say it like that, Mackenzie. I had to make sure. When they were on the floor I felt the rage of what they had done to Gigi spilling out of me. I got carried away."

I threw my hands over my face, squeezing my eyes closed as if that would squeeze the image from my mind. I wanted to be sick.

"Pete?" Blake said, spitting his name through his teeth. "What did he do?" My head shot up. Pete! He hadn't done anything wrong. He wasn't involved at all.

Megan's eyes dropped to the floor. "That wasn't intentional. He kept accusing me. Accusing us. He thought it was you, Kenz. He said you were getting close to Blake so his family wouldn't think it was you. There was an argument and he said he was going to Wright. I followed him home."

She did it. Not only did she plan murdering Courtney and Josh but she did the same with Pete too. And she drugged her friends, hiding behind us to cover her own back.

"How could you do that to us? I thought we were friends."

"We are."

"No. You framed us to get yourself out of the shit!"

"I planned it well, Mackenzie. No one was ever supposed to be arrested for it."

"Then why plant drugs in Blake's room?"

Her eyes flicked to the table. "That was a backup plan in case things started to go wrong. Blake coming along was perfect and when I learned the wake was at his house…" she trailed off, shrugging. "I'm sorry for that. He was a random person none of us knew." Disposable then. "I was going to find a way to get it back if the case was closed, but it wasn't, so I made the call."

"Aaron?"

"I couldn't stand it in the end. I'm not a monster; I do feel guilt. I was a mess, hysterical about going to prison when Aaron found me in my room. He made me tell him and that's when he said he would confess. He'd do anything for the people he loved, you know that. Aaron would be fine in prison. He is fine, but I wouldn't."

"How could you let him?"

"That was a mistake. He said it would be over and I could move on. He said he would act crazy and then get better in a psych unit. That was how it was supposed to go. He was just meant to scare us that day and ramble on, make it look like he'd had a breakdown. Blake was never meant to get hurt; that wasn't part of the plan."

"He'd take a bullet for his friends, he'd do time for his friends," Blake muttered.

I remembered telling him that Aaron would die for the people he cared about when we first met at the cabin. I had no idea what else he would do to protect the people he loved. Aaron loved blindly.

My head felt ready to explode at the latest revelations. Megan was behind everything. Aaron was stupid and his only crime was loving Megan. Blake could have died because of their actions.

"I'm sorry you were both pulled into this. I never wanted to hurt you guys, especially you, Mackenzie. I have to put this right now. I posted a letter to Wright this morning, and I'm so glad I waited to see you. I'm the last link in the chain. It can only end with me." She turned the gun on herself. "I love you, Kenzie."

I gasped. Time stood still and everything inside me turned to ice. "Megan, no!"

The gun went off with a loud bang and the sound echoed through the room. I felt her blood splatter across my face, like I had just walked out into the rain. Megan slumped forward, hitting the wooden table with a deep thud.

My body shook. I stared on in horror at Megan's limp body. Blake jumped up, dragging me with him. He swept me up and carried me into the lounge. He was a little rough. I felt like a rag doll, but I understood his urgency and I was so grateful that he got me out of there as soon as he could.

I was practically dumped on the sofa and then he was calling 999. Megan shot herself. I felt like I did the day we found Courtney and Josh – cold, distant and unable to properly digest what had happened.

She shot herself right in the face, right in front of me. Flashes of the gun going off and blood splatting on the surface behind her plagued my mind. Images of her stabbing Courtney and Josh flash past my eyes. I held my hands up and saw little red spots covering them.

I tried to take a breath but nothing happened. My lungs burned from the lack of oxygen. Folding myself in half, I buried my head in one of the scatter cushions and screamed until my throat was raw.

# EPILOGUE

Blake and I walked along the soft, golden sandy beach in Cyprus. The sky was a gorgeous light blue. The sea was a similar colour and on a really bright day you couldn't see where one ended and the other began. We had been abroad for almost three months, living off savings, some money my parents gave us and the part-time bar jobs we'd landed.

Neither of us wanted to be home after everything that had happened. One day we would have to go back, but we were determined to enjoy our twenties and live it up somewhere hot. I would worry about facing the quiet little village that was scarred by Megan's actions in a few years.

I was still scarred. I saw Megan shoot herself too many times in my dreams. Trusting anyone was almost impossible. Blake was the only person I trusted. He'd been through it too. We vowed no secrets and as hard as it was to talk about everything we made sure we did it. Secrets killed.

Everything was easy in Cyprus, well, easier at least. Blake and I spent almost every second together, messing around, making love, swimming, drinking, dancing, taking boat trips, and working in the evenings. We were living the life you were supposed to have when you were young, finally.

I spoke to Kyle often. He had a new girlfriend that he knocked up almost straight away, but they were happy and giving it a go. We planned a short trip home when the baby arrived. As much as I was looking forward to seeing the only friend that hadn't committed a horrible crime I was also dreading it. Even the thought of being back there made me feel sick. I couldn't handle being so close to where it all happened and I couldn't handle the pointing and the whispers.

Then there was Aaron. He was getting out of prison soon, in just six days. He was made to serve time for perverting the course of justice. I thought about inviting him out to stay with us for a while. After being in prison for almost two years, the sun, sand and gorgeous blue sea would do him good. But Blake was dead against the idea – something about some stereotypical sequel film revenge. Revenge for what I had no clue, Megan was dead.

Blake watched way too much TV. But I had to listen to his fears, even if they were ridiculous. I loved him so much and trusted him with my life. He came first and he always would.

Whatever happened though I was determined to be there for Aaron in whatever way I could, whichever way Blake was also comfortable with. The more I thought about it the more I realised that the only part I was still angry with Aaron about was hurting Blake. Thankfully I knew that was unintentional, but I was still pissed it happened. As stupid as Aaron was his actions were, he did it to protect someone he loved. I believed he deserved a second chance.

I looked up at Blake and smiled. His short messy hair blew gently in the warm breeze. His eyes were alight with happiness and in the gorgeous blues of the Cyprus sky and sea made his eyes a bright, crystal clear blue.

"Cocktail or beer?" he asked, nodding to the little straw roofed hut that started the line of the tourist favourite bars.

I grinned. That was about as complicated as my life got out here and I loved it. I squeezed Blake's hand, smiling up at him and replied, "Cocktail and then you."

He groaned and pressed his lips hard against mine. "We're skipping the cocktail."

# More books by Natasha Preston

## Out Now

### *Silence (Book One)*
Oakley Farrell stopped talking at the age of five and has remained in her own little world since. Her mum is desperate to find out what's wrong with her daughter, but does she really want to know? Oakley's best friend, Cole has stuck by her. Their friendship is easy but as they start to become closer she is faced with a new set of issues to deal with.

### *Covert*
After seven friends take a trip to a secluded log cabin, a drunken night ends in the tragic and brutal murder of two of them. Mackenzie and four of her friends wake in a disorientated state to find the bodies of Josh and Courtney on the kitchen floor. With the police determining that there was no forced entry or signs of a struggle, suspicion turns to the five survivors.

### *Players, Bumps and Cocktail Sausages*
*(A companion novel to Silence and Broken Silence)*
Putting his player ways behind him, Jasper Dane is now strictly a one-woman man. Jasper, desperate to start a family with his wife, Abby, is devastated when she puts their baby plans on hold. Holly has just arrived back in town for the summer, and after landing a job with Jasper, the two form an unlikely friendship. Abby's immediate dislike of Holly and Jasper spending time together causes him to question his wife's fidelity. Broken hearted at Abby's sudden change of heart and suspicious of her reasons, Jasper takes action, sparking a chain of events that make his once well planned out life spiral out of control.
To get what he wants, he first has to lose everything.

## *The Cellar*
### *(Published by Sourcebooks)*

Nothing ever happens in the town of Long Thorpe - that is, until sixteen-year-old Summer Robinson disappears without a trace. No family or police investigation can track her down. Spending months inside the cellar of her kidnapper with several other girls, Summer learns of Colin's abusive past, and his thoughts of his victims being his family...his perfect, pure flowers.

But flowers can't survive long cut off from the sun, and time is running out...

www.natashapreston.com

Made in the USA
Charleston, SC
03 September 2014